Lilly's Angel

Fangs & Halos Book 1

Charlayne Elizabeth Denney

Heavenly Fangs
17003 Blackhawk Blvd
Friendswood, Tx 77546

Copyright © 2013 by Charlayne Elizabeth Denney
Print Edition
Paperback ISBN—978-0-9897685-0-4

Heavenly Fangs and the halo/fangs symbol are trademarks of Heavenly Fangs Publishing

Cover by: Charlayne Elizabeth Denney
Layout by: Paul Salvette, BB eBooks

Book cover and charms: © Dreamstime.com: Seleznyov, Russell Shively, Zts, Kuzzie, Risto Viitanen, Dagadu

Dedication

To my little muse and helper, my granddaughter Haven. Sweetie, you helped me more with ideas and keeping me going with your challenges and questions than I can say. And soon you will grow up and be old enough to actually read the story.

I love you,
Grandma.

Authors Notes

While "Lilly's Angel" is a work of fiction, I have tried very hard to get the history of both 1900 and 2005 New Orleans as correct as possible. In the 1900 scenes, every effort was made to gather the names of the participants in the Storyville area of New Orleans. With the exception of Lilly, Marcus, Jesse, and Abesolom, everyone mentioned in this part of the story existed in the area and could have participated in the activities portrayed. The brothels of the area are long-gone, many of them replaced by the Iberville Housing Project by the 1950s.

In the 2005 portion, I attempted to show the city just after the hurricane within historical context. Hurricane Katrina blew into New Orleans on 29 August at 6:10 a.m. and was out by that evening. While much of the city was left flooded from the storm surge breaking the levies in the canals around the below-sea level city, the French Quarter, part of the city right along the Mississippi River, and most of the Garden District were left unflooded because it is higher ground. The Iberville Projects and St. Louis One Cemetery on Basin Street were minorly flooded and the water was under less than 2 inches deep. The water was deeper further back from the river, knee deep in Canal Street and up to waist deep around the Superdome where thousands had sought shelter prior to the storm. There was widespread looting in the entire city, some taking food and water only, others taking almost anything that wasn't nailed down. Vandalism was high downtown.

The places mentioned, O'Flaherty's Irish Channel Pub at 514 Toulouse was locked up tight for the time and has since, sadly, closed. The house described in the Garden District on Prytania does exist; it is a bed and breakfast. St. Louis One Cemetery is still there, the oldest cemetery in New Orleans and the crypt is there. Jimmy Walker's Sports Bar at 720 Rue Bourbon was, indeed, the only bar open in the city and was featured on many news reports, it too has sadly since closed. The names of the bar folks have been changed. The "Gay Mardi Gras" known as Southern Decadence was scheduled to be held the weekend after the hurricane and was cancelled. But about two dozen residents of the French Quarter who would have been involved in the celebration did parade down Bourbon Street in an unofficial observance. They did have the parade permit and were challenged by a police officer who allowed it to continue. The people involved and the date have been changed—the parade happened on Sunday afternoon, September 4 but I have moved it to the night of September 1. And yes, there have been voodoo altars on the crypts in St. Louis One cemetery, my husband and I found one during one of our visits in the mid-1990s.

There was a lot of destruction of the majestic city that week and many people suffered. 1,464 people perished in New Orleans and a total of 1,836 in the entire U.S. Many people lost everything; some left and never came back. But, the city has fought back and is now well into its recovery*

Acknowledgements

No one ever writes a book by themself. This is one that took a lot of input, research, and permissions to do some of what I've done. So many are owed thank-yous for their assistance in the research for this book: Amanda Bloomfield of the UPenn Historical Preservation Program for the use of their website detailing the layout and historical significance of the St. Louis 1 cemetery, as well as pictures for my website. Robert Nicewander of Onward Brass Band for his assistance with history of the band, jazz funerals, and use of a picture on my site. Mark Farah of Williams Research Center of New Orleans for answers about automobiles in 1900 New Orleans. Octavian Coifan of "1000 Fragrances" blog for help with Lilly's perfume. Mark Griffin Heise of Engaging Causes/YellowSpringer.com for his building and hosting of the website for "Lilly's Angel" and "Fangs & Halos."

I had so many cheerleaders and encouragers for this as well. Jean Stutz for her help with originally naming the books and series, Cathy McNulty for her endless enthusiasm for the project and being there when I got worried about things, reading, editing, opining, and cheerleading. My friends at Paranormal Romance Guild, especially Gloria, Lea-Ellen, Penny, and the associated authors who beta-read, edited, walked me through the process, and answered every little question I had with patience and grace. My writer friends, including Jaz Primo, Meredith Spies, P.n. Elrod and Cj Cherryh, who encouraged me to try again. Those who graciously allowed me to use them as characters, somewhat shamelessly at times: James, Stephen, Mike, Tommy, Paula, Trevor, and Mark. My brother, Arthur Burnett and his wife, Helene, who read the first early stuff and shared experiences. My sister, Lynn, who has told me forever not to listen to anyone about not being able to write fiction. My kids, Michael and Amy, John-Michael and Marcia, Keresa and Andy, and Kimberly, who have heard so much about this and only slightly rolled their eyes at times about mom's "story." Thank-you ALL for everything, you rock!

And then there's my muse, my housekeeper, cook, laundry-doer, and lover/companion of 20 years now, my beloved husband, Bruce Denney. He was there for every step of this and never let me quit, even when things got really dark in my life. I love you babe, thank you.

Also, there's a very special thank-you to those who talked me off the ledge when I was panicking over the layout/design and ready to chuck all of this thing, Chris, Mark, and Vickie Rose, you guys are in my hearts forever. Thank-you!

I know I've forgotten someone but hopefully if I have, you will forgive me. I have a few more of these planned so I can thank you then.

Two words of caution: 1) There is a scene of a violent rape in this book. I have made an effort to portray the scene without graphic details to help avoid triggers for people who could be affected. 2) There is use of historical language considered wrong today but it is used for a reason.

Charlayne Elizabeth Denney
July, 2013

Chapter One

A LONE FIGURE leaned against the railing on the grand riverboat. Marcus Lancaster watched as the shoreline slipped into the predawn darkness. His penetrating blue eyes flecked with gold then scanned the horizon for the beginnings of the glow over the city of New Orleans, his destination. Intense thought wrinkled his brow and made him oblivious to everything else around him.

"Thinking about *her* again?" asked the man approaching and standing next to him at the rail.

"Hmmm" he nodded, undisturbed by the other man's sudden appearance.

"Why are you so fascinated with this young woman?"

"I don't know, Jesse." He pondered. After a long pause, he continued, "I have watched her since I first discovered her in the New Orleans brothel and she's been on my mind a lot. She's beautiful, smart, and talented, yet she seems to hold a strong and innocent quality to her."

"Yes, but sexual talent isn't what will make a relationship." Jesse Cumberlain remarked, turning to face the dark-haired man.

"Who said it was sexual? I've actually never been with her," he remarked, "yet." Jess cocked an eyebrow up at the addition. "I've let her grow and mature, I'm planning, however, to get to know her much better once we arrive in the city. It's time."

Jess stared at his boss and long-time friend. "I never thought it was that profound an attraction." Suddenly thoughtful, "You're infatuated by her then?"

Marcus shook his head but his eyes belied the negation and he dropped his head. "I am. I dream about her during my rest, I smell her perfume. I can hear her voice in my head."

"You're obsessed, my friend." Jesse smiled. "I've not seen you this way in a very long time."

"Yes, I am. And the fact that we've only talked, never even been to the bed chamber together is driving me insane. I find that I want to know more of her, make her mine. I can't help it, it's just almost like she's bespelled me."

"So she's my replacement in your affections?" Said Jesse, wounded. "We won't be indulging in our intimacy any longer?" Jesse asked, slipping his hand down between them, seeking the other man's hand.

"No, Jesse, not replacement, she's an addition. I find I miss the gentle woman's touch as much as I crave yours. So, I just refuse to limit myself." He smiled and squeezed Jesse's hand. "I promise, you will always be with me." Marcus turned back toward the shoreline and turned his gaze up ahead.

Just over the tree line, there was the awakening glow reflecting against the hot, dank Louisiana night clouds. The Crescent City lay ahead as it did, and so did the young woman he was determined to make his.

Chapter Two

LILLY MARCHANTEL SAT relaxed on the settee. Her mocha skin glistened against the ruby satin of her embroidered chemise and bloomers. Her hair was piled loosely on top of her head, random curls falling down, making her look like she just tumbled out of bed. That was the idea, probably because she did. She had already been with four men today and was waiting for Miss Lulu to bring her next client in so she could go back.

Lilly was a prostitute in the famous Mahogany Hall brothel in the Storyville area of New Orleans. She started working there when she was twelve, carrying laundry to the laundress and bringing drinks to patrons for Miss Lulu White, who was known as "Miss Lulu" to everyone, especially her girls and clients. She started off at Miss Lulu's house on Customhouse Street and then later at the leased older house on Basin before Miss Lulu's grand mansion was finished. She had grown up learning to cook and clean around the brothel. Finally, the day came when she turned sixteen and Miss Lulu told her she was going to go to work as one of the girls. She had been with clients for four years now. It seemed like forever. She really didn't know anything else. Miss Lulu was mom and the new, shiny Mahogany Hall was home. The other girls were her sisters and when they weren't working, they had taught her to read, write, dance, sew, and all the other things she needed to know.

Just barely twenty now, Lilly was considered old, even for the society outside the brothel. Unmarried at her age, she was probably never going to marry, much less have children. She sighed.

Miss Lulu came into the room with yet another well-dressed gentleman. Lilly recognized him, she had seen this one here before, several times over the years, but he had never been with her. He had a smile for her when he walked into the room. His blue eyes sparkled with gold and his teeth were white and straight. He looked wealthy and Lilly knew he was. She smiled back. Maybe she could make him part with more of the money than Miss Lulu had quoted him if she worked things out just right. In the past, he had sat with her in the parlors, talking into the night on all sorts of topics, and paid her for that simple act. She would like to talk with him again, for he, unlike most of the others, treated her with kindness and...respect.

"Monsieur Lancaster, you remember Lilly. She is one of our best and beautiful. I hope she is to your liking?" Miss Lulu re-introduced Lilly to the man.

"Hello, Lilly, it is very, very nice to see you

again, please sit." She did and monsieur. Lancaster raised her hands to his lips and kissed them, lingering over them for a minute. "But please, call me Marcus."

"Monsieur Lancaster, would you like a drink or refreshment before you and Lilly get better acquainted?" Miss Lulu smiled at the gentleman, knowing he was obviously pleased with her. He had been here on several previous occasions and always asked for her time for awhile before asking for another girl to take upstairs for an hour of time.

"Champaign, s'ill vous plait, two glasses." He sat down next to her.

Marcus Lancaster looked at the raven-haired octoroon beauty next to him. He had first seen Lilly Marchantel a few years ago; a mere servant girl in Miss Lulu's other brothel. But he had been taken with her beauty, the reports by the other girls of her quick intelligence, and her beautiful smile. He had not had a woman in his life for a very long time and had never thought to find someone he could allow himself to fall for, but this young girl had caught his heart like no other in his lifetime, since he split from his maker, Eadwina.

He had tried to convince himself that his feelings were just lust; he was just looking at her like all the other women he had been with over time. But no other woman held his attention as this girl did. She floated through every thought unbidden. His patience had been rewarded, she had matured into a beautiful, intelligent young woman.

Seeing her now, he knew she was special. Tonight would be the night—his night to finally make his dream come true...

He jolted back into the present as he heard Miss Lulu address Lilly as the sound of the jazz piano flowed in from another room.

"Lilly, take Monsieur Lancaster upstairs." The Madame smiled at her youngest girl, knowing she would do what was asked.

"Yes, Miss Lulu." Lilly smiled at the man sitting next to her. "Would you like to adjourn to my room now, Monsieur, or sit and talk like we have in the past?"

"Please, Lilly, call me Marcus. We have the entire night with you so no clock watching. We have all the time in the world to talk, get to know one another a little more intimately, sip Champaign, whatever we decide to do. Have you eaten tonight? Would you like to go out to eat before we go up?" His eyes never left her face, unlike so many of the men she entertained, who never seemed to see her beyond her bosom.

"I have taken supper, sir. As you know, Miss Lulu would not like it if I left the premises with anyone; she likes to know we are safe here. She would send Abe to fetch us and it might get ugly." Lilly's smile was pained. She would have loved to leave the brothel and walk the streets of the French Quarter with this beautiful man, go to a fine restaurant, and pretend she was a lady for a night. It was a dream she would never realize, however. Girls like her were not allowed in polite society, and even if they made it into money by marriage or inheritance, the women of society would shun you if you were found to be a "fallen dove."

"What are you thinking, sweet Lilly?" Marcus interrupted her wistful imaginings. His hand held hers, his thumb lazily rubbing the inside of her wrist. The sensation created little excited bumps up her arm and she shivered.

"I was just thinking about how nice being with you is going to be, Monsiseu..., I mean Marcus," she quickly recovered. She focused all of her attention on him, taking the Champaign bucket and glasses from Margie, one of the other girls, and started to stand.

Marcus took it from her, sat it on the floor and then did something he had never done in the past. He gathered her into his lap. He reached up, stroked her back and then pulled the comb out of her hair, letting her black hair cascade down around her shoulders. He nibbled across her chin, holding onto her curls, and then moving up to her full lips. He breathed lightly on her neck and drank in deeply of her smell. He recognized her perfume, Le Parfum Idéal by Houbigant, an expensive American brand. He had gifted her with such a bottle the last time he was in town and came to visit her.

He lavished attention on each lip, kissing and nibbling, tasting her spice and heating her for him. His tongue dipped deep into her mouth, exploring her, touching her inside in places like he wanted to be touching her elsewhere. She had heard of his prowess from the other girls in the house and she had wanted to find out if the stories were true. Now, here she was, with one of the most handsome men that ever visited, someone who she had sat and talked with for years, and now she was getting her chance. And his touch did not disappoint. Lilly's breathing began to get faster and more shallow, her tongue reaching out to touch his, going into his mouth, trying to make him warm and horny. She moaned as he palmed her breast through her chemise and wiggled to try to get a better angle on his lap.

Marcus pulled back, a sigh escaping from his lips. "Lilly, we need to take this to your room or we will be showing everyone how skilled you are." He grabbed the bucket and lifted her in his arms effortlessly moving toward the stairs.

Lilly started to object, but he was so warm and she was still soaring from his kiss and touch, she put her arm around him and snuggled into his neck, drinking his scent deep. He smelled of sandalwood and cinnamon, a pleasant combination of scents that set her senses on fire. She had never had such a reaction to a client before and it scared her to think she could be falling for this man so fast from just a few kisses and touching.

She pointed to her door and reached out to turn the knob, realizing that between holding the bucket in one hand and holding her ass in the other, he had nothing to open the door with. She giggled and pushed the door open. It could be dangerous to fall for a client that could lead to trouble and heartbreak.

Marcus looked into her smiling face and

smiled back. "I am glad you find this amusing, mon amour," he purred into her ear as he back-kicked the door shut, walked to the bed, dropped her onto it rather unceremoniously, laughing. "I find your laughter inviting, beautiful, tempting." He put the bucket down and stepped back.

"You will find that Miss Lulu does not want locks in case someone decides to hurt us. She wants Abesolom to be able to come in and rescue us without having to damage things. It's nothing personal and no one will come in unless I scream or yell a certain code. We will be left alone here to explore whatever it is you wish to explore.". She explained as a matter of habit.

"I know, ma petite. I've been here before, re-member?" Marcus reminded her and Lilly, to his surprise, blushed as she sat up and kicked off one shoe.

Marcus put up a finger and wagged it, indicat-ing he wanted her to stop. He picked up the Champaign, opened it with a loud pop and poured it into the two waiting glasses. He handed one to Lilly and then clicked his to it in a silent toast. He raised his glass and tossed back the entire contents. Lilly's eyes widened in surprise at his action but she tried to copy him. She got one good swallow down but the second tickled her nose and she sneezed and spewed bubbly wine across the room, covering the waistcoat Marcus was wearing. He frowned, obviously not happy with the situation.

Lilly immediately jumped from the bed, limped across the room, one shoe still on, to the washstand and grabbed a towel. "I am so sorry, Monsieur Lancaster. I did not mean to...!" She started cleaning up and said, "I will have Abe take it to the cleaner at my expense. If it's uncleanable, I will buy you a new coat. I am so very sorry, sir." She was dabbing at the wet spots and fussing, trying to take the coat off him and wiping at the same time, frantic that he may be furious.

Marcus caught her hands. "Lilly, stop it. Stop!" He looked into her eyes and caught her attention. She looked at him and then at the floor. Holding both of her hands with one of his, he reached up, caught her chin and pulled her face up to look at him again. Then he pulled her in tight and kissed her, his mouth catching her lips, his tongue pushing its way into the sweet cavity where her tongue was. He caressed the inside of her mouth, at first gently, but then more demanding. She hesitated just for a moment and then gave back to him as good as he gave, showing him that she was wanting him as much as he was wanting her. The kiss lasted several minutes, deep, needing, and demanding. Then Marcus pulled back and brushed Lilly's black hair back from her face.

"Let's not allow this good Champaign go to waste. Let's drink to our continued desires and spend some time exploring each other's bodies." He rubbed her bare arm lazily as he poured the elixir into the glasses again. He handed her glass to her again and this time he smiled as he said, "To our desires." He sipped the liquid this time, most likely not wanting to tempt her to try to keep up with his ability to drink. She sipped the Champaign and closed her eyes, letting the cold drink warm the inside of her, loosening her muscles and giving her a bit of a floating feeling.

As they continued to drink, Marcus began to stroke her leg, starting at the foot she had kicked the shoe from, rolling off the stocking and touching her toes before rubbing his way up toward her knee. As she settled into the pillows, sitting up just enough to be able to watch him, he alternated between touching and nibbling on her leg.

"I want to do this to your other leg, my dear. I want to be able to strip your clothing from you, a piece at a time, and worship each part of your body as it should be worshipped." He looked up from nibbling on her knee to see her eyes closed, a calm, relaxed, blissful smile on her lips. "Look at me, Lilly, ma belle. See your lover licking your skin."

Lilly didn't want to open her eyes. The sensations she was experiencing were intense and she wanted to keep her eyes closed to be able to feel each of them. But at his command, she pried them opened and watched as Marcus bent toward her other leg, pulled her shoe off, carefully rolled the stocking off and lay it aside. Then, taking a sip of the Champaign, he reached down and took her big toe into his mouth, sucking and caressing with his tongue, allowing the bubbles of the drink to tickle it.

Lilly started to giggle and pull away, but a firm hand caught her ankle and held her like a vice.

Marcus' piercing blue eyes shot a warning as he moved from one toe to another, licking and sucking each in turn, paying attention and laving each before starting up the leg. She shivered and swallowed the last of the sparkling wine in her glass, her head beginning to spin. She started to pull back, the intensity crashing into her nerves. She moaned and let her head fall back onto the pillow, trying to pull her knee back toward her chest.

"Ah, Lilly, you pull away. I think I need to show you what I expect you to do. But first, I need you to do something for me. I want you to remove my clothes." Marcus stood up from the bed and stepped away. Lilly sat up and started to stand. Marcus took her hand, helping her to stand. Then he stepped back and let her come to him.

She walked forward, put her hands on his shoulders and gently removed his coat, pulling it down his back and arms and folding it, laying it on the wooden chair next to the wall. She then went for his belt, but Marcus guided her hands to his cravat. She pulled the knot loose and removed it, unbuttoned the shirt. She ran her fingers through the dark curling hair on his chest before gathering the shoulders of the shirt and sliding it down his arms and off, putting it on top of the coat and cravat.

Then she reached over to the bedside table and placed a round tin with the words "3 Merry Widows Condoms" on it. No words of explanation were necessary; condoms were a requirement in all Storyville brothels and he was a regular customer.

Marcus grabbed her hair and kissed her deeply before pushing her to her knees. He lifted each foot so she could remove his boots and stockings. She bent and kissed each toe, and then she reached for his belt, undoing it and unbuttoning his trousers, pulling them down to his ankles and off. To her surprise, he was not wearing drawers. He was hard and ready.

She looked up and smiled, reaching, intending to start to stimulate him. Her fingers brushed the tip, wiping the beads of cum off and she licked her finger. Marcus groaned, aroused. Lilly leaned forward, aiming to start pleasuring him with her mouth when he grabbed her hair and pulled her to her feet.

"Right now, Lilly, if you did that, our night might be over. I want to now see you, all of you." Marcus pushed her hands out from her sides and began to undo each hook on her corset, letting it fall to the floor. Then he nuzzled her neck, letting her perfume entice him, lazily licking the side of her neck as he ran his hands under her camisole and brought it over her head, baring her breasts. He bent his head to each dark nipple, licking and sucking them to hardness as Lilly fought to stay upright with her hands outstretched as Marcus had wanted.

Her moans filled his ears; better than any music in the parlors of Storyville. Then he grabbed the band of her bloomers, pulled them down and had her step out. Those he threw behind him. He really didn't care where they landed, as long as they were no longer an impediment to getting to the core of the beauty he was worshipping.

He spun the young light mocha beauty slowly in a circle so he could appreciate every part of her. He smiled. She was exquisite, probably one of the most beautiful women he had ever had the pleasure of bedding. His other visits to Mahogany Hall, when he had watched her, talked to her, had caught his interest, but he had never imagined she would be as beautiful, as playful as she was showing him tonight. He knew he was correct in choosing her. His eyes darkened as he smiled when she turned back toward him.

She started to reach for him and he pulled her arms up again, holding them straight out from her shoulders. "I haven't said you can touch yet, young lady."

Marcus reached out and picked up his cravat, stepping behind Lilly and wrapping the silk material around her eyes. He tied it tightly, making sure she could not see around any of the material. Her breathing shallowed, quickening in her excited surprise. He leaned up to her ear and whispered, "You have never been blindfolded before, have you, darling Lilly?" She shook her head slowly.

He leaned to the other ear. "Good. I will be the first to show you how deeply you can feel when you cannot see, when you cannot touch. Tonight, you will belong to me and you will feel what I want you to feel, you will experience what I want you to experience, and you will find that you like giving over your control to me." He finished the last word and tweeked her right nipple, just hard enough to make her draw in a sharp breath.

He guided her to the bed and lay her face up. He took her stockings, pulled each arm to the posts and tied her wrists with them. He saw Lilly tentatively tested the ties, trying to see if she had any room to pull loose no doubt. Marcus laughed deeply. "Ah, darling Lilly, you cannot escape my ties. You are trapped and at my mercy until I decide to let you go." Lilly shivered and moved her legs together, as if attempting to pull herself into a ball.

"Uh, uh, uh. Put those lovely legs down, open please. I do not want to have to tie those down too." He cast a lustful eye up her body. Even though the mansion had electricity, Miss Lulu preferred the girls to use candles in their rooms. In the light of the few lit candles, she was a beauty. Marcus put a hand softly on her foot, caressing the sensitive instep. Lilly giggled and tried to pull away. "Ah, ticklish, eh?" Marcus's eyes sparkled wickedly. "I'll have to concentrate my attention there, then, and see if I cannot get that to become erotic instead."

He crawled onto the bed at her feet, took her right foot into his hand, rubbed it for a few moments and then kissed it. Lilly's giggle turned into a moan and she appeared to be relaxing into his touch. He rubbed her foot as he licked each toe, the arch, and then started kissing up her leg. He caressed her other leg as he crept up her body, making her shiver and moan. He took great care around her knee, moving her so that he could suck on the tender flesh of the back of her leg. As he did, she gasped a shuttering moan, the tender flesh's assault seeming too much for her to remain calm.

Marcus chuckled as he rubbed the area, easing the jangling feel of his kisses. "I know you like this. You have to relax, ma belle Lilly." He started nibbling on her thighs. His hands roamed higher.

Lilly's head raised and then lay back as she raised her hips, obviously searching for his touch. He was so close to her, he knew she could feel his breath, his warmth and he could tell she wanted him. She arched as his hands and mouth caressed her thighs, teasing her and trying to make her more aroused. He let her pull up and anticipate his touch, looking for him to come closer to her entrance, to ease the ache that he knew was burning within her.

Marcus smiled; he knew exactly what he was doing to her and how it was affecting her feelings, he had done it countless times in the past to other women. He let his fingers of his right hand brush over her lips and she moaned, her hips trying to follow his hand as it moved. She was trembling, hot and already wet; he could smell her musk, her sweet fragrance calling to him.

Her lover placed his hand on her pubis, pushing her hips back to the bed. She groaned as he pinned her down. His lips never left her thigh, but his hands trapped her hips to the bed where she could not move. Suddenly, she felt something pushing into her, hard. A finger? She tried to move, but she was still being held down as the hard item began to move in and out of her. She let her head toss back and forth and she moaned deeply, pulling on the ties on her arms.

"Lilly, dear, don't pull so, you shall harm yourself if you continue. Relax, and just feel. Enjoy." Marcus' voice seemed to wrap around her from everywhere. Relax? How could she relax with his sweet assault continuing as it was? Her nipples were so hard, straining against the air. Every nerve, every inch of her skin was on fire.

Then the finger moved away. Making her heartbeat quicken, his mouth fastened over her core, licking and sucking, pulling at her lips, her nub. She panted, trying to stay on top of the feelings jolting through her. She wanted to move, to rub against him and take the feelings up and over. She felt as if she was going to die if she didn't.

But Marcus kept her still, holding her down as his mouth assaulted her flesh, licking her and nibbling, driving her hotter and hotter. She moaned and gasped. She pulled against the ties, tried to move, mewled, then she began to plead for him to let her cum, let her fly. She begged, she promised him anything if he would just take her over that edge. She began to cry, pleading with him as she continued to try to move under his mouth as he sucked and licked her into hysteria.

Finally, Marcus reached in with two fingers, touched that soft place inside her as he sucked her clit, launching her into an orgasm that had her screaming. And with that scream, Lilly didn't even notice when he turned his head and bit into her thigh, his fangs striking her femoral artery, flooding his mouth with her warm, sticky and sweet blood.

Lightheaded, Lilly began to come down from the height that Marcus had sent her, just to have him crawl up her body further. He took one hard nipple in his mouth and suckled, rolling it around with is tongue and biting it gently, then taking the other in his mouth for the same treatment. Then he nibbled up her neck and put his mouth over hers, kissing her deeply. She could taste herself on his tongue, a sweet tang but with a coppery overtone she didn't recognize. Her head swam when his kiss heated her again, his weight making her want him in her. She could feel him, hard and wanting, just outside between her legs.

"Lilly, darling, are you ready?" he whispered into her ear as he finished sucking on the lobe. Her mouth twisted into a question, her eyebrows rising under the blindfold. Marcus growled, the blindfold now obstructing his pleasure rather than making it better for both himself and Lilly. He reached up and ripped it from her face.

She opened her eyes, blinking against the dim light in the room.

He looked into her deep brown eyes and smiled. "Hello, darling," he purred, just before he buried his shaft deep within her. Lilly gasped, her eyes widening as he filled her, the condoms, unused, forgotten by her. She was far from virginal, but the invasion could not have been more like taking her virginity again—the suddenness, the force, and the passion combining to surprise her.

Marcus began to move, pulling almost totally out and then gliding back in, picking a rhythm that was neither slow nor fast. Lilly felt the beating of her heart matching the rhythm and gave herself to it. She began to raise her hips and matched his movements, both of them meeting in the air as they came together.

Marcus reached up and released each of Lilly's hands as he slid in and out of her, never breaking stride. She winced as she moved her shoulders down and then placed her hands on his back, bringing her fingers onto his strong, tight ass, clutching it in an effort to push his stride faster. Her need was rising again, her core heating as he continued to glide in and out to the rhythm of her heartbeat. But he would not go faster.

"My darling, patience. Allow me give you pleasure as I take my own. Relax and just feel us," he whispered as he covered her lips with his own, his tongue mimicking what his rod was doing.

Lilly relaxed, letting his body rock hers back and forth, her hands rubbing his back, running through his hair, holding his body to hers. She made love to him, giving him the touch he seemed to want, playing his body like a lover who knew him well would. And as she did, her own desires, her own longings, began to climb and she rode the energy he was giving along with him. She matched him again, stroke for stroke, touch for touch, mewing and moan with the deep feelings beginning to burn within her again.

Marcus caught the feeling and stepped up the pace, allowing his own passion to rise and his own need to begin to peak. Both bodies linked in a dance, heat rising.

Suddenly, Lilly's passion peaked again, her body arching under his. She grabbed for him, pulling him into her as she clamped down on his cock with her vagina, pulsing and throbbing as she tumbled into the magical place Marcus had prepared for her.

His own passion triggered, he raised up, plunged into her once, twice more, then pulled back, ready to push another time. As he did, he opened his mouth, his fangs sliding from his gums, and he sank them into her neck. He flooded her with his seed as he took her blood, moaning and growling in his own daze of pleasure. He lost all time as his body spent itself in her and her blood filled him.

Marcus raised his head slowly, opening his eyes and looking around. Blood had pooled under his cheek on Lilly's shoulder and he lazily licked it off and then sealed the puncture wounds he had made on her neck. He took his time with them, making sure that they healed up so they would not be seen. Then he lay his head back on her shoulder as he disengaged from her body and rolled off of her. He pulled her over to him, placing her head on his shoulder and kissed her lips.

She did not kiss him back. Her entire body was limp, her head rolling to the side. Marcus stopped and listened; he heard no heartbeat. He swore. "Damn it!" He put his other arm up to his mouth and bit into his wrist, opening up the skin and letting the blood drip fast. He then put it over her mouth, against her lips, forcing the blood into her mouth. He stroked her throat with his other hand, trying to get her to swallow.

"Come on, darling. Drink. Take what I offer and drink to live," he encouraged her. She wasn't breathing, wasn't swallowing. "Come on, Lilly. Drink!" He got more forceful and held her up, tearing at his wrist again to get more blood. He put it back down to her mouth and pushed it against her lips, making the blood fill her mouth as he stroked her throat again. If his heart was beating normally, it would have been racing, but it was as slow as it had been for centuries.

Instead, it felt as if it was breaking. He had taken too much. He would have to pray he could get enough of his blood down her to turn her. He tried to get more to her, but as he sat up to try again, his head spun. He had already given her a great amount. He was weakened and would have to stop. He gently lay her down and covered her with the blanket.

"My darling Lilly. My sweet, darling Lilly. Oh, ma belle! I am so sorry. I never wanted this. I would have turned you eventually, if you wanted it. And I would have stayed with you, but I never wanted your death." A blood-red tear fell down his face and landed on her cheek.

He brushed it away and kissed her tenderly one last time. Then he dressed, and with a last look back at her still beauty, walked out.

Chapter Three

A S THE MORNING wore on, Miss Lulu wondered why Lilly had not come down to eat. No one had seen her all morning. Finally, she asked Belle, one of the youngest and newest girls, to go up and check on her.

Miss Annie, the cook and housekeeper came out to talk to Miss Lulu about the day's activities when a scream split the air. Both women went up the stairs quickly and down the hall into Lilly's room where Belle stood over the bed, screaming and crying. Lilly lay still, gray, with a small dried trickle of blood at the corner of her mouth. Annie went to her and put her head to the girl's chest, checking for a heartbeat while Miss Lulu pulled Belle back toward the door. "Belle, go get Abe, girl," she slapped Belle to get her to stop screaming, "Pay attention. Go get Abe, NOW!" Belle backed out of the room, still crying, and fled down the stairs.

Annie looked up, "She's been dead awhile, I think. She's cold and stiffness has set in. Did she have a client last night?" She pulled the blanket over the girl's head.

"Yes, she was with Monsieur Lancaster last night. I never saw him leave but I doubt he would do this. He seemed very fond of Lilly." Miss Lulu said. "Either way, we cannot tell the officers that he was here, I cannot afford to lose such a well-paying customer. We tell them she was alone, sick last night. Be sure to wash her good before they get here." Miss Lulu turned just as Abesolom, the house guard came up. A big man, dark black with a bald head and large muscles, he was the one person that Miss Lulu could count on to take care of any problem that she had, not only completely but discretely.

The mute man rumbled in, his hands flying in an attempt to communicate, belying his nervous manner. He saw the covered body on the bed and crossed himself hastily.

"Go to the police and let them know we've had a death in the house. It is Lilly Marchantel. She was ill yesterday with her stomach paining her, as it had been for a few days, and she went to bed last night. We tried to wake her this morning and she would not wake. I need them to send the undertaker so that we can plan the funeral and such." Miss Lulu was very matter of fact about how she wanted things handled. The story would be adhered to as she told it, no deviation would be tolerated and Abe knew it. Annie took a piece of paper and pencil, hastily writing a note for Abe to take with him.

Taking the note, he nodded his head and put his hand on his heart and then onto her chest in a gesture of love, he liked Lilly a lot because she was always so kind to him, never teasing him about his inability to talk. Abe shook his head as he turned and went down the stairs.

"Annie, I'm really not sure what happened to Lilly. But we need to make this look as much like an illness as possible. We need a basin and some vomit. Which of the girls can do that for us?"

Annie looked at her boss like she could not believe she was hearing this. "I think Margie could, she drank a lot last night with several of her clients. I'll step..."

"No, you keep cleaning; I'm going to go get her in here. Just make sure there's no sign of a client and make it look like she's been in bed for a while and sick." Miss Lulu went across the hall, opened the door and woke Margaret Nicoles. She was still sleeping and looked much worse than the night before.

"Miss Lulu, my head is pounding and I do not feel well. Can I take a few hours off? I will work later and my day off. Please?" Margie tried to turn over and pulled the pillow toward her head.

Miss Lulu grabbed the pillow and then pulled Margie to her feet. The young woman groaned and looked like she might fall any moment. Lulu walked her across the hall and into Lilly's room. Margie swayed and Annie stepped up to her just in time with the basin before she vomited. Once that occurred, Lulu handed her a glass of water and told her to go back to bed. Margie did not even notice the covered body on the bed or question why she had been dragged into Lilly's room or dismissed so suddenly after getting sick to her stomach. All she wanted to do was go to the water closet and then crawl back into bed. "I hate tequila." she complained softly and moaned on her way out. She shut her door very quietly.

Annie had taken the basin and, using a washcloth, placed some of the foul contents into Lilly's mouth and dribbling it down her front and across the bed. As she put the basin down, she sloshed a bit more onto the floor. Then she took the washcloth, rinsed it out in the bathroom, and put it into the pocket of her apron. "I think we have it as set as we can." she said as she drew the blanket back up over Lilly's face. The room, already warm from the late season heat, was beginning to smell bad.

Miss Lulu smiled sadly and took her friend's hand, "I liked that girl. I wish I knew what happened. I do know that Marcus Lancaster will be closely scrutinized if he ever comes back here. Let's go wait for the coppers, they should be here soon."

JUST AS ANNIE brought the coffee service into the parlor, Abe came back with three policemen following him. He stepped aside and let the officers step up to greet Miss Lulu, even though introductions were not necessary. Miss Lulu was known as the "Queen of the Demi-Monde" and every police officer and elected official in New Orleans knew her. Mahogany Hall was known as the most luxurious in the city and the women the most beautiful. And Lulu was known more professionally too, she had been jailed quite a few times since coming to the city. So she knew the men who now stood before her, holding their caps in their hands.

"Hello officers. I wish this could be a social call, I miss seeing you here. But we have had a sudden death of one of our girls and I need to let you know before we call the undertaker to come." She smiled but did not get up. "Would you want some coffee while we talk?"

"No, Miss Lulu, I just have a few questions before I go up to where the body is." Corporal Stephen Boyard stepped closer and sat down on the divan. He looked at his officers, "Louis, Joe, you two go with Abe up to the room and look around. Talk to the girls and see what you can find out. But don't touch anything yet, I want to have a look at it before we move anything." Officers Therence and Tholmer looked to Abe, who led them up the stairs.

"Now Miss Lulu, tell me what happened last night. Who was the girl with? Where is he now?" Officer Boyard took out a pad and a pen. He scribbled something on the paper and looked up at Mahogany Hall's madam and smiled.

"You know, Stephen, she wasn't with anyone." Miss Lulu called him by his first name in a show of familiarity. "She has been ill for the last few days, some sort of stomach malaise. We let her rest; I'm not an evil woman, Corporal. Annie was tending to her, checking on her as needed. She wasn't feeling well last night when she went to bed. Sometime in the night she vomited and this morning we could not wake her. We tried but she's gone. It is that simple." Miss Lulu dabbed her eyes with a handkerchief and shook her head. "I loved that girl and she's gone." she broke down and cried. From other parts of the house, Stephen could hear crying. Lilly Marchantel was loved in Mahogany Hall by all appearances.

"I will go up and look things over, Miss Lulu. If everything is as you say, I do not foresee any trouble and you can probably call Emile Lebat to come get her body for embalming." Corporal Boyard stood up and stepped toward the sweeping mahogany staircase. "What floor is her room on?" he asked, looking back at the still weeping woman.

"The third floor, to the right hand side of the hallway." Miss Lulu dabbed her eyes again daintily. "I will send you up alone, sir, I can barely stand the thought of that poor girl dead, I can't bear the sight of her so still." She watched the policeman disappear up the stairs.

Miss Lulu was thankful that the three officers that had come to this were the only three black officers on the force. They were known in Storyville and one of them was a customer. She knew, at this point, that the investigation would be cursory for sure; not that it would not be without them, most of the New Orleans police and government did not look too closely at what went on in the sporting houses and cribs of the red-light district. Unless it was a customer who died, and even at that it had to be a white customer with some means, they really did not bother to investigate too closely. Any threats to the sporting house were taken care of quickly, especially the largest ones on Basin Street, which had enough money to pay the bribes to keep things quiet and swept well under rugs to never see the light of day, or night, again. Miss Lulu had that kind of ability, she just did not want to use it unless necessary.

Corporal Stephen Boyard found the room with the body easily, there was a crowd of people gathered in the hallway, his officers talking to each of them about the girl who lay dead in the bed inside. The women were all crying and talking about how Lilly Marchantel was a good girl, a nice person who became everyone's friend in the house. The officers stood by, taking notes and nodding. The man introduced to him as Abe stood silently watching, leaning against the wall just past the crowd. His eyes passed over each of the women and back over each policeman like a dog guarding a herd of sheep with a couple of wolves nearby.

Stephen stepped into the room with the body. The smell in the closed, hot room was almost overwhelming. The sickness was apparent, it appeared that someone had tried to clean up after her, but the girl had been vomiting on the bed, on the floor, and into the basin beside the bed. Miss Lulu must have told them not to move anything until after the investigation because the clean towel was laying on the edge of the chair next to the bed. He pulled down the blanket covering the body. Fresh wails of crying came from the hallway as someone obviously was watching when he did. The body was gray, blood was probably already pooling on the backside, although he didn't turn her over to look, and the hair still damp and plastered to her head. She smelled like sickness. There were no marks he could see on her, no bruises on her neck-she hadn't been strangled; no protruding tongue or discoloration that might indicate poison. He looked a little closer. There were a couple of small wounds on her thigh, like an insect bite, still red. A spider? It didn't look like anything bad enough to kill though. She died of whatever illness she had picked up. Natural causes is what he would put in his report. He covered her and went back into the hall.

"Ladies, if I could have your attention for a moment. Did anyone see or hear anything unusual in the past few days concerning Miss Lilly Marchantel?" he asked, looking at each of the women, who shook their heads in turn. No one volunteered any information. He looked to his officers, "I'm satisfied, Louis, Joe, let's go let Miss Lulu know what the opinion is so she can go ahead and send for the undertaker. Good morning ladies." Corporal Boyard smiled, more of a grim half-smile than anything, and turned, going down the stairs.

He stopped on the landing and turned toward his officers, "Did you get anything from them before I came up?" he asked quietly.

"Well, Most of them said that they knew she

was ill but had not thought that it was bad. The girl, Margie, was getting over her own drunken night and said she did not know that Lilly was ill. But the housekeeper, Anne, said that she was sitting with her off and on all night and Nellie came to sit with her about 4:00 a.m. so Anne could get some sleep. Nellie had gone to the water closet in her room and when she came back, that is when she found Lilly had vomited. She called for Anne and they tried to get her awake but they could not do so. That is when they came for Miss Lulu and she sent for us." Joe Tholmer detailed.

"None of the other girls had anything to add." Louis Therance said.

They came down the stairs and into the parlor again. Miss Lulu was still sitting where they had left her, patiently waiting to speak to them. Her eyes were red, a bit swollen from crying. It struck Stephen Broyard that Miss Lulu White actually cared for Lilly Marchantel and mourned the girl's passing. It wasn't just a work relationship with her. "Miss Lulu, I think we can close this one as a natural death and let you go ahead and make the funeral arrangements. I will send the report to the recorder's office so that it's registered that she has passed away." Corporal Boyard shifted from one foot to another, suddenly wanting out of the sporting house and back into the daylight, away from the sorrow in the house.

"Thank-you, Corporal Boyard. And please thank Recorder Henry Lanauze for me. I will send him a payment for the record as soon as we have her buried." Miss Lulu held her hand out to the police officer, who shook it. He took then looked back at his fellow officers, who each shook her hand as they turned and left the hall, the man Abe following them and shutting the door, locked it.

Miss Lulu stood, still shaking, and looked at Abe, and at the girls who now lined the staircase. The whole house had a feel of death, a death none of them had any idea how it happened. Lulu knew that the story she gave the police was false but she didn't know what did happen. She knew that Lilly had spent the night with Marcus Lancaster, a man who had been at the Hall many times over the years but had left before dawn and as far as everyone knew, Lily was alive. Lancaster was a gentleman and a frequent guest at Mahogany Hall, he was never rough with any of Miss Lulu's girls.

Miss Lulu looked at Abe, "I need you to go to Joseph Ray, the undertaker up on North Rampart, take this letter to him, and get him to come down here with a decent coffin and the items to set up a wake. Nellie, Corine, I need you two to get dressed up nice and you are going to that church that Lilly always went to, I think it's St. Augustine over on Governor Nichols Street, and tell the priest I need to talk to him immediately, that we've had a death. He needs to come here. Don't take any lip from him, don't take any excuses, I need him to come here; he needs to tend to his flock. Make yourselves presentable for a church call, all of you. For the next few days, we're going to be presentable ladies of the city of

New Orleans. Now go on, get dressed and clean up your rooms and this house."

Miss Lulu handed a note to the big bouncer and then started up the stairs to her room as Abe went out the door and closed it. She looked around the expanse of the lowest floor of Mahogany Hall, the finest sporting house in New Orleans. She was proud of her house, her home, and her girls. And she had been proud of Lilly, who had been with her for many years. Now she was gone and the house would feel that much emptier.

Most of the funerals held for the girls of Storyville were quiet affairs as befit a less-than-honorable side of society. But Miss Lulu White was no ordinary madam and she knew an opportunity when it died in her house. As she waited for the undertaker, her mind was whirling with plans to throw the biggest funeral Storyville had ever experienced. The talk, the opening of the brothel to mourners, and the gossip about the funeral expense could fuel the curious new patrons coming to see the house and the madam of the dead girl. She calculated that the publicity for the affair would more than pay for the outlay she would make. Even the newspapers of New Orleans would carry the story, which could be very lucrative indeed. She only had to play the part of the grieving mother figure.

It was almost noon when a teamster wagon pulled up in front of Mahogany Hall. Abe rode in the back and jumped quickly off. The driver, a medium sized man with dark hair and blue eyes climbed off the front, locking the wagon brake. The two men carried two ornate saw horses up the stairs to the front door. Abe knocked and the door was opened by an older lady who then opened the opposite door to allow both men to move their burden into the Hall. Miss Lulu stood inside the entry, awaiting them.

"I am glad you came, Mr. Ray. I knew Abe could bring you here to us in this time of need." She reached out to shake his hand, forcing him to put down the saw horse. As he shook her hand, Abe took the item and stood by. "Abe, put that in the main parlor, in front of the fireplace. We will hold the wake there this evening." She turned back to the undertaker and smiled a grim smile, still holding his hand, "Our dear girl, Lilly, has passed very suddenly and we need to have her ready to be buried tomorrow. If you could handle that for me, I will pay you handsomely."

"Of course, Miss White. I have brought the coffin you asked for, it is in the wagon. If I may have the assistance of your man, Abe, until I get things to where I can manage them?" Joseph Ray smiled at the madam of Mahogany Hall, knowing that this was going to be a very good payday for him.

"Certainly. Abe, follow Mr. Ray's instructions until he dismisses you today. You are to help him however he needs." She waved Abe back into the entry. "Sir, Miss Lilly is on the third floor. Abe can carry her down for you. The girls have cleaned and dressed her and fixed her hair and makeup. Anything else you need, we can do or help you do." She touched her handkerchief to her eyes again, the tears threatening to run down her face. "Lilly was such a sweet girl and we had no idea she was so sick."

"I am sorry for your loss, Miss White. Let me get started." Mr. Ray waved to Abe and both men went out to the wagon. They brought in planks of wood and a folded piece of black material, laid the planks between the sawhorses and covered it all with the black material. Then they went back out and returned with a nice mahogany coffin with brass fittings, placing it on top of the black bunting. When Mr. Ray opened it, the blankets and pillow were a beautiful shade of pink. An angel was painted on the inside of the top in gold.

"Oh, that is perfect." Miss Lulu gushed. "Miss Lily will look beautiful in it and it is just what she deserves. Thank you so much for your kindness in bringing it." She ran her hand down the silk blanket, admiring its beauty. She turned as Abe came down the stairs, Lilly's body in his arms, draped in the sheet from her bed covering her. He walked to the coffin, stiff legged as if he was afraid of what he was doing to her, afraid she would awake and jerk away. Joseph Ray carefully lifted away the sheet from her, dropping it on a nearby chair and smoothing her dress down before taking the body from the big man. She was not embalmed. Not everyone was, it was an extra cost as well as a disturbance to the body that some considered sacrilege. Ray wondered briefly which was the reason this beauty had not had the treatment. She was not stiff from the rigor mortis, which was unusual, he thought but he didn't want to upset Miss Lulu so he didn't mention it. He arraigned her hands on her abdomen, her eyes closed as they had been moved when she was found. He carefully laid her into the coffin, fixed her hair on the pillow, smoothed her dress further, and then turned to the women who had been assembling in the room behind him.

Weeping, Belle Downing, a young, blue eyed octaroon beauty dressed in a gray gown with black orchids came up to the coffin. She slipped a pearl rosary into the folded hands and then kissed her forehead. Holding her handkerchief, she walked fast back to the other girls, who folded her into their arms and let her sob. Miss Lulu came up, touched her back and smiled, then whispered to Annie, and then stoically led Joseph Ray into the front parlor to take care of the business that needed to be handled. Behind her, Abe and the girls began to set up chairs for the wake that would be happening later in the day.

"Thank you so much, Mr. Ray. Your kindness in this matter has touched my heart. I think that this will cover both your materials and time sufficiently." Miss Lulu handed the undertaker a stack of bills. The man flipped through them and smiled. "Yes, this does nicely. I'm sorry for your loss, Miss Lulu. If you will send Abe to my shop once the funeral is done, I will come and pick up my equipment. There is no rush but I will get them out of your way once you are ready." He shook her hand and left the mansion. Lulu turned, wrote a quick note, and called for Abe.

"Take this to the social club. I want the Onward Brass Band put on notice we will need them for the funeral tomorrow evening. If they have questions, bring someone to me for explanations." Abe nodded and left the mansion again.

Just after Abe left, Corine and Nellie returned, a priest dressed in black robes following behind them into the mansion. He looked around hesitantly, almost like he was unsure whether he was supposed to be there or not. He was very uncomfortable and out of his element. It was obvious that he knew what sort of place Mahogany Hall was and he wasn't sure he liked being in the mansion.

Miss Lulu stepped up to him with a smile and a hand out. "Thank you for coming, Father. I am Miss Lulu White."

The priest grasped her hand, "I am Father Louis Henrionnet of St. Augustine Church. You sent for me?"

"Please, let's go to the front parlor and talk." she shook his hand and then led him into the side door and to a chair. He stared at the room around him, trying to figure out how much of his consternation was founded and how much wasn't. Then he sat down after she did... "Father, we've had a death in the house. Miss Lilly Marchantel, as you may have been told, died last night of a short illness. She was like a daughter to me, precious to me, and it has affected everyone. I know she attended mass at St. Augustine's and I was hoping that you could say a mass for her and then perform her burial. It would mean so much to all of us." Miss Lulu dabbed at her eyes dramatically.

Fr. Henrionnet sat forward, rubbing his chin. "I am sorry; I don't think I remember her. You say she was one of our parishioners. Do you have a portrait of her that I could see, maybe that would remind me?"

Miss Lulu stood up, "I can do better, Father, she is in repose here in the house, in the main parlor. Please come with me. We plan to have her wake tonight." She walked out with him and into the main parlor. They stopped before the mahogany coffin. The priest looked down into the face of a pretty octaroon woman wearing a blue dress who seemed to only be asleep, a rosary in her hands.

"I've seen her at mass many times. She comes, sits in the pews and prays but has never taken sacraments. I've often wondered about her, why she never took communion or came to confessional. I guess I know why now." He bowed his head, saying a silent prayer for her soul and then placing the Sign of the Cross on her forehead, turned to Miss Lulu. "I would like to say mass for her but she died without confession and sacraments, in a state of sin. I cannot do it in concordance with the laws of the Church. I am sorry."

"Father, you do not understand, there was no time to summon you while she was sick for her to confess. I know she did not like to do what she did for a living but that was what she felt she had to do, as do we all. She would rise early every morning and dress and go to your church to pray, every day, to try to make herself a good person. I asked her why once, why she went when she knew that the churches look down on the way we live, and she said that it was what she knew, and that while she knew she could not participate completely, she always prayed that God would understand even if man didn't. And now you are saying you cannot give her a decent funeral and burial because of your rules. You are telling me that your rules outweigh that dead girl's faith." Miss Lulu stroked Lilly's hair like a mother with a lost child, tears flowing.

"I wish I could, Miss White. They are not my rules. I have others to answer to." Fr. Louis Henrionnet faltered when talking to crying women. He did not know if it was her tears or her words that caused him such discomfort.

"Father, I am not without means. Could I pay for an indulgence, maybe you cannot say mass for her but could you say some words for her at her tomb and then pray for her soul for a few weeks? I could pay for that for her. Can you see your way to do that for her, for us? Please?" Miss Lulu took both of his hands in hers and looked deep into his eyes. Father Henrionnet gazed back for a moment and then blinked. He closed his eyes and then opened them again.

"Miss White, what I will do is accept the indulgence and I will come tomorrow and go with the casket to the tomb. There I will say a few words and lead a prayer, but not as a Catholic priest. I will wear civilian clothing and do it as a layman, praying for a woman who needs prayer. And, I give you my word that I will say prayers for her soul for as long as I am able. She seems to have been a remarkable woman and one I wish I could have helped her... But this is the best I am able to do." Fr. Henrionnet smiled at the woman, shook her hands, and then backed away. "What time tomorrow do you plan to have the entombment performed?"

"I have sent for the Onward Band to come tomorrow evening. I have not heard back from them yet but once I do, I will send word to you about the time. Is that enough notice?" Miss Lilly wrung one hand around a handkerchief that appeared from her pocket.

"Certainly. I will hold the afternoon and evening in readiness and I will come here when needed. Thank you, Miss White. I am sorry for your loss." The priest raised his hand, blessed the woman, turned and left Mahogany Hall, passing a florist and his assistant carrying in armloads of flower arrangements.

Miss Lulu looked around the room trying to figure out what she was missing for the wake. Her eyes settled on the piano in the corner of the parlor. Smiling, she directed the florist to the main parlor, where Lilly's coffin was. Looking up the stairs, she called, "Nellie! Come down here, I need you to run an errand!" Nellie came running down the stairs, pulling her hair back into a bun with pins as she descended.

"Yes ma'am?" She said around the pins in her mouth.

"I need you to go over to Frank Early's Place and go upstairs. Talk to Tony Johnson and tell him we need him here tonight to play piano for the wake. Tell him that I am going to pay him whatever he normally gets for a full night's work plus a bonus but I need him here by 5:00 because I want him playing when everyone begins to arrive. And tell him I expect him to be his dapper self when he comes." Miss Lulu instructed. Nellie nodded, went up to the stairs, changed her clothes into something more appropriate for the street, put on her best hat and left the Hall.

The afternoon seemed to pass quickly. The florist was kept busy with deliveries from all over the French Quarter and New Orleans, as well as nearby towns, bringing sympathy flowers and bouquets from merchants, past and current patrons, and politicians. While Lilly Marchantel may not have been well known, Miss Lulu White was, and when someone in her house passed away, everyone wanted to court favor with the Demimonde. Wreaths of black and pink flowers were placed on both of the front doors of Mahogany Hall, a sign of mourning to all who passed. Some of the restaurants and cafes in Treme and the Quarter sent food to help with the preparations for the wake.

Some of the girls were put to work putting black cloths over the mirrors in the rooms and arranging the flowers around the first floor. When Abe returned with the answer from the band, confirming they would be at Mahogany Hall to escort the coffin to St. Louis cemetery an hour before sundown on the next day, Miss Lulu sent one of the girls to Fr. Henrionnet to let him know the time. Abe went to Tom Anderson's with the wagon to pick up more chairs.

EVERYONE STAYED BUSY as the sun began to slide behind the tall houses on Basin Street. Tony Johnson came in looking as dapper as always. His pre-performance ritual was executed in silence and with a somber flair that befit the occasion. He placed his signature grey derby atop the upright piano. Next he shrugged out of his coat and hung it on the nearby coat tree. He adjusted his black sleeve garters on his black silk shirt, tugged his charcoal and midnight blue checked vest and straightened his matching midnight blue ascot. And as a gesture of completion of ritual, he touched the large glittering diamond stickpin in the ascot... The black silk shirt shined in the low candle light, the flickering catching the diamond stickpin in the ascot. He sat down and began to play hymns that he had heard in church, slow, quiet, somber music.

The sun slid behind the ornate buildings, the shadows deepened, and the first mourners began to arrive. As Lulu White could have predicted, the who's who of the Storyville District came through her door, not so much in memory of Lilly Marchantel but to greet her madam and keep up appearances with the grand courtesan. Miss Lulu took station next to the coffin containing the deceased girl but her presence commanded center stage. She filled the room, in her elaborately voluminous black silk mourning dress, three diamond necklaces lay on her bosom, and diamond bracelets graced each arm over her sleeves. In her copious coif nestled a diamond tiara with a generous length of black embellished with shining gems. In her hand was an enormous black lace handkerchief. The other hand held an ornate black and onyx fan that she periodically fanned herself with, for dramatic effect. To finish the ensemble, each finger was adorned with an audacious diamond ring. She was the very exaggerated caricature of a rich, mourning widow, except she had not lost a husband. But, as it would be remarked in countless parlors in the city for weeks to come, Miss Lulu White was a great showgirl and she never let a chance to show that side of herself pass by. Even the death of a friend.

Abe and Annie served as the host and hostess, Annie greeting guests and Abe handling the duties of making sure the grooms that Miss Lulu had hired were taking care of the carriages and horses. There was a table of libations set up in the fourth parlor for those who wished to partake and Miss Lulu had even seen to it that the gentlemen mourners had a place to have a cigar and brandy if they wished in the back parlor. The ladies were given the two front parlors to visit outside of the parlor where the wake occurred.

Tom Anderson and his business partner, Billy Struve walked down Basin Street from Tom's restaurant, The Arlington to Mahogany Hall. With them came Josie Arlington and her beau, John Brady, and Hilma Burt. Josie and Hilma greeted Miss Lulu graciously, being fellow madams of houses on the mansion row. Tom and Billy both shook her hand and murmured words of condolences. They all passed by the casket and then took seats. Others came, madams of other houses such as Fannie Lambert of The Phoenix, Countess Willie Piazza, Margarite Angell and Yvonne LeRoy of the French House, each bringing a few of their girls and paying their respects to Miss Lulu and then to Lilly.

Pauline Avery then came swirling into the Hall, her perfume and red hair announcing her arrival. She ignored Annie and walked, almost ran, straight to Miss Lulu and swept her out of the chair with her large arms. "Oh, Lulu, I am so sorry you have been so thusly burdened by the loss of one of your girls. I cannot imagine how you can cope like this without just crumbling into bed and stayin' there, you sweet soul!" Pauline laid the sentence thick with a southern accent that could pull a Georgia peach off a tree at ten yards. "Sweetie, how are you coping?" She kissed her on both cheeks and then practically threw Miss Lulu back into the chair. A sharp intake of breath from the assembled mourners was heard and then a hush came over the room. While Miss Lulu White was known to be a genial hostess, she also was known to have a hot temper when crossed and everyone wondered just how she was going to take Pauline Avery's arrant greeting.

Lulu closed her eyes for a second, dabbed at them dramatically with the large handkerchief, and then waved the fan in her face to cool herself. She sighed and then opened her eyes again, looking for the world like a small, put-upon mother mourning a child, despite the fact that she was neither small nor a mother. Then she smiled slightly and said, "Hello Pauline. I am coping like anyone else. I sit quietly and pray, and I take comfort in my friends. I'm glad they have come to sit with me, and I know you came to sit too."

The wryness of the statement was lost on Pauline, who seemed to overlook it. She smiled and said, "Of course I have. I could not leave my friend in her time of need," and then she patted Lulu's shoulder and then went to take a seat. She took a chair near to Fannie and the Countess, who plainly moved over to the next row to avoid the offensive woman. It was a public slight that could, in weeks to come, start trouble in Storyville.

Miss Lulu turned to Hilma Burt, who was sitting close by, and said, "I guess I should be thankful that it is Pauline who came and not Emma Johnson." Everyone in Storyville knew Johnson, madame of the French Studio, was known to use girls all the way down to age 10 and also animals in her "sexual circuses." Most of the more reputable madams, including Miss Lulu, were disgusted by the older, masculine woman and did not invite her to anything in an effort to run her out. Miss Lulu thought to herself that if Emma had come, she would have had to make a scene, have Abe probably bodily remove her, and that would have caused trouble that she didn't want to have with so many in attendance.

Many others came to Mahogany Hall to visit, to mourn, and to be with Miss Lulu. A commotion and loud sound came from the road as a horn honked. Horses neighed nervously and the groomsmen could be heard shouting. Then voices were heard and the door opened. Four men came through the door, dressed finely in dark suits. Annie recognized them immediately, the mayor of New Orleans, Paul Capdeville pulled off his hat, handing it to Annie, who greeted them as they entered. With him came the coroner and the councilman of the 4th Ward, the Storyville representative. The buzz from the assembled group quieted as the men entered the mourning hall. It was not often that the people in Storyville had a visit from those who governed New Orleans. It wasn't to pay regards to Lilly that they came, it was to Miss Lulu and this fact was not overlooked by anyone assembled. Behind the foursome, the fire chief and the police superintendent came in. They handed their caps to Annie and then joined their compatriots in the room set up for the wake, taking the hand of Miss Lulu and expressing their condolences.

Everyone began to settle down and quietly talk until Annie came forward and stood next to Miss Lulu. She bent down and spoke quietly and then Miss Lulu nodded, wiping her eyes with her handkerchief and beginning to fan herself with her ornate black hand fan. Annie straightened and then spoke. "Welcome to Mahogany Hall. We have been very heartened to see such an outpouring of support from so many friends in our time of mourning. Lilly Lenora Marchantel was with us for a very long time, having come to live with Miss Lulu as a child, an orphan. Miss Lulu had her schooled at the Ursulin School, she paid her way and made sure the nuns took good care of her. Lilly was taught reading, music, and other subjects that have served her well as an educated woman." Annie went to describe some of Lilly's other traits.

Corine Velergage could not listen anymore. She stood and walked quickly to the door, opening it and stepping out, trying not to shut it too hard. She burst into tears and buried her head in her handkerchief, sobbing. Her brown head bobbed as she cried, letting out the pain and anguish she felt at losing her friend. She looked up and stepped down the stairs to the place both of them had called home for years and she hid in the shadows of the staircase, seeking a dark place to allow herself to mourn. The night air was thick and still very hot, even with the sun down. The windows and doors had been left open to entice a cooling but nonexistent breeze inside. She could still smell the oppressively sweet flowers that had been delivered all day and filled the entire lower level of the house. Corine could hear Tony Jackson's beautiful piano hymns being played, actually covering some of the words Annie was saying from outside.

"Mam'selle, why do you cry?" A deep voice

whispered into her ear. Corine startled and began to scream but a gloved hand covered her mouth gently. "Shh, mon ami. I will not harm you. I just wish to know what disturbs your heart." He took his hand down and gently stroked her arm, trying to calm her.

"Oh sir, my friend has died and I cannot bear to be in the wake. It's just so very sad. She was so young!" Corine began to sob again. The man turned the woman toward him and cradled her gently against his chest, letting her spill her tears. As her tears began to slow, he took her handkerchief and wiped her tears. He smiled at her with a plaintive smile, almost drinking in her sadness. She knew the man had been a client at the Hall but she had never been with him and did not know his name. She had seen him sitting in the parlor at times when Lilly had been there.

"What is your name, Mam'selle? I would like to walk with you for awhile and try to ease your sorrow." His smile and his blue eyes spoke of kindness and she relaxed.

"My name is Corine. Corine Velergage. And yours?" She tried to smile but it faded before it really got started and she hung her head again.

The gentleman gently took her chin and lifted her face, looking at her. "My name is Dane." Marcus gave a name he hadn't used in years, not wanting anyone else associated with Mahogany Hall to connect him with Lilly and last night's misadventure. "Corine, walk with me, please." He proffered his arm, she took it gratefully and they slowly strolled down Basin Street toward Canal.

"Who is it that you are mourning, Corine?" he asked her gently with another of those gentle smiles.

Corine thought that Dane could feel everything, every sad feeling she was having. He could understand losing a friend, someone who was like a sister and he was someone she could trust totally. She relaxed with him, "A close friend of mine, someone who has been like a sister for several years. Her name was Lilly. She got sick last night and they couldn't stop her from dying. I had last night off and had turned in early to bed. I awoke to her being dead. She was young, so young. Not even twenty one yet. I am going to miss her so badly." Her eyes filled with tears again and threatened to spill down her stained cheeks.

Marcus nodded. Even as he smiled sadly at the mourning woman, his mind reeled, trying to figure out what went wrong with the turning. Did he get enough blood into her after he drained her? He couldn't remember. She should have been coming around by now. It didn't take much over twelve hours most times. He had not meant for Lilly to die the final death. He had meant for her to die and then be reborn into his world, the world of darkness and pleasure at a different time, after he got to know her as the rules placed on the vampires by the angels demanded. He knew she would, eventually, agree to be turned. But his ardor had clouded his mind, he had taken too much blood and killed her. To hear that she had never awakened, that she had passed from this world and beyond his reach sickened and confused him. How could that have gone wrong? Did someone do something to hurt her, to kill her once she started to awaken? Did someone suspect her rising as someone undead? Had he failed to help her enough in his panic at her death?

No doubt the angels would be sending someone to let him know what would be his punishment for breaking the rules. Whether it had been an accident or by intent, it did not matter. The angels took great delight in the process. He looked at the top of his right hand, briefly noting its pristine condition.

Corine was watching him intently. They had stopped walking as he thought and the puzzled look on his face had caught Corine's attention. "What is it? Are you familiar with Lilly or know something about what happened to her?" she asked.

Marcus's smile disappeared, he took Corine's arm in his hand and steered her into a small passage between two of the enormous houses. He stood in front of her, his eyes smoldering and jaw hardened. "No, Corine. While I was a visitor to the Hall, I was never with your friend. Why would you think I knew what happened to her?" He tried in vain to calm his thoughts. Was there talk about his visit and supposition about his involvement in Lilly's death?

"Oh, I'm sorry, just the way you were sounding, I thought you might have known her or you had been one of her visitors. I didn't mean to say you had done something to her. Miss Lulu said that Lilly died of a very quick illness and the police said it was illness." Corine dropped her eyes toward the ground, then looked up again, into Marcus' eyes.

"No offense taken, my lady." He had been able to lie to her and obviously the madam had covered up his visit sufficiently. He slid his hand down her arm and then lifted and kissed her hand. "I was just lost in thought about how loved she must have been to have such a well-attended gathering." He smiled again, trying to reassure the trembling woman. "When are they going to do the burial?"

"Tomorrow at sundown. Miss Lulu wants us to gather everyone together about 6:15 at the house. We are going to walk with the coffin to St. Louis One Cemetery where there is a priest who is going to say a few words before they put her into the crypt. She has got one of the bands to go with us, everything. Miss Lulu is giving Lilly a big funeral. It is so sweet." Corine started to cry again, letting Marcus once again hold her against him as she let herself dissolve into mourning.

Once she had cried it out and began to relax, Marcus began to talk softly to her in her ear, stroking her back and holding her close to him. She had to be hot in her mourning dress, August in New Orleans was never cool and this night seemed to be closed in with the humidity. Marcus should have been hot as well but he really didn't have trouble with heat or cold either. He kept whispering to Corine, calming her and taking her into a light trance. As her heartbeat slowed and her breath started to grow shallow, Marcus allowed his fangs to drop and he bent down to kiss her neck and then bit, taking her blood for just a few moments, then licking to heal the wound. He then bent and kissed her hand. In the last moments of her trance, Marcus planted a different mental picture of himself in her mind, as a short, blond man with a slight German accent. That should throw off any inquiries if she was questioned about who she talked to.

Corine smiled lazily at Marcus and hiccuped. She covered her mouth with her hand, "Oh my, I'm so sorry! Excuse my manners. I sometimes get the hiccups when I cry or laugh."

Marcus smiled at her. "Should you be returning to the wake, mam'selle?" he steadied her with his arm as he turned her back toward Basin Street. They walked arm in arm back to the sidewalk and then Corine began walking up the stairs toward the front doors of Mahogany Hall. Singing met their ears from inside.

"Thank-you, Dane. I feel like I can make it through this now." She turned and smiled at him.

"My pleasure, Mam'selle Corine. My condolences for your loss." he tipped his hat and then turned and walked off into the night.

THE WAKE LASTED well into the night and people from around Storyville and New Orleans came and went from Mahogany Hall most of the night. Miss Lulu wasn't open for business as such but did not turn down gentlemen if he was willing to pay enough to make it worthwhile to get one of the girls. Most people who came were there to talk with Miss Lulu and Annie and drink the copious amount of alcohol that the madam supplied.

Saturday dawned hot and humid. Most of Storyville slept in, those who had attended the wake slept; windows open in their rooms, trying to catch a breeze in the stifling heat. As the day progressed, the streets began to fill with carts, wagons, carriages, and an occasional motorized vehicle as people went about their usual Saturday business.

The flowers on the black wreaths on the doors of Mahogany Hall began to wilt in the heat and the windows on the bottom two floors were closed and covered with dark curtains. No one came or went from the building as usually happened. It was like the building itself was in mourning. The residents of the area would glance at the looming edifice as they passed, almost as if they could not believe the quiet of the area. Everything appeared locked up tight and there was no movement near any of the windows on the upper floors. Mahogany Hall was as dead as the corpse lying in the casket in the main parlor within.

As the afternoon waned, the big brick building woke up. Curtains were pulled back and windows were opened. The doors were opened and what air was moving was allowed to flow through. Annie was seen wearing her black mourning dress sweeping the front steps and the landing. Livery boys started to gather on the sidewalk nearby and

Abe was taking trash to the bins. A piano was being played inside, a classical piece with a somber tone to it. Soon, people began to come to Mahogany Hall to visit with Miss Lulu and to wait for the procession to the cemetery.

The crowd gathered both inside and outside of the big four-story brick house, women waving fans to try to keep cool in the brutal heat while wearing black dresses. The men just sweated. Several were overheard to say they were at least glad that Miss Lulu had planned this burial for sunset; the heat of the day would be less by that time. Just as the sun was retreating behind the buildings, the Onward Brass Band arrived out front of the mansion. A carriage pulled up and a man in a dark frock coat got out and went inside.

Father Henrionnet found Miss Lulu sitting in the main parlor next to the now closed coffin, visiting with people who had come to be part of the burial. The people surrounding her parted and he walked up to her, taking her hand. "Miss Lulu, I am here as we discussed. I've planned what I will say and I think you will be pleased."

Miss Lulu smiled broadly, "Thank you, Father. I know this is quite irregular but I am grateful for what you can do for us. I have planned that we will walk the procession to St. Louis 1 Cemetery since it isn't very far from here. I would like to get there, have the service and then be back before it becomes too late. Is that acceptable to you?"

"That is acceptable. When do we need to start?" Fr. Henrionnet looked out the parlor to the open doors. It was already getting into late afternoon and sunset looked to be soon.

"We need to gather everyone now, I guess, and get going." Miss Lulu stood and turned to Annie, "Sweetheart, would you please get the girls together and go out front. I need the gentlemen who are going to be pall bearers in here to bring out the coffin. Once we're out, we will get everyone together and go."

Annie went through the house, gathering the house girls along the way and they followed her outside. Six gentlemen, including Abe, came in and, after shaking hands with Miss Lulu, they carefully lifted the mahogany coffin by the brass handles and carried it out of the place Lilly had called home for the last time. They formed up behind the band and Fr. Henrionnet. Miss Lulu and her girls came behind the coffin with the rest of the mourners behind them. Dusk was just settling in long hot shadows in Storyville.

The band stepped off to the tune of "Nearer My God to Thee" and the funeral parade started down the one block and a half to the cemetery. As the procession walked down the street to the sounds of the funeral dirges, people began to fall in behind the mourners. One of those was a man dressed in black, carrying a black valise, his hat pulled down over his forehead. He trailed behind, following the in the crowd, singing as they went. At the gate, the group separated a bit, the band and most of the second line mourners stayed outside while the main family mourners following the priest and casket into the cemetery and down the right hand side, along the St. Louis Street vault wall to the tomb that Miss Lulu had purchased space in from a broker. The family who owned it had died out and the tomb was ready for new occupants. The man slipped in behind them.

The tomb stood open and ready, the heavy marble door removed so that there would be easy access to the interior. The pall bearers stopped and Fr. Henrionnet marked the top with holy water. The mahogany coffin was slid into the frame, then the marble door was replaced. Just as it was settled, it slipped from the hands of the two men moving it and the bottom right corner broke off, leaving about a five inch gap. Fr. Henrionnet and several of the mourners who were Catholic made the Sign of the Cross to ward off any evil, the breaking of the door believed to be a sign that the soul of the person inside might not rest like she should.

"Dear friends and family of Miss Lilly Lenora Marchantel, she has passed from this world and awaits the call to judgment. As I understand it, Lilly was an educated woman who had a deep faith and, while her circumstances prevented her from living all the precepts of that faith, she was a believer in God and Christ and she came to celebrate the Mass every day that she could. She is a good example for all. We remember that all who die are past the trials and tribulations of this world and now rest with the Blessed Mother. Lilly is now past the pain, the sickness, and sadness of this world. Please, let us pray..."

As Fr. Henrionnet prayed, in the shadows of the twilight, the man with the valise knelt a few tombs away. He held a bloody handkerchief in his hand and bloody tears ran down his face. Marcus Lancaster mourned the life of the woman he intended to join him forever. She was now forever out of his reach. Once the prayer was over, he stood up and wiped his face, wiping away the blood. He walked behind the mourners, a safe distance back. As the group met up with the band outside the gate, he slipped out of the gate and, instead of following the procession that was now playing "As the Saints Go Marching In" and dancing down the street back toward Mahogany Hall, he walked down St. Louis toward the Mississippi River.

When Marcus reached the river, he was met by Jesse. The look on Marcus' face told him that things did not go well. He raised an eyebrow, giving Marcus the chance to tell him if he wished to.

"I lost her, Jess. I think I may have not gotten enough blood into her. She never rose. She was dead, the true death, and they buried her." His eyes welled blood but he fought to hold on to the tears. There would be time for that later in private, and in Jesse's comforting arms.

"I have secured passage for us in one of the ships as you've asked." Jesse said. They walked down the line of ships tied to the piers until they reached one that was getting ready to sail.

"Where are we headed then?" he asked as they passed a sailor who was working the rope.

"Galveston. Two days out." Jesse said as he watched the rope being tossed to the ship Then the sailor walked back toward the boarding plank.

Marcus and Jesse followed him up the ramp and onto the boat. Soon those on the dock saw the gangplank pulled up, the ship begin to catch the current as the steam engines fired up. Marcus was seen standing along the side with his friend, watching, as New Orleans slid from view.

Chapter Four

THE HEADQUARTERS OF the Host Assignment
Department (HHAD) was a busy place.
Monitors flashed pictures of places all over Earth
and situation boards held an ever-changing list of
names of people, places, and things that were in
need of intercession by the various departments
of angels that worked out of the HHAD. Across the
room, angels with large colored wings conferred
with others and names changed and other angels
flew in and out of the apertures in the gigantic
space.

A group of angels with larger wings than the
others were grouped up on a balcony, discussing
what was going on. Mikhail, the Archangel who
was head of the Warriors and supervisor of the
hosts at HHAD led the group. "How is the world
response at the moment?" he looked at the others
gathered near him. Most were Archangels and all
were in charge of departments.

Gabriel ruffled his large gold wings, "The Messengers have been going back and forth between
all the various crisis points. We are working with
Uriel, as usual; making sure that everything that

is happening around the world is reported up and is being covered here." Uriel nodded, letting Gabriel fill in the details of the crisis that his Shadows had been covering, his brown wings folded around him. "We have five major problems across the globe at the moment that has our departments working extra. There is a Typhoon named Talim/Isang hitting China and it looks to be heading to Taiwan next. Guardians are out in force, as are messengers. Barachiel can't be up here answering for the Guardians because she's had her hands full making sure that there are enough Guardians in the field to cover all the things going on along with all of the regular action that happens. She asked me to report for her." Mikhiel nodded.

Gabriel continued. "We have the aftermath of that flood in Romania and Europe where we had 42 die, people are still trying to find their homes and animals," he nodded at Azrael.

Azrael's dark eyes fastened on the red-winged leader, his voice deep, "We have cleared the bodies from that crisis, we have 15 in China being taken at the moment, There is a cloudburst in Mumbai, India and we've sent a contingent to pick up just under 1500 souls from there, most from drowning. We'll have a few from disease as it runs its course. We've got between 1800 and 2000 dead in the United States Gulf Coast area from Hurricane Katrina, we've sent another contingent down to take care of that situation."

"Cheil has been asking for extra Guardians to send to both Mumbai and the United States for these two situations. The amount of people who need help is very high and there are a lot of requests from people coming in." Gabriel reported for his friend.

Mikhail spoke up, "We are going to have an incident in Baghdad, Iraq, someone is going to stampede on the Al-Alarmmah Bridge and trample 2000 people in the next couple of days. Azz, you're going to have to be ready for that and I'm going to have to have a few of my guys there to help settle the situation down." Azrael nodded.

Mikhail, as the Senior Angel in Charge, or SAC, usually had insight into crisis situations before they occurred. He was not only in charge of the H.H.A.D., he was responsible for continuing the earthly beings, the humans, and trying to keep them from destroying themselves.

Rafael looked around the group, opening his blue wings and settling them again. "My healers are spread pretty thin with all of the things going on. It's busy on any day but the crises have pushed our ranks to the limits. But we'll keep working. Any group that can lend a hand, it's appreciated, of course." he smiled.

Mikhail's eyes rested on Raguel, the one who had yet to give his report. Raguel never smiled, most of the angels usually said his demeanor was as gray as his wings. "All of the paranormal beings are behaving themselves, if that is what you want to know. Those in the path of Hurricane Katrina moved on days ago for higher ground, except for the ghosts, who don't really care if it comes a gale or not. The Chinese group moved out and sought some time in a drier place. I don't think anything could make those in India move unless they wanted to but they are behaving themselves so I haven't had to do anything about them. And there aren't any paranormal beings in Iraq right now, most of them don't like getting shot at. Oh, a few ghosts hang out there but..." he shrugged his shoulders. Mikhail shook his head; it was about as normal a report as he usually got out of Raguel. But then the Enforcer Angel raised his hand, "Oh, I forgot. We had a French vampire go rogue last night; he decided that trying to eat his way down the main street of Berlin was a good way to satisfy his craving for German. We did kill him, took his head and burned the body rather than just mark him and take him to hell whole. Azz got the soul down to storage, and we managed to get the Germans to back off the international incident before we had to call you to stop a war." He shrugged again.

Mikhail's eyes narrowed. "I'm glad you thought that was important enough to inform me of, after the fact." Raguel just shrugged and stood there frowning. "Ok, sounds like everything is in hand at the moment. I know we're busy, again. Let's keep it tight and keep the planet from exploding." Mikhail's wings fluttered as he strode into his office. The remaining leaders floated to their respective areas and began to check on their boards.

As time wore on and angels came and went, the boards filled up with needs and assignments. A brown-winged Shadow angel floated through one of the apertures and down to where Uriel stood next to his command center. She walked up to him and waited to be acknowledged. Finally the leader turned and looked at her, smiling. "Parisa, you have something for me?"

"Yes sir. I've just come from New Orleans. I've picked up two new paranormal signatures; neither of them has been tuned by the Enforcers. I could not follow them because of the situation in the city but they are close to the Iberville Housing Projects."

"Why didn't you send this information in by a messenger? You came in yourself to report this. Is there something urgent about these two signatures that we need to move on immediately?" Uriel's eyes narrowed. Parisa closed her eyes and then opened them again.

"No sir, it's just that, um, with the chaos in the city of New Orleans right now with the storm and all the flooding and the death, I could not find a messenger to send back with the information. Everyone is so busy trying to keep people alive and keep things from getting even worse, I just..." she put her head down.

"It's ok, Parisa. I understand. It's a crisis situation, all hands on deck, as it were." Uriel looked across the room and mentally sent a call to Ranguel. The Enforcer leader looked up and strode across the room, his dark demeanor flowing like his wings.

"What now, Uriel? Did we find another rogue vampire?" he groaned.

Uriel raised an eyebrow and nodded to his

messenger, she was going to have to explain it, much to her horror. "I found the signature of two untuned paranormals in New Orleans about an hour ago, sir. I came to inform Uriel so an Enforcer could be sent to check it out." she stood straight and tucked her wings tight against her back.

Ranguel scowled at her. "You did, did you? You want us to send an Enforcer during a hurricane to track down a couple of lost paranormals? We have those all over the globe and some are not behaving. We will check the report out but after the weather clears so we're not adding to the chaos. To let you know, almost every paranormal being hates being out in things like hurricanes so they will usually hide until the storm passes." He turned to Uriel and nodded, and then strode back across the room to his department and punched on his board and had his assistant write a new situation on the list.

Uriel smiled at Parisa, "Never mind Ranguel, he's just that way. Go get some ambrosia and rest before you head back. You did ok. Thank you." She smiled at him and then rose toward an aperture, passing a gray-winged Enforcer on the way out.

Sullivan landed a few feet from Ranguel and walked over. He clapped the lead angel on the back, stunning many of those who observed it. Ranguel look at Sullivan and almost smiled, another look that probably shocked a few of those observing.

"Hey Ran, you summoned, I'm here. What's up

this time? Do I need to go all Ghostbusters on somebody?" Sullivan rubbed an apple on his wing and then bit into it, crunching noisily. Ranguel rolled his eyes. Sullivan was way too fond of the human's culture. And where did he get that apple?

"No, no 'ghostbusting' this time. We just got a report of a couple of untuned vampires down in New Orleans. One of the Shadow's caught their signatures in the middle of that storm, somewhere around the housing project near the French Quarter. It looks like the storm is passing so I'm sending you down to track them and tag them or get rid of them, either way, I don't really care. Just make sure they aren't causing any trouble. I would send Essex with you but he's busy on another case. The city is a big mess anyway and with the trouble that is breaking out, a couple of dead undead won't really matter. Just don't let them make any more or add to the havoc, ok?" Ranguel sounded like he was chewing on glass.

"Sure. I'll find them and tag them. It'll be fine. Hopefully things will be ok with the Big Easy; I could use a bit of R&R time and Bourbon Street sounds like just the place to unwind." Sully said around the last of the apple he was chewing as he tossed up the core and it disappeared. He wiped his hands on his jeans and smiled. "Don't worry, boss, I'll get it done." Ranguel just waved his hand, signaling to the erstwhile angel to leave. Sully opened his gray wings and rose, aiming for and exiting out the nearest aperture, heading toward Earth and the beleaguered city of New Orleans.

ON AUGUST 29, 2005, one of the strongest hurricanes to ever hit the United States had just passed over the Gulf Coast, leaving New Orleans a tattered, flooded mess. Windows in the high rise buildings of the central business district were shattered, water stood in 80% of the city, some up to the roofs of the houses of the 9th Ward, trapping those who had not heeded the mandatory evacuation warnings and tried to stay behind or could not flee due to various reasons. People stood on their roofs, having cut holes in them to crawl free of the attics. Bodies of animals and people floated in the fetid, dangerously poisoned waters.

Down on Poydras Street, the famous Superdome, scene of many football celebrations, was now a peeled and leaking mess containing thousands of desperate people who had sought shelter there from the storm. No electricity, no water, no sanitation, no food. Rumors of rapes and murders, shootings. Once the wind and rain stopped, people poured out onto Champion's Square between the dome and the broken windowed Hyatt Regency Hotel to escape the darkness and fear, only to face the heat and sun and still no supplies or sanitation.

Gangs of people roamed the streets on that

first day after the storm, getting into anywhere they could. Some broke into grocers, taking anything they edible that might be safe. Some took carts of meat that had been sitting in uncooled shelves for hours growing who knew what bacteria. Others grabbed drinks or alcohol, or even things they didn't have need for but thought they could trade for something they did. There were people breaking windows on flooded Canal Street, carrying off electronics that could not be used without electricity that would not be available for weeks or months. They grabbed carts full of shoes, clothing, and anything else they could take. It was open season on every shop.

Houses were broken into and ransacked. Pharmacies were pillaged for drugs that were taken to escape or sold or exchanged for food or alcohol or goods. By sundown, a blackmarket economy began to blossom.

Within the Iberville Housing Project on Basin Street, most everyone was gone. Windows not boarded up were broken from the wind and debris, wetting down carpeting and walls within. Items left behind had been picked through by the looters who had stayed behind. Anything not wanted was generally ruined, smashed or torn, left to rot. Food that had not spoiled had been carried off, rotting refrigerated food was left behind, the doors to the now useless box left open and the stench was practically overwhelming to anyone still in the building.

It was in this atmosphere that four enterpris-ing young men in their twenties had combed the

building only a couple of hours after the residents
had left. They had taken food, items they could
sell later after the storm, and anything that even
appeared to be drugs. Most of the drugs were
useless, leftover antibiotics, heart medications,
and various other non-narcotics. But the guys did
find a small bale of grass in the top of a closet
behind a stack of books, wrapped in a raincoat.
They were still smoking it hours after the hurricane had passed, empty liquor bottles and snack
boxes strewn around the dark third floor room
they had taken residence in. Someone had gone to
the trouble of nailing wood over the inside of the
window in an effort to keep out the weather. It
wouldn't save the glass but if the wind stayed
down enough or from the right direction, maybe
the room wouldn't get so wet. It was a good place
to hole up during the big blow that was Hurricane
Katrina.

Matthew, known as "Chewie", was finishing off
a bottle of rum. He let the liquid roll around in his
mouth before swallowing and taking a drag of the
joint in his fingers. "Y'all know, now that the
storm's gone, we gotta get some money to get
outta here, go somewhere that we can get some
good stuff goin' on." He laid back on the pile of
pillows. "Everyone else is hittin' the stores on
Canal, we gotta figure out somethin' else to
do 'cause I'm not gonna challenge them crazies for
that junk. So, think. What are we gonna go get
nobody else ain't." Chewie grabbed another bottle,
whiskey, and pulled the stickers and opened it,
taking a big swig of it.

"W…we could hit the porn sh…sh…shops on B…b…Bourbon." David, "Dark" fumbled through the words and then bit into another hand full of cheese puffs. He ran his fingers across his short, dark black hair, leaving orange streaks in it, and then said, "Everyone w…w…wants p…porn."

Willem "Razor" smacked Dark on the back of the head, knocking cheese puffs out of his mouth. "Ah, nah, man. Youse dumb as hell, Dark! Not porn. Besides, they's still people on Bourbon that ain't gone nowhere. Maybe we needs to go down ta Royal and get in them fancy anti-cue stores and take that stuff."

"Nah, that won't work either. Royal has alarms and people still working and living down there. And we cain't carry that shit anywhere and sell it, it's heavy and big and we ain't got a car neither," said Lips, whose real name was Phillip, not that anyone remembered that because he had been called Lips since he was small because of his large lips that didn't seem to fit his small face.

"We…we could bbb…b…boost a car." Dark countered, swigging a large mouthful of Jack Daniels and following it with more cheese puffs. "Shshshsh…ould be eeasy since nobody's around much."

"What cars'us here ain't runnin' because a' the flood, dummy." Chewie countered. "We ain't takin' antiques. Think, people. Something small enough to carry off, and somethin' someone wants that we can pick up here and take somewhere's else to sell. There's gotta be somethin'."

As the marijuana smoke got thicker and the

alcohol disappeared from four more bottles, the guys thought about what would get them some money. Then Razor smiled, "I 'member talkin' to a guy who was lookin' for someone to get some stuff for one of those voodoo women. He said she wanted bones, heads, hands, whatever. She said that there were peoples in New Orleans and out payin' big money for real stuff."

Chewie sat up, rubbing his eyes, "Yeah and there ain't nobody guardin' the graveyards right now. We could go in, grab what we want, look for jewelry and shit, and then take the bones. Sell everything. That might work." Chewie stood and walked toward the other end of the room by the boarded window and pulled one side loose. "Gonna be dark soon. We might as well go out and get started. I figure a couple a'tire irons, a bat, and Razor's knifes should work. We'll strip the pillows and use the covers for sacks. Y'all kay wit that?"

The others nodded and kept on eating, drinking and toking. Chewie walked up to Dark and kicked him in the side, "That means get ready, dumbass. We need to put shit up where it's not gonna be found while we're gone. Find some place to hide our stash, Get movin'." The other boys moved, griping about Chewie and about having to give up their stuff. But soon everything was out of sight and they were on their way out the door with tools and bags in hand, climbing down the dark stairs to the ground floor and out of the door.

The water came up to their ankles on the

sidewalk on Basin Street. They slogged through the dark, smelly mess the block to the side gate of St. Louis One, the oldest cemetery in the city. The gate was closed, checked and locked up well before the hurricane by the guard who always was on duty. The side gate was never usually unlocked, the tourists had to enter and leave by the front gate but there was no one to stop them as the four young men climbed over the wrought iron side gate and began to search the above ground tombs for anything that could be sold on the black market or online on Ebay. They used the tire irons to pry open the tomb doors and Dark, even though Chewie was the smallest, climbed in to find the things they wanted, Chewie never, ever got his hands dirty, he always made the other guys do the work, he considered himself the 'brains.' Some tombs were empty, just dirt or little bones left, a bit of brass or silver from the handles of old, rotted coffins. The water was coming up a little into some of the crypts, making it harder to sift through the dark piles inside the crypts with very little light and the red light coming from the cellophane-covered flashlights. The red would preserve their night vision and give them a little light but it would also keep others from noticing them right off as well. It just didn't work as good for the crypt interiors, especially with the flashlight's dying batteries. It was by touch only for the most part.

They came around the corner on the northeast side, near the wall paralleling St. Louis Street. Suddenly everyone stopped, Dark plowing into Razor's back. Then he looked at why they stopped, eyes growing wide, and took three steps back, crossing himself.

"You're not scared there, Dark? Are ya?" Chewie teased him.

What made Dark scared was sitting on a brick and concrete step-tomb with a rusted cross embedded on top. In front of the cross was a card stood upright to the cross with a rock. Two jar candles, one purple and one white, were still lit and glowing in the darkness, casting shadows on the wall tombs and nearby structures. A lit cigar, a pack of Pall Mall cigarettes, two styrofoam cups with a dark liquid in them, coins, some peanuts, rice, beans, and corn piled in small cup lids, a battered black top hat, and a bottle of rum with something floating in it stood before the picture.

"I want the rum" Razor called out, running ahead and reaching out to grab the bottle.

"NO! Don't t...touch ANYTHING on th...th...there!" Dark stammered, yelling and trying to grab Razor and missing, but Razor did stop. "Do you know w...w...what th...that is?"

"It's some fucker playing with satanic shit" Chewie said, stepping up a little closer to look at the stuff on the top of the tomb. "So if you don't believe in it, it can't hurt you, dumbass fuck."

Dark crossed himself again, "Oh, y...you are S...S...SO wrong. My grand-mere w...was a voodoo w...woman and she sh...showed me this st...stuff. That's Baron Sa...Samedi, the Loa of the Dead. S...Someone's b...been trying to contact him. Everything th...there is HIS and you don't want to f...fuck with it because he w...will fuck with you if you do. I've s...seen th...things from f...fucking with the Loa and I w...won't even do th...that s...shit." Dark's hands were jammed down hard into his sagging jeans pockets, out of sight, just to prove he wasn't going to touch anything.

"Coward." Razor scoffed. He reached out and grabbed the rum bottle and opened it. It looked a little funny; some orange things were floating in the liquid. He raised the bottle to the others, as if in a salute, and took a big swig of the liquor. His eyes teared up and he tried to inhale while trying to swallow at the same time he started to blow the liquid out of his mouth, all at once. The rum bottle fell from his hand and rolled toward the tomb, still open. The spewed liquor made the candles flare high and then Razor started coughing and bending over, sweat pouring off of him. Then he started vomiting. He moaned, a strangled sound that had no form and no real sound to it. Then he grabbed the rice and the beans and shoved them into his mouth, chewing furiously. Then he grabbed both of the cups of dark liquid and drank them down, collapsing where he stood. Tears ran down his face, his lips were red and swelled, and his nose was running like he had the world's worst head cold.

Everyone else turned to Dark, who was shaking his head. "I t...toll you not to drink th...that shit! Th...that's the Baron's Piman Rum! It's got twenty-one hot p...p...peppers in it that has b...been s...s...sitting in there for months. Looking at the color, I guess they used them damned habineros, they's hotter th...than anythin'. And you drank his coffee, both cups, and ate his f...food too! I t...toll ya the Baron didn't like his sh...shit messed wit." Dark picked up the rum bottle and bowed, mumbled something, and placed it back on the altar, then crossed himself again. He backed away, not taking his eyes off of the place where the candles still burned brightly.

"That's mumbo-jumbo, dumbass." Chewie finally found his voice. "Damn near poisoned Razor, though. We need to leave this shit alone and continue what we're doing." He helped Razor up and steered him toward the next aisle. Before leaving, he grabbed the top hat and put it on his head and then, picking up the bottle of peppered rum, corked it and took it with him. It could be fun to fuck with Razor later.

They opened another six tombs and Dark had to crawl into them and bring out the items that were on their shopping list. The stinking water, the smell of old death, and the mud was hanging in everyone's nostrils except Razor's. His were still trying to drain from the rum.

When they next stopped for a break, their bags were only about a quarter full despite having been out in the dark cemetery for over five hours. The wet and hot weather was combining to make everyone grumpy.

Grumbling overtook the silence as Dark hit his head coming out of the latest crypt he had crawled into. "Man, I'm not goin' b...back in th...there. somebody else gets to." He stared at

Chewie, daring him to tell him no.

Chewie looked at him, "Chickenshit," he threw the word like a curse and turned to Lips, "Your turn, you get to go into the next one and look around." Lips raised his bat like he was going to hit Chewie but the little guy didn't move, stared at him like he would kill him where he stood, and Lips lowered the bat.

That's when they heard a rustle in the aisle behind the crypt next to them. Using hand signals they all understood, Chewie told Razor to go behind one way and the others went with Chewie to the other side, making enough noise to get the attention of whatever, or whoever, was on that aisle. What they saw stopped them and Chewie smiled, a broad, white-toothed grin that could be taken only one way...evil.

A very tall, broad, and muscular man in a long gray coat stood next to a tomb, one hand on it, a big winged ring with a dark stone on the middle finger. He didn't seem to notice the three men facing him until Chewie cleared his throat loudly and then he raised his head and looked at them. He had piercing gray eyes that seemed to look through the three robbers. He let a cocky smile cross his face. "Well, now who are you?" he asked in an Irish brogue, his head tilting to the side.

Chewie twirled the tire iron in his hand, "Nobody you need to know about. But you need to know you're not getting out of here with that pretty coat, that ring, or anything else of value. So start handing the shit over."

The man stood there, looking intensely at each

of the three men. "I guess you three think you will be taking it from me if I don't hand it over, right?" he took one step to the right to position himself in the middle of the aisle. "I have no intention of just handing anything over so I guess we are going to...what is it called, rumble?"

"Your language is WAY out of date, man. We're going to put you down and take it. And since you are choosing to fight us, we won't hold back, you'll be dead and we'll take everything. Your choice, man." Chewie kept smiling as Lips and Dark walked up next to him and then stepped in front of him. They closed the distance fast and started hitting the man with their bat and tire iron.

The man in the coat wasn't easy to hit, he side-stepped the blows and deflected the blows easily. Grabbing his assailant, the tall man hurled him, almost effortlessly, down the open aisle. The next assailant was shoved into one of the crypts. He was obviously strong, maybe stronger than he looked. The man grabbed the ironwork fencing around the tomb he was near and wrenched it out of the ground, wielding it like a battering ram, thrust the third assailant across the walkway and into the side of a tomb. The fencing shielded him from Lips' ineffectual bat swings. The sound of the hits echoed off the tombs and into the darkness, metal hitting metal. Dark roused and crept around the tomb where Lips was pinned. Emerging from the shadows, tire-arm raised, he struck the man hard on the hand. Grabbing the fence from his slackened grip, Dark threw it beyond reach. Then both stepped toward the man again, weapons ready. The man grabbed Dark and flung him across a step tomb to the ground. Lips swung the bat at the man, who deftly ducked and grabbed Lips' leg under the hem of the baggy shorts. He yanked hard and pulled him down to the asphalt, a well-placed kick to the head left him stunned. Then he turned back toward their leader.

He stepped toward Chewie and then had to re-throw Dark, who had recovered to come at him again. He edged closer and closer to Chewie, who never stopped grinning like a death's head and never made a move to hit the man, just motioning to the man, throwing him the "come on" sign like he was waiting for him to make his move. Chewie was nothing if not cool in a fight, he never panicked and he always bragged to others about not ever getting beaten. As he maneuvered toward the grinning thug, Dark and Lips hit him from two sides, one up top and the other around the knees. The football-like move had been calculated to drag the stranger down but he stayed upright despite efforts.

Chewie watched, fascinated with the fight the big man put up. He seemed to be standing up to everything the gang could put out. Without an equalizer, they might just lose this fight. One against four and they might lose.

"Oh HELL no!" Chewie said. He stepped up, holding the bottle of Piman Rum at his side, looking for a chance to use it somehow.

Suddenly, from behind and above, Razor

dropped onto the stranger's back, both straight razors open in his hand. He reached over and cut the man's neck. The stranger tried to reach around to grab him but Lips and Dark struck at him at the same time, pounding his knees backwards with hard swings that should have pulverized the joints. He let out a strangling and wet scream and stumbled but did not fall as expected. Razor hung on with one hand and pulled the coat down the stranger's shoulders and arms, effectively pinning the man's arms down.

The move exposed his back, allowing Razor a look at two large, gray-feathered appendages that looked like wings. The appendages moved and Razor, still holding the coat, reached up with his right arm and cut deeply into the muscle coming from the joint in the man's back. This caused the stranger to shriek in pain and attempt to reach for the person behind him again but his hands were tangled in the coat. He tried to spin but the pain in his legs slowed him down. The other robbers were raining blows down on his torso and it was all he could do to protect his middle.

Then Razor reached up and cut the muscle on the second feathered appendage. Blood, red and sticky, was flowing from both wounds as well as the one on the man's neck where Razor had cut him. Any normal man would have been dead by now. But this man wasn't normal. Everything the robbers had put the stranger through, this one was managing to stay alive and on his feet. Chewie, still watching the fight, was amazed by the strength of will the man was showing.

Chewie saw this as his chance. He stepped up close enough to reach the stranger. He lifted his arm and swung the bottle as hard as he could. It landed across the man's head with a thud and the man staggered. Renewing his effort, Chewie swung the bottle again, connecting with the skull of the seemingly invincible man.

The bottle shattered, casting the pepper-spiked rum across the man's head and down into his eyes.

This had the desired effect. The man screamed a pained scream as he clawed and tried to pull his arms up to try to wipe the painful liquid off his face and eyes. His arms pinned by the coat, he spun in circles to try to dislodge the person behind him who was holding his arms down.

Chewie yelled, "Get him now!" Dark and Lips picked up their weapons and swung for the fence, Dark connecting with the tire iron on one side a second before Lips smacked him on the other side with the bat.

The man dropped like a stone. The three assailants continued hitting and kicking the prone man until he ceased to move.

Then Chewie motioned, Dark and lips picked the man up to a slumping standing position. Razor continued cutting and the pulled the wing-like appendages from the body, blood flowing down the man's back.

Razor reached up, put both of his hands into the cuts in the muscles he had just made and pulled down, back, then up as hard as he could, ripping the muscles the rest of the way and pulling the feathered appendages off completely. This violation brought the man back to the fight as the pain in his back escalated, he shrieked again. This time it was obvious that he felt his wings tear from their sockets, the pain blinding. The stranger fell, going down on one knee and then got hauled to his feet again. The four young men surrounding him laughed, someone stepped up, from the sound. The man was still blinded and the pain had slowed his thinking. Once again, Lips hit the stranger in the head and for a moment he probably saw stars as pain exploded across his brain. Then everything went blessedly dark for the man as the he fell against the door of the crypt, shattering it with his back and shoulders.

"Take the coat and that ring off him. Check him for a wallet, cards, anything. He only thought he could handle us." Chewie ordered. "And what the hell are you holding, Razor?"

Razor held up his prizes, smiling broadly, "I don't know how or why, but the guy was wearing these wings. I had to cut them to get them off of him. I don't think they are real but they did have a blood sack or something because they did bleed. I'm not taking them with me, they smell funny." Razor threw the wings to the ground.

Chewie reached down and pulled a long gray feather from the severed appendages and popped it into the band of the battered top hat he wore. "Well, we're done for the night. Let's go home and we can do St. Louis 2 tomorrow night. I'm hungry and need a hit before I get some sleep." Chewie turned away from where the stranger lay, broken and bleeding on the steps of one of the crypts. "Leave him here, something will eat him." The men grabbed their sacks and walked down the aisle toward Conti Street and the gate they had climbed over. The thought of a dry place to relax with food and alcohol sounded good. They joked with each other on the way across the graveyard, laughing and cutting up, oblivious to anything going on around them.

The wings began to steam in the hot August night and became liquid almost before the assailants got out of the cemetery. One lone gray feather lay next to the body of its owner.

Through the rubble of the marble crypt door, two small, brown hands reached under the big stranger's shoulders and quickly dragged his body into the dark, forbidding grave. Then a hand reached out again and snagged the feather and disappeared. A piece of wood was slammed up against the open hole, sealing it shut. The sound of rocks being placed against the mahogany panel came from inside the tomb. Suddenly, the graveyard was silent again except for the sound of distant laughter as the grave robbers left the dead to their rest.

Chapter Five

THE BIG MAN was dragged into position on the upper area of the vault on the faded pink mattress and pillow. Even though his legs were long, the woman in the ragged and dirty blue dress managed to get him completely up on the platform. She carefully arranged his arms comfortably on his chest and crossed his feet. Then she dragged a long, dirty pink and white sheet up his body to his stomach. She frowned as she pulled it up a little higher and noticed that it slid over his boots and ankles, leaving them exposed.

"My, you are a tall one!" she exclaimed, shaking her head. She turned away and reached down and scratched the ears of a very large, long haired, tortoise shell cat. "Hey Baron. I have a job for you. I am going to need a big nutria brought back here constrained so that it's not going to get into trouble. I'll wait to eat until you get back and we'll share, but make it quick, if you please." The big cat's eyes glinted bright gold, even in the darkness of the tomb. The woman moved a couple of the marble rocks and slid the mahogany cover open enough for the cat to leave. He exited the space slowly, making a show of waving his big, fluffy tail in the dark space a few times as a farewell. The woman laughed and threw a small bone at the appendage "You show off! Go on." She slid the door shut the moment the fur was past the opening.

The small space was dark and damp. And miserably hot in the aftermath of what obviously had been yet another hurricane. Not that she really felt it, she didn't really feel temperature. The little crypt had held up just fine, the wind and rain never really reaching inside, always tight and safe from the elements. Until the big man lying in her bed had broken the door, it had been rather air and sunlight tight too. The little broken bit at the bottom left of the door had never been a problem; she had a big rock that fit just perfectly. It may not be much, but it was home and it was hers. She had enough to eat, she had Baron to visit with, and she had Marcus whenever he felt like talking to her. Reaching down under the sleeping platform, she grasp a white ball-like item on a wooden box. She pulled it out and sat down on another box.

It was a skull. There was a bit of black hair still clinging on the top of the head and most of the teeth were still there, the jaw held on by pink material tied around the mandible and through holes on the skull that had been crudely cut. She looked into the eye sockets like she was looking into the eyes of a lover. "Marcus, I need to ask some advice. I have a big human that got dropped, literally, on my doorstep. Baron and I are hungry and human is very tempting. I've sent

Baron for a nutria to help me feed the human once he's awake. Am I doing the right thing? Is this really all right to do?"

She sat in silence listening to the something that only she could hear, nodding periodically. "I knew you would have the answers, darling Marcus. I will share our supper with you after we finish. Thank you!" She closed her eyes and gently kissed the skull. Then she reached and placed it back on the box under the bed. She occupied her time straightening up the small space she called home. She retrieved the stained bowl she used for Baron's food and set it on the floor near the bed. She grabbed a few rat bones that she could find that Baron left around the room and slid the door open and threw them out, grimacing as she did so. Baron was clean at everything but his eating and he always left the carcasses around after supper.

As she was preparing to close the door, she heard a small growl and Baron poked his head through the door. She opened it wider and Baron strutted in, behind him walked a very large, filthy rat-like creature. Probably about 25 pounds, it was brown and smelly with a long nose with whiskers and a long, naked tail. Baron had brought home the required nutria. It was entranced, walking into the room and then over to a corner and sitting down, eyes glazed over and oblivious to anything else but seemingly the end of its nose.

Closing the door and securing it with the rocks, the woman turned back to Baron and scratched his ears again, "You, my dear feline, are marvelous. That's a magnificent specimen of nutria and will work very well. Now, are you ready for your supper?" She picked up the bowl, made of the top of a skull, and turned toward the unconscious man on the bed, then she bowed her head and said "Bless us, O Lord and these gifts which we are about to receive from thy bounty, through Christ our Lord, Amen." She rolled him to the side so that she could see his back. There were two very big, deep cuts on it, still weeping blood lightly from the knife that had been used. The woman reached out, dragged a very sharp fingernail across the top cut and placed the bowl down below, catching the blood. Before she could stop the blood flow, Baron jumped up to the bed and began to bathe the cut with his tongue. The cut began to close and then stopped bleeding. He bent down and bathed the other cut, stopping its bleeding as well. The woman smiled and moved the bowl and picked up the heavy cat and placed both on the floor, Baron going straight to the bowl and lapping at the warm, red blood.

Then she climbed up on the bed, rolled the man back over, and climbed over him to his left side. She lay down in the crook of his shoulder and listened to his heart beat for a few moments. She noticed a cut on his head and wet her fingers and ran them over the cut. Despite the cuts, burns, and the bruises, he was obviously very handsome. She ran them over his face, memoriz- ing the look of his strong cheekbones and then his lips. With a sad smile, she stroked his hair and then sighed. She closed her eyes for a moment and then leaned up on her elbow. She opened her mouth and bent down to his neck First she licked the gaping cut and kept going until the ugly gash closed.

"Eww, what is that? Owwww!" she said as she first tasted the skin. Then her lips and tongue began to burn like a fire was on them. She rolled down and grabbed an urn from the floor beside the box table. She turned it up and drank from it, seeking to quell the pain. After a few minutes, she grabbed a piece of old cloth that might have been pink at one time, and wet a corner of it. She returned to the body and began to wash the neck to remove the offending coating.

She wrinkled her nose, "Rum, with peppers. Somebody has been messing with voodoo." She said to Baron, "I can begin again once I get this all cleaned up."

Once she was sure things were clean, she bent down and put her lips over his jugular vein, which had been missed when the slice to his neck had happened, and bit down into the flesh. The man moaned and brought both arms around her as she drank from the open wound. She drank deeply and for what seemed to her a very long time, it had been many, many years since she had tasted human blood and she was almost unable to pull away from the sweet, coppery taste. Finally she licked the wound closed and sat up. The man was still totally unconscious, his movements more a reaction than a thought. She breathed a prayer for the man's soul and crossed herself.

She smiled at him, her cheeks bright pink and her lips red, and she pulled her wrist up to her mouth and bit, opening up her own vein. Then she placed it on the man's mouth and opened his lips with her other hand. "Drink, sir. Drink and live." She spoke the words that she remembered that were said to her. She squeezed the blood into his open mouth and massaged his newly-healed throat to get him to swallow. Then he grabbed her arm and pulled it to his lips, fastening on to it and sucking, swallowing in desperation like a man that had not drunk in weeks. She allowed him to drink for a few minutes and then, gently, she pulled her wrist away and licked the wound closed. She bent down and whispered into his ear, "Shhhh. Rest now. You can drink again in a little while. Rest now, let your body heal. I will wake you soon and we can talk." The man relaxed, the tension easing out of his face.

She slipped over him and down to the floor again. Going under the bed, she grabbed something and crossed over to the still-quiet nutria. She raised her arm and in her hand was a white knife-shaped object. She plunged it into the neck of the animal and across, severing the artery. Blood welled up and then started to spray. She fastened her mouth over the dirty hole and allowed the blood to flow down her throat, replacing the blood lost to the sleeping man on her bed. Once the blood slowed, she picked up Baron's bowl, caught more of the blood for him, laying the dead animal on the floor. Baron would probably feed on it again before she had to throw the carcass out of the door; he earned it because he had gone to retrieve it. She pet the sleeping cat's fur and then climbed back onto the bed, over the man, and back onto the place on his left shoulder. She laid her head down on him and, almost instinctively, his arm curled around over her, across her waist. Drawing the cover over her, she closed her eyes and slipped into an oblivious sleep just as the sun rose over the ruined city of New Orleans.

Chapter Six

SULLIVAN'S EYES POPPED open, instantly awake. He strained to figure out where he was as his head tried to chase the last of what had to be a killer headache away. He smelled blood, then rum and peppers. And he was laying on something hard and holding something soft and cuddly...

He sat up abruptly, bumping his head on the ceiling of the crypt. His movement dropped the woman he was holding onto the palette and she sighed as her eyes came open and she yawned, waking. He looked down at her as he rubbed his head, turning on his side toward her. She was a small thing, very light brown skinned with long dark hair, brown eyes and the cutest little nose Sully had ever seen. Wait, did he just look at her nose?

"Hello. Who are you?" he asked, trying not to notice her lush lips. What was his brain doing? This was not his normal train of thought.

She smiled at him. The smile was genuine, beautiful. "My name is Lilly. Lilly Lenora Marchantel. What is your name?"

Her voice was pretty, light and musical, Sully

noticed. Then he wondered what was going on with his brain, again. This fascination with her was becoming disconcerting. He smiled back at her, "My name is Sullivan."

"Oh, Sullivan what?" there was that smile again. It lit up the little room like a light switch had been tripped.

"Just Sullivan. I usually just get called Sully by my friends. May I call you Lilly or do you go by another name?" he smiled back, hoping his smile was a warm one and not touched so much with the pain he was feeling in his head.

"Lilly is fine. Are you feeling all right? You weren't doing too well when you came in and I thought I heard you hit your head as I awoke." her language was formal, not at all like most of the New Orleans residents he encountered. It was like she was very well educated or spent a lot of time reading old novels and watching old movies. It was charming, though.

He started to look around the room but he didn't seem to be able to take his eyes off of her. Where was this coming from? He never had feelings like this, ever. "I, uh, my head hurts, looks like I hit it on the ceiling but, uh, I think I will live." He had a vague memory of...what? "What happened" floated across his conscience and then left him. He took a second to glance up at the ceiling and then back at her. Then back at the ceiling with a larger look. It was close, too close, it looked like there was about four feet between the boards he laid on and the stone ceiling; it was not even enough room to sit up completely. He looked at Lilly again. "This is a very small place. Do you live here?"

There went that smile again. She didn't just smile with her mouth; she seemed to smile with her entire face, and body. He couldn't help but stare at her. "Why yes, Mr. Sullivan, I live here. It's not much but it's home to me, Baron, and Marcus."

"Please, it's just Sully. Drop the Mr. It makes me feel, I don't know, old or something. Care to show me around and introduce me to your housemates." Sully was hoping that this Baron and Marcus weren't close friends with her, or were ugly and old, or not intimate with.... What the hell was going on with him?

"Certainly. If you would excuse me, I can crawl over you and get down and then show you whatever you wish." She leaned up and sat cross-legged, curled up small enough to sit and face him. She was petite, she must not be much over five feet tall and her ebony hair was haphazardly tucked up on her head in an attempt at a bun but much of it had escaped and cascaded well down her back. "I will need you to turn to your back so I can cross over you easier, sir," she gestured with one nicely shaped small hand.

Sully hesitated. The thought of Lilly's body on top of his, sliding across him, bodies touching intimately. He was suddenly aware, overly aware, that his fascination with Lilly had produced something very unexpected. He was extremely uncomfortable in his groin area. His jeans had been tight before, now his penis, hard and throbbing with need and want, was painful. He reached up to loosen them and then stopped, his eyes fixing on Lilly's face. What the hell was he thinking; he couldn't take the jeans off in front of a human woman. He bit his lip and then rolled to his back, moaning. Trying to keep her from noticing his huge boner, he took both hands and put them on his head. "Go ahead and cross, my head just hurts." He lied. He lied? Wait a minute, he was incapable of lies. What...

Lilly put her hands on his thighs and slid over his knees, apparently not even noticing his discomfort in his groin. She jumped down, and motioned for him to come with her. "Be very careful sitting up; don't hit your head again. I don't know if you are too tall to completely stand up and, unfortunately the floor is wet because of the storm we had, but I have a couple of boxes we can sit on. Come on down." She took his arm as if to be able to help him. If he fell on her, he would squash her flat with his weight.

He partially sat up, leaned back, and slid to his feet. He could stand up straight, his head touching the ceiling. Looking around, he figured out where he was, inside one of the crypts in the cemetery he was at when...when, what was it that happened again in that cemetery? He strained to remember and his head hurt even more.

He could visualize people, men, a fight, and pain in his back. He didn't remember exactly what happened but he had a pain memory and he flexed his back muscles to pull the wings from the space in his back. When nothing moved and he felt a strange empty feeling, he began to panic and reached back and tried to feel where his wings would attach. His skin felt smooth, there was no wing lock, no armature joints. His wings were gone, his back felt like what he thought a human's might. "Lilly, would you please raise my shirt and look at my back?" Not only had his hard-on gone down, he forgot all about his new crush on the woman in the panic he was feeling about his wings.

Lilly stepped behind him and raised the bloody, shredded shirt. She ran her hands across his back softly. "Everything looks good back here. I think you've healed really well." She smiled at him as she pulled the shirt back down. He turned toward her and caught the smile but it didn't make him feel any better.

"Healed? What happened to me? What did you do?" Sully stepped toward her, grabbing her shoulders and shaking her more violently than he meant to. His eyes searched hers, trying to find the answer to the question that was making his heart race and his breathing shallow. "What did you do?" he roared, anger blossoming out of nowhere. A small voice in the back of his mind tried to tell him that this wasn't normal, he didn't react like this but he pushed it away. He let the anger flow over him and out every pore of his body. He was furious.

She blanched, her honey-colored skin getting as white as coffee with too much milk. She bit her lip and went limp, terrified at Sullivan's sudden anger. Tears welled up and spilled down her cheeks. "I didn't do anything to hurt you, I promise. I saved you."

Sullivan shook her again, "Bullshit!" He roared, "You did something that took my wings. Now, for the last time, what did you do?" His entire face had gone from soft handsome to very hard and full of hatred. She could feel the anger coming off of him in waves. She hung her head and when she looked up again, the tears were flowing down her face… blood tears. He recoiled from her, screaming in rage and horror. "A vampire? You are a vampire?" Nothing but innocent bewilderment registered across her blood-stained face.

"Did you turn me? Did you? Answer me, bitch. You did, didn't you? DIDN'T YOU!" The accusation seemed to carry out of the small room, out of the area, and across all of New Orleans, a shout of anger, fear, and complete heartbreak. Sullivan raised his hand and slapped Lilly across the cheek, knocking her against the wall. She continued to cry bloody tears, curled in the heap of torn faded blue rags where she landed while Sully looked at his bloody hand.

He thought his heart was beating fast and hard but when he stopped to listen, it was his imagination. He stopped his heaving breath and found he didn't need to do that either. Neither bodily function was necessary anymore. He was dead. Or, to be more precise, undead. He put both hands on his head, grabbing his hair and pulling, and screaming in abject frustration. He fell to his knees, bending over with his head to the wet, slimy floor of the room. Lilly scrambled backward under the bed chamber and grabbed the skull and bone knife off of the box. She hugged the skull to her, seeking the solace of her good friend. The knife she held out toward Sullivan in case he came toward her again.

Something shot past her out of the dark and jumped straight up, then landed with an ungodly howl on Sullivan's back. The man shot up like a rocket, reaching behind him attempting to reach whatever had landed and attached massive hooks into the muscles in his back. The pain was blinding, and then there was a very sharp burning bite on the back of his neck that felt like the cords of his muscles were being severed. Sully whirled in circles, reaching behind him, yelling, trying to get a handle on the thing. Then he turned and slammed hard backwards hard against the marble wall. His only thought was to stop the attack. Whatever was on him turned loose after the collision with the wall and fell to the floor. It shook and walked, wobbly, to Lilly and lay in her lap. Sully stopped and drew back a fist, his gaze fixed on the thing in her lap.

"Sullivan. Stop. Please. Don't hurt us again. We want no trouble. Go if you want, leave us be. I am sorry. But stop." Lilly's voice was small, almost child-like. She was afraid. She was afraid of him.

The thought stopped the angel, former angel, whatever he was now. Confused, angry, hurt, the big man sank once again to his knees in the bloody muck and stared at her, all the anger draining out of him. The two of them looked at each other for a time, saying nothing but each trying to assess what the other would do next. Lilly cuddled the skull in one arm and stroked the big cat with the hand holding the knife, never taking her eyes off the man facing her. Finally she laid the knife down into her lap next to the large cat, who she continued to stroke.

Sully tried to calm down and assess what reality was now. The tracks of the beautiful girl, uh, vampire's blood tears had dried on her face, her eyes no longer happy but haunted. The gold eyes of the big calico cat blazed with hatred, it never took its eyes off him like it knew he was now evil, ruined. Lilly clutched that skull like it was her last friend in the world. HE had done that. He, one of the Enforcer Angels, had lusted, had lost his temper, and had beaten a woman. He had sinned, fallen. He did not know what had happened, how he came to this point. This scared him more than the fact that he had no wings and had fallen from grace. As he sat, numbing, trying to remember what had happened to his idyllic life, tears began to flow down his own cheeks. He tried to wipe them with the back of his hand and his hand came away bloody. He moaned, the moaning cry of the damned and put his face in his hands, shutting out the world, trying to shut out everything that he had done. He sat, crying into his hands, silently mourning all that he had done and the loss of his life.

LILLY WATCHED SULLY, her heart breaking. She had thought she saved his life, not taken it. She had been beaten before, worse than the mere slap and yelling he had given her but this had hurt so much more, she didn't believe she had deserved his anger. He was dying, bleeding to death. The bite and transfusion should have made him better, not made him into a vampire, whatever that was. He was angry at her. For saving him!

She bent to the skull and whispered as quietly as she could, "Marcus, what should I do? This was not what we discussed. I know we saved him, he doesn't get that, he thinks I did something else to him, I hurt him somehow." She sat, looking like she was listening to the skull. She didn't see Sully watching her from between his fingers, his heightened hearing having caught the whisper.

"But what do I do? He's not going to listen to me, he's too angry to listen. I can't make him listen, he's bigger than me!" her voice began to get a bit louder as she argued with the skull.

"Shut up!" Sully growled. "You look stupid talking to that damned dead thing. I hear you, I can hear everything. I'm not going to hit you again but I don't care to listen to any more of your whining shit. You didn't save me, you DAMNED me, don't you realize what you did, you stupid woman? I would not have died from a little blood loss. I didn't need your brand of *help*, I needed left alone to heal so I could go back to work." his eyes were as red as the tear tracks on his face.

"I did not mean to harm you, Sullivan. I thought I was doing good. I am sorry. I am sorry I pulled you in to protect you. I am sorry I stopped your bleeding and I hid you from those men who tried to kill you. I'm sorry I ever tried to help you. I want you to go, now, and find your own way. You no longer want to stay here and you have nothing you can learn here, so go." As she talked, Lilly's back had straightened, she had raised her chin and she held the skull in her right hand like a talisman, her entire demeanor changing, her aura stretching to show someone who intended to take no more grief from the man.

Sully became interested, despite his anger. He had to admit, Lilly was a very strong woman, despite her quirky actions. Where was the anger coming from, he had never been angry like that? He had every right, admittedly, with the change, but that would have never happened without it. He had lowered his hands and then sat, watching her watching him. That damned cat was watching him too. It yawned, like it was bored already with the standoff and Sully got a look at why his shoulder hurt so much, the fucking cat was a vampire. Fangs that looked like a sabre tooth came out of the mouth and he swore they dripped blood, his blood.

Where did that thought of the use of the word "fucking" come from? Another something he had never done. It was a morning/night/whatever of a whole lot of nevers.

"So, are you going? Please leave my home,

Sullivan." When he didn't move immediately, she remembered how Miss Lulu could verbally handle any man that got out of hand in her house. Lilly straightened herself and in the most powerful voice she could muster said, "Or I will have the Baron and Marcus escort you out." she snapped at him, raising one eyebrow that made her face look a bit lopsided and a whole lot more interesting.

"No, I'll go when I am finished figuring out what is going on, finished figuring out what to do, and finished with you." He tried to hold on to the growling, angry Sully but the Lustful Sully began to come up within him, and that was awkward. Why couldn't he just be Sully without all the enhancements?

"You think so? As I said, this is *my* home, you are not welcome and I am wanting you to leave. You can do your self-assessment somewhere else, anywhere else. Baron, give him two minutes to gather himself and then make sure he gets out. Marcus, assist him, if you would." She said the second set of instructions to the skull she held in her hand and Sullivan had no idea what she thought was going to happen with that.

He turned his head toward the door as his ears picked up laughter and conversation coming from outside, within the cemetery but not very far away. He rose to his feet, crouching, and turned his head back to Lilly, his finger on his lips to quiet her.

His movements having stopped, she did not quiet but rather raised her voice to assert her dominance once again, "You will not silence me, sir! Leave now!" His head whipped around and the look on his face was one designed to close her mouth without saying a word and it had the desired effect for a minute. Lilly could tell he was serious about wanting silence. Then she heard what he had, voices carrying across the area. She motioned to him to come back under the sleeping area, into the only partially hidden area in the room. She knew what those voices were, they belonged to the men who had hurt Sullivan before and they were not nice men. She had sat inside the small tomb listening in fear as the man next to her fought for what turned out to be his life. She knew they had to be very quiet so they would not be discovered. Sully wasn't moving and she silently got up and took him by the arm and tried to move him under the bed into the darkness. He finally moved, crouching against the corner in the darkness and wishing he had something to use as a weapon.

Lilly walked over to the dead carcass of the nutria, laying by the box that had held her things. She grabbed it and dragged it toward the door, placing it across the opening, about a foot back. Using the bone knife, she cut the head, tail, and legs off, putting them under the box. Then she made a slice on the belly and pulled the skin, running her bone knife across the flesh to loosen the hide until it came off as well. It went over the box. She took the skull from the floor and rolled it on the bloody meat, covering it with gore. Reaching into the belly, she pulled the intestines loose and draped them across the body and around the skull. She looked to Baron and motioned him up to the skull and gore.

The cat did not need more instruction; he walked up to the mess and started eating, growling and making as much noise as he could. He put one paw up on the skull, holding it down and showing his large claws as he tore pieces of meat from the dead beast. As he ate, Lilly slipped back into the darkness next to Sully, settling as close as she could. Sullivan put an arm around her protectively and pulled her close. They sat, quietly, Sullivan hoping silently that the voices would go away instead of coming closer, he did not feel like having another run-in with the men who had beaten him and cut him. He didn't remember all of what happened but it had led to the loss of his wings, the loss of his life, and the loss of his virtues. Having time to think about it, his anger was misplaced, Lilly wasn't at fault for what happened. In reality, it was those voices out there, getting closer, cussing and swearing, sounding drunk as they hit and broke various things, laughing that were responsible and Sully promised himself that the four would not get away with what they had done, since he was dammed he might as well take advantage and get a little revenge, for himself and for the way he had treated Lilly. He looked down at her and hugged her a bit closer.

Lilly was confused. One minute Sullivan was nice, almost to the point of seduction, something Lilly was very familiar with. Then he was yelling at her, hitting her, and blaming her for everything that had happened. And arguing with her. Men didn't argue with her, they tried to woo her, charm her. But not Sullivan, he berated her. And then he changed and was now holding her again and smiling. She shook her head, trying to figure him out was going to give her a headache.

Chapter Seven

CHEWIE FOLLOWED BEHIND his guys. Everyone had a huge buzz, having discovered a virtual goldmine of cocaine stashed in an abandoned car in the projects and had liberally sampled the goods before hiding them for future "testing and distribution." But, as they were downing the last of the liquor they had liberated from a closed bar on S. Robertson, Chewie started remembering that strange guy they fought in the cemetery the night before or whenever it was, he couldn't remember with all the booze making his brain fuzzy. He had fought hard until Razor had cut those weird feathered wing-like things off the guy, then he went down like a pussy. When they went back, he was gone and Chewie knew the guy wasn't able to walk off. So, either somebody found him and carried him off, or, more likely, he crawled into one of the closest, opened tombs, and either died or was dying. And Chewie wanted him not only dead, but he wanted a piece of the guy. Maybe a hand, or, even better, his scalp, like the old warriors did to enemies.

So, once again, they were armed with their

crowbars, bat, Razor's knife, and this time a gun Dark had found with the cocaine, walking through St. Louis One cemetery, breaking into graves, taking skulls and other bones, whatever else they could get, and looking for that strange man.

"Chewie, m...man, y...you be crazy tonight. W...we got... we got enough b...bones, m...man. Let's just go get s...some more b...b...booze and go home an get loaded again." Dark complained.

Lips smacked him on the back of the head with his hand, "Chickenshit!" and he clucked like a hen.

"You are such a pussy, Dark, since you saw that damned grave with the candle on it." Razor taunted the man, dancing around him, waving his hands like he was dancing.

"Well, w...well at least *I* didn't dr...drink the offering f...from the altar to the Baron Samedi!" Dark tossed back.

"Shut the fuck up, asswipe. I didn't know what it was, and I was thirsty. Besides, I got paid back. My stomach still hurts and I can't taste anything, and you should be wearing my asshole, it burns like someone has a hot poker shoved up it. Burns to fart and really burns to shit. Hell, it burns to sit even!" Razor made a face as he rubbed one butt cheek.

"Quit whining. You deserved that for messin' with the voodoo.

"Like you didn't?" Razor shot back, pointing at the top hat that Chewie wore.

"Fuck you, Raz." Chewie spit, "Now, we need

to find that tomb we had the fight at. I want to see if that guy is dead or if he's gone somewhere. I don't want the cops trying to find us when this is over because he was alive and talked. So, let's find him—or his dead body—so we can go on and get out of this damned place. I'm tired of the stench in this broke-down-ass town." Chewie said, walking on ahead to the place he remembered being.

He spotted the blood on the crypts first, splatters made by the gushing from the cuts that were made in those weird wings. It was all over the side of the double crypt that bore the name "McCall-Jones". In front of the crypt was a drying puddle of goo where they had left the wings. One side was still sealed with the original marble door but the other was covered from the inside with an old piece of dark mahogany wood.

"From the inside!" Chewie said aloud, confirming what his brain was seeing, "Guys, this is it. Kick that son of a bitch in and let's see who's in there." He smiled in spite of himself. The guy had to be in there, someone had to have put that board up on the door space.

Lips stepped up, bat in hand, ready to swing like he was going to hit a major league pitch. "No, Lips, not with the bat. Move it to the side with your hands so we can see what's on the other side." Chewie said, stopping Lips in mid-swing. Lips snarled and threw the bat down, moving in to move the wood to the side with his hands. The wood moved easily, sliding to the left with little effort. Chewie's flashlight beam shined past Lips and into the dark crypt.

"Holy Jesus, Mother of God!" Lips screamed as he crab-walked back from where he had fallen on his ass as he caught sight of something inside.

"You dumb fuck, it's Holy Mary...Mother of..." Razor started to correct him and stopped. He made the Sign of the Cross and stepped back, his voice a mere whisper, "What the seven Hells is THAT?"

The red light shined dimly into the small space to reveal a very bloody, mutilated body, the entrails pulled out and spread across the body. The skull lay at the top, bloody with the eyes removed. A very large, multicolored cat sat facing them, looking at them, a gargoyle with bloody gold eyes, both front paws bloody and on the body, and the mouth chewing on a strand of intestines. The minute they looked at the cat, it let out a long, menacing growl. Never dropping the gore in its mouth, the cat stood on its back legs and pulled up to its full height, showing how very big it really was.

"If that's your guy, Chewie, he's not gonna tell nothin' to nobody" Razor said, taking a couple of steps back. Everyone had done so, leaving Chewie out front facing the cat. Chewie was watching the cat and trying to figure out if the body was, indeed, the stranger they had met up with the previous night. His eyes kept going from the cat to the body to the skull and back to the growling cat. Something was not right but Chewie was not sure just what it was. It took a bit for his coke-addled brain to slow enough to process the scene.

Then he looked at the skull again. The thing was gray and had blood on it. It wasn't a fresh skull and there was a whisp of hair. It was a plant. Someone wanted them to think it was someone. And the body didn't look human, more like animal. "It's a fucking trick. That's not human. That bastard is alive and around here, probably watching us and laughing his ass off, making fools of us. Lips, use that bat on that cock-suckin' cat and then Razor, get in there and check that tomb, I bet that son of a bitch is in there." Chewie was almost hysterical, screaming his frustration. The other guys stood, mouths agape, staring at him.

"No way, man. I am not going after that big cat. It's already mad; I am not becoming cat food for you. You want it bashed, you go get it and hit it." Lips threw the bat to Chewie and stepped back further.

Chewie caught the bat with one hand and took a step and raised the bat like he was going to coldcock Lips with his own bat. Then he turned around to face the crypt and the cat. Looking at the situation, hitting the cat with the bat was going to be the hard way to settle the situation. He turned to Dark, "Gimme the piece, boy." he stepped up and took the gun from Dark's shaking hand. Putting the bat at his feet, Chewie reached up and aimed the gun toward the cat and squeezed the trigger. The 9mm Beretta boomed, spitting out the bullet that raced into the tomb and toward the cat, who, amazingly, dodged it with a yowl and sprung out of the tomb. It landed on Chewie's outstretched arm with all claws extended and planted its fangs and teeth into the thugs face close to the eyes. Biting, scratching and growling simultaneously with Chewie's shouts and attempts to pull or shake the cat off him. The other thugs stood, transfixed by the scene, not making a move toward the cat or Chewie. Finally, the big cat leapt off the now bloody and wheezing man and came to rest on the roof of a tomb, the bloody golden eyes and dripping bloody mouth making a very horrifying sight. The cat let out a very loud yowl, a war cry aimed at the men standing behind the writhing body on the ground. Dark did not need a second scare; he grabbed the gun from beside Chewie, turned, and ran down the row of tombs back toward the Iberville Projects. Lips followed him, leaving the bat behind.

The cat growled low and deep, looking at Razor with an unblinking malevolent gaze. "I'm not afraid of you, cat, but I'm not going to do anything to you. I just want to get my friend and we'll get out of here. You can have this damned place, we ain't comin' back." he cautiously scooted up to Chewie, leaned down, and picked the man up, putting his arm around the mutilated body and grabbing his bloody mangled hand. Chewie let out a scream and the cat yowled again, louder than ever. Razor didn't look back but took off running, dragging Chewie along with him.

Baron, not willing to give up the taunting of the stupid humans, followed along behind them, growling and yowling, from tomb-top to tomb-top until he was satisfied that the four were gone over the gate and out of the cemetery. Then he jumped down to the path and with a flip of his tail, he strutted back to the tomb where Lilly and Sullivan waited for him.

AS BARON SAUNTERED back into the crypt he was flipping his tail from side to side and, Sullivan would swear, grinning like the Cheshire cat from Alice in Wonderland. Lilly stood up and grabbed the cat around the neck and hugged him, bloody fur and all. "You great and wonderful feline! You are brave and strong and smarter than any other cat on the planet. Thank you for chasing those awful men away. When we can, I'm going to find you the biggest fish and treat you to something special." She picked him up and hugged him to her. The cat was almost as big as she was, it seemed, and the look he gave Sullivan was one of begging to be helped. He may be Lilly's cat but he certainly did not like the "good kitty" treatment.

"Uh, Lilly, I think we need to gather your things and get out of here. It's not safe anymore." Sullivan prompted, in part to save Baron from further humiliation as Lilly started raining kisses on the cat's nose, causing the gruff old cat to sneeze, and in part because he honestly believed that it wasn't safe to stay in St. Louis One. He knew guys like Chewie, now that he had been humiliated and the only way he would be able to regain his lost status was to return and kill Baron and anyone else who might have viewed his disgrace. "Lilly, you need to decide what you want to take with you and we need to get out of this cemetery right now before the sun comes up." he said again, stressing the need to move.

Lilly stopped kissing and cooing over the cat and set him on the floor. She straightened up and looked up at Sullivan. "What makes you think I would be leaving my home to go with you?" she wiped her sticky and furry hands on her ruined and faded dress and put both hands on her hips. Then she raised one eyebrow. It was a set of gestures that made Sully want to smile. She wanted to look menacing but was managing only to look totally adorable and he fought to keep from grinning.

"Well, looking at it like this, I was wrong to lose my temper earlier, I'm sorry I slapped you, I need to make it up to you, your home is ruined, those idiots know where you live and will be back, your cat doesn't want to be here either, and now we can't seal this one up and be safe. I hope those are all reasons to get you to get your things and go with me. I have a place we can go, a real building with a bed, a bathtub for a nice, hot bath, safe and out of the sun. And the goon squad won't be able to find us." He smiled at her and held out a hand.

Lilly chewed on her lip with her front teeth; it was a habit he was coming to know as her "thinking pose." Finally she let out the breath she was holding, dropping her arms and reached out to take his hand. "Ok, you may be right on this. I need to bring a few things with me. Let me get them and we can go." She let him go and went to the sleeping area and grabbed her pillow and blanket. She stuffed the small blanket in with the pillow. From an edge of the headboard, which Sullivan could recognize now as part of a casket, she carefully took down a rosary and placed it in the pillowcase. She moved the nutria skin from the box and took out two worn books, sliding them into the pillowcase as well. Then she grabbed a ragged piece of cloth and picked up the skull and began to wipe off the bloody nutria gore. The last sprig of hair fell off the skull as she wiped, leaving the thing bald.

"You're not going to take that thing, are you?" Sullivan tried to keep the revulsion out of his voice. The thought of travelling with a skull just did not settle well.

"Of course, Marcus saved our lives and we're taking him with us. He's been invaluable to us and he'll help us stay safe. He's a wealth of information and he stays awake even when I sleep. He goes or I stay." Lilly looked at Sully with a challenge in her eye. He just shook his head.

"Oh, all right, bring him along. And don't forget your bone knife. That thing will come in handy as well. Do you have have something I could use as a club, just in case we need it?"

Lilly dug around in the bottom of the crypt, under the bed area and came up with a long leg bone and slipped it into the pillow case. She picked up the knife, handed it to Sully and he slipped it in the belt of his jeans. Sullivan pulled his shirt down over it and patted it, smiling. "Is that it?"

She turned around; taking a long, last look around the room. As she turned, Sullivan caught the shine of tears in her eyes and a sadness he was lost to understand. It was such a hovel, not a real home at all. It was dirty, cold, wet, and lonely. But she was reacting like she was leaving somewhere that she treasured. He decided to ask her about it once they were safe inside where he was going to take her. He took the crook of her arm and helped her out of the tomb, taking care to step over the bloody gore of the nutria. Baron followed them and, once everyone was outside, Sullivan pulled the mahogany wood across the crypt door and led them away, toward the main gate of the St. Louis One cemetery.

Coming around the northeast edge of the cemetery, they found a step tomb with a cross on it and candle. A picture of a skeleton in a tuxedo and top hat lay face up next to the cross with scattered lids, coins, and other items nearby. There was the pungent smell of rum and, was that hot peppers (?) filled the air. Lilly took a step backward out of Sully's grasp and made the Sign of the Cross with her right hand.

"What's wrong?" Sullivan asked, following with his own Sign of the Cross, as much to put her at ease as anything else.

"Voodoo." she whispered. "Someone has called the Baron Samedi to this place. He is hunting Souls."

Sully's education in religion included the African-Caribbean religions and he was familiar with the Baron, who Lilly seemed afraid of but yet she had named her killer of a cat after. The woman was a dichotomy of superstitions and beliefs and she was amazing. "We won't disturb the voodoo, Lilly. We are just passing through." he smiled, trying to reassure her. He looked around trying to get his bearings when he noticed she was not wearing shoes. Her brown feet were tough and dirty but they were no match for the broken glass. "Here, let me pick you up and carry you over this glass and past all this mess. I don't want you hurt." He stepped back and lifted her slight body up into his arms.

She fit against him like she was made for him and he once again noticed that his jeans were fitting much too tightly in the crotch. She didn't put her arms around him, she held on to the skull and the pillowcase she had, like she trusted him not to drop her. Trust. He hoped she was beginning to trust him after all the other things that he had done. He looked down into her brown eyes and smiled at her. "I won't drop you, let's get out of here." he said as he strode off toward the gate. He had not completely thought out how he was going to get out of the cemetery or across to his friend's pub but he knew he had to get Lilly out of the confines of the place and into somewhere safe. He looked at the wall and tried to find a way out as he strode along.

Reaching the main gates, he found them in the condition he thought he would, chained and locked. He would be able to climb it but Lilly was small and would never make it over. He could toss her over but, uh, scratch that thought, tossing her would not lead to being able to snuggle with her and maybe even have sex... Sullivan shook his head violently. Where were these thoughts coming from? His brain was acting like a human teenager. Angels didn't have these kinds of thoughts.

"Are you feeling unwell, Sullivan?" Lilly looked up at him, questioning the sudden movement. He smiled at her and tried to keep the thoughts to what was going on and not on her lips.

"I'm fine, just trying to think of a way out of here. Let me think a moment." he walked back behind the caretaker's house and found a brick tomb that backed up to the wall around the cemetery. It was crumbling so he would have to be careful but it was short enough to climb with Lilly and go over the wall, just stay away from the middle of the top and the very edges, the bricks did not look too solid. "Here's what we're going to do, Lilly. I'm going to step up on this tomb and then up onto the wall and jump down. I think you should put at least one arm around my neck and hold on tight." He shifted her up enough that she could put her right arm around his neck and pulled herself onto his chest tightly.

Sully stepped up on the edge of the crumbling tomb, gingerly testing each step to keep from falling, or having the decaying tomb fall in under his weight and throw both of them into a dark hole, again. A couple of bricks wobbled but he moved quickly and went over the wall fast, landing on his feet. "There, we're out of there." he smiled. "Now to get to Danny's place where we'll be safe." Baron went around the guard's shack and squeezed through the bars of the gate as he had done many times and he ran to catch up with them.

"Are you sure your friend, Danny, won't mind us chancing by? Shouldn't you get a runner to go with a calling card and make sure that we are properly announced first?" Lilly wasn't sure that she was ready to meet anyone, especially dressed in ragged and bloody clothes as she was. She was very aware of the time she had spent in the clothes, the lack of bathing facilities in her little room, and such. She was certain that Sullivan was being incredibly kind in not mentioning her smell or looks.

"Danny is out of town. He evacuated when the city told everyone to get out before the storm. Everything is locked up tight over there. But he has told me where he hides the emergency key and I can get in. We will have a nice room; hopefully there will be things for us to use to clean up and such. I will have to go out for supplies but it will be a very safe place to be because no one will be expecting anyone to be there." His strides, as he talked, carried them across Basin Street and down toward the French Quarter. The sound of his voice and his Irish accent lulled her into feeling safe, even though being out in the open was frightening.

She was looking around and nothing, except a

few of the buildings, looked familiar. There were things with windows and wheels, painted in many colors, parked along the street. They looked vaguely like the horseless carriages that were just coming into New Orleans when she was working for Miss Lulu. The houses looked the same, though, like time had stood still. As they progressed down St. Louis Street, something making a very loud sound came down behind them, lights shining in her eyes as she turned to see what it was. Terrified, she clutched at Sullivan's neck with both hands, almost dropping Marcus in her fright. Blue and red and white lights flashed, blinding her and the thing, another of the metal carriages screamed as it flew past them and continued on into the darkness of the Quarter.

"Hey, it's ok. It's gone. We're ok. Nothing to be afraid of. That's the good guys." he laughed as he caught the skull and dropped it back in her lap, taking her right hand down and placing it on the top.

"What was that thing? The good guys? It didn't sound good, it was scary." she said, pulling Marcus close to her and shivering. It was far from cold in the post-Katrina mugginess; her shivers were from fear because the temperature did not bother her.

"It was a police car. The policemen drive them now. They are like horseless buggies, but much faster. They talk on machines that send sound through the air from their station to the car. The sound was a siren meant to tell other car drivers to move aside so they can go past. The flashing lights are to get attention as well. That policeman has somewhere important to go and wanted us to move so he could go by and not hurt us." Sullivan recited patiently. It had not occurred to him that Lilly did not know what a car was. What else did she not know about the time she was living in? "Lilly, how long did you live in the cemetery?" he asked, trying to keep it very conversational.

"I came to live in the little cemetery house in 1900. I remember working at Miss Lulu's last in August, late August of that year. I must have gotten sick and they must have thought I died so they buried me in the little house." She was looking away, like she was looking through time.

"Didn't you leave and go back to Miss Lulu's or try to find another place to go?" he was being as gentle as he could with her memories, still working his way toward the place he had in mind to stay.

"No. At first I was not able to get out of the coffin they put me in. When I finally found the way out, I was too weak to get the door open. I hid inside. The door had a hole in the corner. From time to time rats and other things would come in and I would eat those, I could put out a skull to catch water, but I found I could not drink water very well. As I got stronger, able to move the stone door, I found I had set up my own little home and I didn't want to leave it, so I just stayed." She turned and looked into his eyes and a soft smile split her lips.

He was getting answers but there were many more questions. "How did Baron come to live with you?" He asked as he stepped across a street and back onto a sidewalk. He looked around and, yes, the cat was shadowing him, about a half-block back, like his backup. It was a bit comforting, that cat could fight as well as some people Sully knew.

"One day he wandered into the house, chasing a rat. It was more like squeezed into the house; he was already so big he almost got stuck in the hole in the door. I pulled him in and gave him the rat. But then I was so hungry—" Her voice trailed off and she looked down, almost as if she was ashamed of what she did, "I was so hungry I picked him up and I bit him and drank. I could hear his little heart beating, fighting to live and I finally stopped but it was too late. I had killed him. I didn't mean to, I was so hungry!" Her voice broke and small red tears began to trickle down her face. She looked up into Sullivan's eyes, searching for what he could only think might be condemnation.

He hugged her lightly and patted her shoulder, "It's ok, Baron is ok, whatever you did brought him back."

"I bit my wrist like I remember Marcus doing when I was sick and I opened Baron's mouth and dripped my blood back into his mouth. I rubbed his throat and tried to get him to swallow. I had to work hard to get him to swallow because he was limp and not breathing anymore. I cried and begged and kept trying to feed him blood until he suddenly blinked and pulled up out of my hands. I reached under the box I had put together and grabbed another rat and hit it on the floor and laid it at his feet. He pounced it like he had never eaten and sucked down the blood from the rat until it collapsed flat. Then he snuggled up with me and slept the day away. He became my friend and I found we could communicate and we could talk to each other in a way. Like pictures in our minds. He shows me what he wants me to know and I can think a picture at him and he knows what I am trying to say. We are friends." She smiled. Sullivan listened and smiled, but he wondered if the vampire rules considered a vampire turning an animal as a violation. He had never heard of it happening.

He looked around and got his bearings. Everything was so very quiet, unlike when he had been to the city before. He had quite a bit of experience hunting paranormals in New Orleans; the city seemed to be one of the preferred headquarters for many different groups. When he wasn't hunting, he had come down to watch humans and try to figure them out. New Orleans was a people-watcher's paradise normally, but with the passing of Hurricane Katrina, it was too quiet, like the entire city was wounded and mourning. He crossed the street, walking toward the tall spires of St. Louis Cathedral, spires that had weathered Katrina just as they had so many storms previously. The venerable old cathedral was protected; he was sure, by some of the Boss's best, from even the worst storms. Just before Jackson Square, Sully turned right and walked once again toward the mighty Mississippi river.

"Do you know where you are going?" Lilly asked, watching the scenery around her. The shuttered buildings looked familiar, nothing had changed as far as she could tell, and the architecture had not changed. In the distance, when they crossed the longer streets, she could see shadows against the sky that could have been very tall buildings but nothing could be as tall as she was seeing so she dismissed it as her seeing things.

"Oh yes, darlin', I know where we're going, we're almost there. Just across this street and it's that building ahead of us across the parking lot." She followed his gaze and saw a building. There was a cement field next to it with lines on it, a few, what did he call them, cars, sitting between some of the lines. Everything was dark and vacant looking. Other than the police, they had seen no one in their walk across the Quarter.

He walked up to the wall and set Lilly down on one of the cars. "I need to find the key to the building. My friend, Danny O'Flaherty had one made just for emergencies and has it secreted here on this side of the building." Sully touched the bricks until he found one that made him smile, then he started counting and touching, changing angles and moving across the building until he found a brick just within reach about halfway down the building. He ran his fingers along the mortar lines, then pulled gently. The brick slid out. Sullivan laughed and turned the brick around; it was hollow and he drew out a key from the core and then he put the brick back. "I knew Danny was going to leave me the key." he smiled as he picked Lilly up and walked around to the front of the building. He unlocked the doors and stepped in. "You might call Baron in, he may not be happy to be left outside without us and I don't think he will answer to me." Sully remarked.

As if called, Baron came strutting around the edge of the building, looking around him as if to say "I know, I'm here. Just checking out everything." He flipped his tail at Sullivan and sauntered into the entryway of the pub. Everything was locked up, both the music room and the pub/kitchen area. When Sullivan looked out into the patio area, the scene was chaos, tree limbs laying down from the big tree that had shaded the area, tiles from the roof, other debris that had come from who knew where. The small building that had housed the Irish souvenir shop was boarded up and looked to be intact. Sullivan turned and looked up to the second and third floor windows of the main building. Most of the shutters were closed tight and everything looked to be intact. Like most buildings in the French Quarter, this one had been there for over a century, maybe longer. It would take more than a Hurricane Katrina to bring it down.

"Well, looks like we have us a good, safe place to hold up until we can figure out where to go. It's got food, drink, a roof, and a bed. I don't know if we have electricity—I doubt it with the force of the storm, and I'm not sure about running water, that may be out as well due to the lack of electricity. But at least it's dry, safe, and out of that cemetery." Sullivan unlocked the doors to the pub and walked Lilly and Baron into the main room, taking care to lock things behind him. He grabbed a couple of glasses, a bottle of scotch, a large key ring with several keys that hung on a hook, and took them around back to the staircase most patrons never saw. They walked silently in the near darkness on the creaking wooden staircase to the second floor and then crossed over the entry to the back of the building where the number of windows were fewer. Sullivan unlocked the last door and let them into a dark one-bedroom apartment that had obviously been abandoned in a hurry.

There was molded food on the stove, plates sitting on the table. Pictures had been pulled off the wall, dust from the walls showing where they had been hung. An empty television stand stood in one corner with books piled on it, obviously having been moved from a bookcase on the wall. The bedroom wasn't in much better shape, dresser drawers open, some things hanging out, others missing. The dust on the dresser indicated where things had been taken when the residents left. The closet held some clothing, both female and male but nothing that would fit either of them. The bed still had sheets and blankets and a couple of pillows so there was something nicer than the remains of a hundred-year old coffin to sleep on. Sullivan nodded as he looked around.

"It's not paradise but I think it'll do. I will need to get rid of the stinky leftovers but other than that, we should be cozy here. What do you think?"

Lilly looked into those smiling gray eyes. He

was trying so hard to make her happy, even in the middle of a destroyed city and despite what she had done to him; this man was trying to make her happy.

Why didn't she feel anything for him other than gratitude and amusement? Why did she still pine for a man who had probably been dead for over 60 years, a man she fantasized about to the point of talking to in the form of a skull? This thought crawled up out of her heart and walked across her mind in a lucid moment of clarity before leaving her back in the wreckage of the past.

"I think we may be safe here." she picked up the skull and looked deep into the eye sockets, "Marcus, what do you think, is this somewhere we can all be safe and hidden until we can come up with another idea?" Her hands held the skull like a lover would hold the head of a paramour.

Sullivan watched Lilly's actions with the skull with increasing confusion. Didn't she understand that the thing was a lifeless bone? There was no "Marcus", only a hollow cavity and no voice. But she talked to it like Marcus was right there with her, listening to whatever voices in her head answered her. Her eyes lit up like she was happy with the answers she was getting and a smile crossed her lips. Her left thumb carefully caressed the forehead; she nodded in silent agreement with the words she was hearing. As they "chatted," Sullivan tried to figure out what was going on with her. As an angel, he had confronted a lot of vampires and had never run into one who was so introverted, one who had not interacted with the human population and come up against the Enforcers quickly after their turning. So many vampires were tagged quickly and just as quickly messed up so badly that they were given their passes to Hell without so much as a notice by most of the rest of the population. Occasionally there would be one who would go so terribly rogue that there would be headlines in the newspapers and rumors and stories of dead bodies. He had been called in on the Jack the Ripper killings in London in 1888, sadly that lousy bastard had slipped even the Enforcers detection somehow and had never been brought to justice and was still out there, somewhere. He had been in New Orleans for the Axeman killings as well, back in 1918. They had caught that vampire and he had been judged, marked and was now in Hell. Both sets of killings were the work of very twisted minds.

But Lilly was not showing signs of psycho-pathic acts. She was gentle, nice, and actually believed in God. She was probably more human than any vampire he had ever met and this was throwing off every bit of training he had been through. And that innocence that she put out was a turn on, Exciting. An excitement he had never experienced, sort of like the old "moth to the flame" cliché he had heard before... He wondered if he would singe his wings.

Wings. Another sore subject. Sullivan had a score to settle with four punk kids and he wanted to find a way to do it before he took Lilly out of the city to safety. Those guys had his wings as well as his ring, the only way to get a word back to Headquarters and let them know that there was a problem with tuning both Lilly and Baron and he needed to report the fact that, somehow, an animal had been turned, a first as far as he knew. Would Lilly be judged for turning him? And, she had turned Sullivan without securing his permission first, that was a big offense and one that would count toward her three-strikes on the way to Hell.

He glanced at her right hand. It was so small and delicate, and unmarked. But that was because she was untuned, the job he had been assigned to do. No one knew at HHAD what had happened; they had no way to know what was going on here in the city. He guessed he could hunt down one of the other angels and see what could be done about getting word to them but that might create more problems than it might solve. How would he explain the problems he had run into and how he ended up in this mess to begin with, much less some of the things he had to do to since coming down here? What a freaking mess.

He came back to the present in the room when Lilly stopped talking. He looked up and she was looking at him. So was the skull, she was holding it an angle where it looked like the thing was staring right at him, disconcerting. Not for the first time, Sully wished she would have left the thing in the crypt. And the cat, Baron, was sitting on the bed, his gold eyes fixed on Sullivan's face.

He resisted the urge to check his fly to make sure it was zipped.

"We like it here, Sullivan. You brought us to somewhere nice. Now what do we need to do for you?" Lilly smiled at him, a smile that made him wonder just what "what" she had in mind.

"I know we don't have a lot of time tonight to get much done. We need supplies and you need clothes. I think tonight we stay here, rest, talk, and get to know each other better, then I'll head out tomorrow night and get things picked up for us. I can head downstairs and raid Danny's kitchen if you want something. I don't know what's good down there, if anything. Electricity has been off so anything in the refrigerator has been gone for a few days but he may have some nonperishable things I can open for us. And there is always alcohol. O'Flaherty's is an original Irish Pub and I happen to know Danny keeps this place stocked with a lot of great stuff."

Lilly had that same confused look she wore when she asked about cars and Sully went through the statement he had just made to try to figure out what had not made sense to her. "What did I say that didn't make sense this time?"

"Referigitator?" she completely mangled the word. He chuckled. He had been around humanity and their inventions for as long as they had been around and he had no frame of reference for not knowing what things were. She had, essentially, awakened in a whole new world.

"Ice box. But it doesn't work with ice, it works on electricity. The storm knocked out the electricity and so everything got warm and isn't good. But there should be canned food around, I think. And the booze never gets ruined. We can go down and rummage around the pantry and see what you feel like eating." even as he said the words, he realized he didn't feel like eating anything but that he was very thirsty.

"We can go look, maybe something to drink would be nice, and Baron needs to go out to hunt before dawn." Lilly smiled at the cat who had come up to her and was walking back and forth, rubbing against her bare legs.

Not for the first time, Sully noticed just how threadbare the dress she was wearing, well, almost wearing was. When it was new, it was probably very conservative but it had been ripped to the point that most of the skirt was gone, coming up to almost the top of her thighs. The sleeves hung in tatters and the bodice was thin and see through. She was beautiful under it, the rags serving to highlight the curves she was built of. His cock surged awake again, reminding him that he had not alleviated the lust he was feeling. He needed to get this set-up going and then tend to that itch; it was going to be a joy to scratch it, with her.

He took her hand and went back down the stairs. "If we let Baron out, will he be able to take care of himself if we don't get back down to let him in before dawn?" asking her as he led her down. The sound from the cat, a deep growl, let him know that it may have been a stupid question. The cat walked to the door and went out the door into the courtyard, ignoring the humans left in his wake.

Sullivan, grinning like a man stupid in love, went behind the main bar of the establishment and started going through bottles, setting some up on the polished surface as he did so. Two or three bottles with amber liquid, a couple of smaller crock bottles, and a couple of glasses were put on a tray Sullivan picked up and adroitly lifted over his head. "I think we can say this part of the mission is successful, let's hit the kitchen." He led the way into the dark room. Amid the pots and pans, he found a couple of cans but looked at them, then back at Lilly. "I don't know if we are going to find much that will be good to eat. O'Flaherty kept a great kitchen but most of it was fresh stuff. The chef went to the French Market daily for a lot of the ingredients. Anything we find in the cooler is spoiled so it's going to end up being whatever we can find in cans." he shook his head, putting down yet another can of tomatoes in disgust.

"I can deal with not having anything like 'food' right now, we can deal with going out tomorrow and finding something or I can send the Baron out for something we can both drain, he's really good at bringing back dinner." She smiled and her fangs were showing. Sullivan's chest felt a twitch as he remembered that he was no longer an angel, no longer even human. He was a vampire. That meant no more sneaking off to enjoy food from some of the best restaurants on Earth, he wasn't sure how much vampires could enjoy the human food he could eat, while they could eat, it didn't seem to nourish at all.

Sullivan and a few of the angels he was friends with, including his best friend and fellow Enforcer, Essex, were known to take a night off occasionally to "do it human." They would disguise themselves as regular humans and go places together to eat, drink, and enjoy together those things they didn't normally get to do. Sullivan had cultivated quite the culinary palate and a distinguishing love of liquor. Never drunk, he was known to enjoy a drink or two as most angels were. There was nothing to prohibit them from eating, drinking, going to movies, or other things most mortals enjoyed. The only rules were not to indulge in excess, the inability to take responsibility for ones actions and the rule of never harming someone. The angels who got into trouble with "The Boss" were the ones who broke those rules.

"Let's grab the liquor and go on up, then." he smiled as he wandered up to the door and opened it. Baron wandered in, hesitating in front of Sullivan to whip his tail back and forth in a manner that Sullivan knew was an editorial comment by the cat. Baron never seemed to be a regular cat but rather more human than feline and Sullivan. The cat most definitely conducted himself more like a human than a cat. Or rather, a vampire.

He grabbed the tray and put one arm around Lilly and led her back up the stairs to the apartment they were going to call "home" for a few days.

With a flourish, Sullivan kicked the door closed and set the tray on the table as they came in, then he grabbed two of the bottles and waved them in Lilly's direction. He clicked the light switch, which didn't work. While it was dark in the room to most people, he had noticed that, probably because of the vampire change, he could see like it was almost daylight. He didn't need electric light. The way she moved, he figured she had the same vision capability.

"I didn't even ask you if you liked Irish whiskey. I have two of the best here. Do I need to go down and get you something else?" he smiled at her. She was sitting across the table from him, hands folded in her lap, her hair falling in ringlets down her face and neck. He closed his eyes momentarily, trying to commit the beauty to memory like he wouldn't ever see it again.

"Oh, I like Irish well enough. That would be fine, whichever you think is best." she said softly, amiably. Sullivan put the bottles down, opened the Jamisons 18 year old bottle and poured the glasses full.

"Sorry, there's no ice, electricity is out." he shrugged as he handed a glass to her. Not that he drank his whiskey with ice; that was sacrilege to him. Pure taste, pure liquor was the only way to go.

"I don't mind. I like it either way." she took the glass and took a deep drink of it. Sully watched on with interest. She didn't seem to have the aversion to drinking straight whiskey that some women had. She put the glass down and he poured her another one. Then he tossed back the one he had and poured a second one.

"This place has a lot of memories. I used to come here on the times I would be here for work. I found out there was an Irish pub in this French-i-fied party town and made it my favorite hangout. Between the music, the liquor, and the best food this side of the pond, this pub was probably the best taste of home I could get." he tossed another glass of Jamisons down and then poured a third.

"Home? Where was home for you?" Lilly asked, drinking as she finished the sentence. She seemed to be matching him glass for glass, which was going to have to slow down because humans couldn't keep up with angels when it came to drink; angels didn't get drunk like humans.

"Well, I tend to think that Ireland is home for me. I wasn't born there but it is my favorite place on this planet. It's green, pastoral, and just beautiful." he looked off, past her, like he was remembering.

"Where were you born, then?"

His gaze came back to her eyes. How to ex-plain this one? "Not really born. I was created whole and as an adult from the beginning. Angels aren't born as humans and those of us who work are not 'made angels,' those turned when they come from humans. They are not made to work for the host; it's thought that since they had to live as human, being made to work after they get to Heaven is a bit too much to demand. So, we, the original angels, get that assignment."

"So you were an angel before you came to be with me in the little house? Where are your wings, you mentioned those before? Do you have a halo?" she smiled, drinking from the glass in her hand.

"Yes, I was an angel, before. The men who attacked us obviously did something with my wings since you didn't see them. As for halo, those are reserved for the 'big wigs' in the Angel world. The average working angel doesn't get one. I am an Enforcer Angel, one of those who keep the paranormal beings in line and keep them from taking over the planet." he tossed another glass full of the whiskey and then poured a fourth, "Or, I used to be."

"Paranormal? What is that? And how did you come to be in the cemetery near my little house?" Lilly sipped the liquor.

"Those who are not 'natural humans.' Beings like vampires, werewolves, ghosts, and such. I was sent to New Orleans because some of the angels who were here helping with the dead and injured from the hurricane reported finding the energy signature of a couple of unregistered vampires. I was supposed to find them and give them the rules, then adjust their energy so that it registers with us." he didn't think that telling the information was going to cause any problems, she was the one he was sent to deal with.

"So you were seeking me from the beginning. You said 'a couple' of vampires; do you know who the other one is?"

"No, I found you but am not really sure who

the other one is. I would be able to tell if I had my wings and my ring. The ring would glow around a paranormal that was unregistered so we know we have someone to deal with and then it stops when we get the registration done. Do you know of another vampire in that cemetery that we haven't run across yet?" Sully chalked up the question to professional curiosity. He would have to eventually deal with it.

"No, just me and Baron. There was no one else in the cemetery at night."

Baron. The Cat. Could it be that this animal was showing up on the energy signature as a paranormal and that is who the second vampire was that was reported? The animal was not 'normal' as most animals were, more human, and vampire, than feline. Sullivan weighed the thought and tried to see if that would have been the case. He looked at the cat, who was sitting on the couch near the wall, looking back at him with those gold eyes. Maybe, just maybe that was the case.

"Ok, well, I was supposed to meet you and then let you know that you couldn't be making more vampires without asking, you needed to leave the humans alone except to eat as you needed and leave them without memory of it, and you were supposed to keep out of trouble. Then I would have reached into you and 'tinkered' with your energy so that you would show up as 'registered' and we would know you had been warned. When we get word of a paranormals going rogue, we can track them down and deal with them without having to upset the human population, the energy signature will change to show problems." he tossed the fourth down and poured yet a fifth glass.

"I came here a lot when in New Orleans because it reminded me of Ireland. I spent a lot of time in Ireland, a lot of my work as an Enforcer was done there because the whole island is full of ghosts, banshees, fairy folk, and other paranormals. I took the name Sullivan after a man I knew there, my angel name was Eistered." Lilly was listening intently to his story, he observed.

"He was a very learned man for a potato farmer. We were in Connaught when I met him; he was getting old even then. He had raised five sons and four daughters with his wife on that little plot of land. But there was this potato blight that had settled on the crops and people who were tenant farmers like Sullivan were unable to pay their rents, much less feed their families. My friend saw three of his children leave for America to escape the starvation; he lost four more to it," The angel took a sip of the whiskey, letting the warm liquid relax him.

"I came to visit the day his wife spent her last day on earth. Sullivan had tried to save her, giving up his meals to her, bartering everything he could. They were losing the land; their landlord had said that they were going to be evicted. Sullivan was a proud man but it didn't stop him from begging the landlord for time to make the next harvest, to save the farm and his family. The landlord wasn't listening and the word had come down that they would be evicted by the Sheriffs on the next Sunday. Mabb was dying and Sullivan was beside himself. I sat with him, tried to comfort him as he watched her take her last breath." He looked down into the glass.

"After she passed away, I stayed with him through the funeral and burial. We were standing by her grave when he looked at me like he had seen me for the first time and said, 'I know you're an angel and you couldn't save her. Not even God cares what happens to the Irish.' Then he reached into his pocket, grabbed his knife, and slit his own throat on his wife's grave. I couldn't save her, I couldn't save him. But I vowed to remember..." his voice trailed off and he looked away, red tears falling freely from his eyes. He grabbed the glass, drained it, and poured another, slamming it down as well.

"I vowed to remember the man who had given his whole life for his family and I chose to by taking his name. I couldn't save him but I could save his memory." he ducked his head into his hands, his shoulders shaking with the tears he was shedding at the memory.

Lilly reached across the table and put her hand on his arm. When he didn't react, she pulled her chair around to his side and sat with her arm around him, holding him as he cried. She sipped whiskey and let him vent the emotions he obviously had held for decades.

He looked up at her as the episode passed. She just smiled at him and said, "You are a good man, Sullivan. You could not stop what happened but you have made them live forever."

"I'm sorry, I didn't mean to get maudlin on you." he wiped his bloody face on his sleeve. "What about you? You told me about living in the brothel but was there anything else?" He tried to change the subject.

She thought a moment and then smiled, a sad, resigned smile. "I wanted to be a nun. I had been sent to the Ursuline School by Miss Lulu and I found myself drawn to the religious aspects of the Church. I wanted to leave Miss Lulu and go to live with the Sisters. But Miss Lulu didn't want me to go and the Sisters weren't sure about taking in an orphan who lived in a brothel. So I stayed and when it was time, Miss Lulu put me to work with the other girls. I had talked to her, to the Sisters, and to Fr. Subileau, the priest of St. Augustine's Church where I attended Mass, but no one would give me the chance to move out of the Hall and become a nun. So, I stayed and worked. Fr. Subileau would not allow me to take communion but I still went to Mass daily when I could, it was the only way I could keep my heart from breaking." she drank the rest of the whiskey in her glass and poured herself the rest of the bottle. "I do not know if God would care about me because I could not keep the commandments exactly as they were set down, but maybe He knows I tried." One red tear slipped from her eyes and dropped onto the bareness of her dress.

Sullivan shook his head and took her hand. "I don't think God really cares about what we do, day to day. It's the big things we do or don't do that get the attention. You kept your heart and intentions pure, no matter what your body needed to do. And that is what counted."

She sipped the remaining whiskey and noticed how cool his hand was. Then she noticed his mouth, the smile he gave her. Her heart pulled toward him, wanting to taste those lips. She stopped for just a few moments and then took the chance. She leaned in and put her lips to his, a tentative, small kiss. She pulled back almost minutely, catching her breath that she no longer breathed.

Sullivan wrapped his arms around her and took her lips again. His body took over; he became unaware of everything but her, her taste, her feel. His tongue parted her lips and slipped into her mouth, searching to feel her, to convey just what his whole being was shouting at him. She touched him back with her tongue; the kiss became a dance, each surge of energy between them heightening the need they both felt.

He stood up, never breaking the kiss, and lifted her in his arms. He walked, still kissing her, into the bedroom and placed her on the bed. His hands searched her hair, ran down her shoulder and onto her breast as he continued to heat inside from the kiss that had taken on a life of its own. Her hands reached around and caressed his neck, running into his hair and back down. She moaned as his hands sought her nipples, rubbing them into aching, taut points.

Her moan urging him on, he reached up and tore the remnants of her dress, tossing it aside. It was no more than a rag anyway and the thought of getting her jeans flashed through his head before he lowered his mouth to her breast and all thoughts of anything else vanished as she arched her back, urging him to take her. The bulge in his jeans pushed against the buttons of his fly, pushing his need even harder. He let his hands brush down her sides as he reached to loosen his own clothes.

Lilly reached his shoulders and stripped the shirt from him in one sharp pull, throwing it out of reach. He growled, then wondered vaguely where that came from as he kissed his way down her belly. He leaned back and looked at her as he popped the offending buttons, relieving the pressure building behind it. She licked her lips in anticipation and then sat up, grasping the edges of his jeans and pulling them down off his hips to his knees. Her hand reached for him, almost automatically, grasping his cock gently at first, playfully, then wrapping all her fingers around him and beginning to slide up and down.

"Oh Lilly!" he cried out, leaning forward and grasping her breast as he pulled her head up to kiss her again. He could not quit tasting her lips; it was almost more heady than the liquor they had been drinking. His head spun inside, dizzyingly, and he fought the urge to just push her down and enter her right there, right then. He wanted to take his time with her but she was driving him crazy.

"If you keep that up, it's going to stop us from doing anymore." he breathed, pulling back from her lips just enough to get the words out. Her hand stopped, then reached lower and caressed his balls, her index finger sliding up and down the seam between them and then back behind them. When her finger reached the skin behind them, Sully pushed her over onto her back and rubbed his cock against her, his voice husky and deep, "Woman, I want to kiss you until you melt, I want to nibble every part of you and I want to hear you scream my name over and over." He gazed into her eyes, seeking to see her soul. "Tell me you want me." he urged.

He was on autopilot. This was all academic until this moment, he had watched humans have sex before, he knew what went on and how to do it. But he, personally, had never experienced it. He knew he should be worried about how to do it right, hell, how to do it at all. But his body seemed to know exactly what to do and again the thought was fleeting as he ran his fingers across her clit and fingered the waiting lips below. Lilly raised her head, moaned, and threw herself down on the pillow again. He nibbled on the edges of her breast gently, sending shivers through her. He smiled as her skin reacted, puckering into a million goose pimples.

He ran his fingers across hers and then down her arms softly. His fingertips reached the soft area under her arms and she started to giggle. He raised an eyebrow, trying to focus on her reaction and did it again. She giggled.

"Tickles!" she said through the giggle. While he knew that sex was supposed to be pleasing but laughing was not in his knowledge base as a response to intimate touch and it baffled him. His sudden cessation of movement caused her to open her eyes and look into his, the puzzlement evident.

"Tickles? But I wasn't trying to tickle you; I was exploring your body with my fingers. I don't understand how that turned out to be tickling, that's not what I was going for." He said, confused.

"It's ok. It's just that a woman's armpit isn't generally known as a sexual zone and I am ticklish there. I never thought you would go there." she smiled at him but the confusion seemed to linger in his eyes.

"So, there are places where I shouldn't explore on you? What other areas are ticklish so I can avoid those, the giggling seems to slow my sexual responses down a bit."

Lilly raised up on one elbow and smiled. "You didn't know that? Sully, you're not very experienced at this, are you?" As beautiful as he was, it was hard for her to believe that he was new to sex.

"No, I'm afraid not. I've watched enough but I've never participated." he tried returning the smile, not something easy to do. He didn't know why he was feeling so timid around her now; it wasn't like they were new to each other. But his emotions were in a jumble, he didn't know where to start, what to do, and how to act with her with this new situation. His head spun, he was having trouble thinking, but his genitals were straining so hard he was almost unable to think of anything but taking her down on her back and screwing her to the bed. Then he shook his head, wondering again where that thought had come from and why the image of her under him was so strong.

"You've watched. You have never made love to a woman." she said quietly, taking in what he was telling her.

"No, I've never made love to a woman. Or a man either, for that matter. This is, I'm afraid, an all-new experience for me. I was hoping that having watched would have made it easier to do but obviously I have not either observed enough to find out how or I'm missing something." Talking about having sex was beginning to take care of that strained feeling in his groin.

"Oh, ok, you're a virgin. I've dealt with this before. I know exactly how to handle it." she smiled at him, not seeming to mind at all that he was telling her how new he was to sex. This also baffled him. "What we need to do is trade places. You need to slip those trousers off further, get rid of them, and then lay down here on the bed. I'll show you what to do." She talked to him softly, sitting up and guiding his hand down to the pants around his knees as she slid away from him and got to her feet on the floor. She put out a hand and helped him stumble out of the bed and kept him from face-planting as he got tangled up in the offending pants.

He stepped out of them and then turned to her. He reached out with the intention of putting his hands on her waist, pulling her to him, and starting to kiss her again. Even looking at her naked, standing in front of him made him stiffen in total lust.

She took his hands and turned him, pushing him back to the bed. He backed up against it and waivered. "Go head, lay down. Let me guide you through this. I promise it will be good." she purred. Nothing of her training back in Mahogany Hall had left her; she still knew how to please even the shyest of men. She held his hand as he laid down and tried to arrange himself for her. She reached down and took the pillows, fluffing them and then handing them to him. He leaned up and put them behind his head. She was touching him on his chest as he was doing this, running her fingers through the fine, dark hair there. Once he was settled, she pulled herself onto the bed beside him, half laying on his left side, and started running her hands through his hair and nibbling, kissing his ear gently, pulling his earlobe with her teeth. He started to turn his head and kiss her but she put her hand on his face and stopped him, "Let me." she whispered into his ear with a small kiss.

What that was doing to him was driving him crazy.

She nibbled down his neck, licking along his chin, then kissed him deeply. His hands flew to her hair, her back, trying to hold her to him and keep her doing just what she was doing. She seemed to know exactly what to do, she was all over him and yet not. His entire body became aware of her and he felt his groin harden further, if that was possible. He felt like if it tried anymore, it would explode.

Lilly pulled up out of the kiss and started kissing him down his breastbone, starting to run her fingers, then her mouth on both of the small nipples peaking hard against her touch. Sully pulled her hair gently, trying to pull her back up to his mouth but she gently reached up and pushed his hand to the bed. "Let me show you." she whispered as she bent her mouth back to his right nipple, sucking it, running her tongue around it. He moaned, pounding his open hand on the mattress in frustration at not being able to touch her.

She left his nipple and set his skin afire with her lips as they traced the trail of hair down to his groin. His erection was strong and she smiled. This was something that she knew how to do, even after the decades without a man in her life. She took it firmly in hand and kissed the top of it, slowly licking the pearl of wetness from it, tasting him.

"Lilly!" he shouted, slapping the bed again. "Oh my God! Do you know what that feels like?" he bellowed.

"Shhh, let me." She bent to kiss and lick it again, popping the head into her mouth and running her tongue around it. This elicited a low, growl, groan, moan, from him. All he could think of was what she was doing to him and how much it was driving him crazy. His cock responded with a fire that threatened to set his very soul alight.

She lifted her head and then opened her mouth and tried to completely swallow him, his cock sliding deep inside her mouth and throat.

He could not help himself. He grabbed her head, holding her to him and thrusting. The feel of her lips and tongue sliding up and down him was maddening and so very, very hot at the same time. He could not stop himself.

She reached up and removed his hands from her hair and lifted her head, leaving his cock feeling very cool and very alone. She followed the shaft down and then kissed his balls, popping one into her mouth and gently sucking. Sullivan swore, trying to find just the right words to tell her how it felt but there were not words, his mind was swimming, there just was no way to think further than what he was experiencing.

Then she rose up again, shifting to her knees. She raised her left leg and then straddled his belly, rubbing her warm lips against him. She laid over and held a ripe breast over his mouth, tempting him. He lifted his head and sucked the proffered nipple into his mouth, sucking, rolling it with his tongue, and nibbling it with his teeth. His hands slid back up, rubbing her back as he teased the soft mound in his mouth. She pulled away and offered him the other nipple, which he promptly took and laved with his tongue as he looked into her eyes. She had the most beautiful smile, from her eyes to that luscious mouth; everything seemed bathed in an inner light.

Damn, she was beautiful.

She lifted her body from his and then, very

slowly, centered her nether lips on the top of his hard cock and slid down, impaling herself on him. Sully thought he was ready for this, ready for the feel of her sheathing him with her inner folds, but he had really no idea just how this was going to feel. He cried out as she settled, then began to rise and fall on him, slipping up and down his shaft. This was heaven, never mind the place he had lived. Nothing was any comparison to what he was feeling. He was dying, going to Hell and Heaven at the same time.

She stopped, just for a moment, to smile at him. The look on his face was one of pure incredulity, he was happy. She rolled her hips, moving him closer to climax but then backing off again, knowing just how much to push him before needing to slow things down. She was going to make this last as long as she could, she wanted him to experience all the emotions that good loving could give him.

That's when he sat up, threw his arms around her, and rolled, putting her under him with a deep growl. He latched onto her lips with his mouth as he pushed his cock deep into her, pinning her to the bed. He lost total control of his thoughts; the only thing in him was the need pushing up from the center of his being, through his erection. He pumped into her, over and over, harder and harder.

Then he felt it.

He felt his fangs slide down from inside his gums and anchor themselves, with a surge of need behind it that completely overwhelmed him.

With a roar, he buried his fangs in Lilly's neck and felt himself come at the same time, filling and emptying him in the same moment. Her taste, her sweet blood, filled his mouth and he swallowed greedily.

"Oh Marcus, yes!" she squealed, crying out with her own orgasm squeezing him tightly. Then she sunk her teeth deep into his shoulder, drinking him in as he did her. He momentarily stopped swallowing, hearing the name of his now-rival on her lips in her climax. But then he passed it off and kept drinking.

Then things began to slow. He felt himself begin to go flaccid as his need for blood sated. He pulled his lips and fangs from her neck and then simply licked her over and over until the punctures closed up. Somewhere in the back of his mind he wondered how he knew to do this but he wasn't up to asking about it. Lilly pulled her fangs out of his shoulder and licked as well. Then he rolled them to their sides and pulled her into his arms, her head resting on his shoulder.

"Oh Lord! That was fantastic." he sighed, kissing her gently on the top of the head. "Thank-you." They held each other, the energy and heat dissipating like the darkness outside under the dawn. Before he knew it, he drifted off to sleep, cuddling her.

Chapter Eight

R ANGUEL WAS CONCERNED. All of his Enforcers were working, accounted for. Except for one. Sullivan had been dispatched to New Orleans to find two vampires in a cemetery and disappeared. One second the transponder was working, the next it was out. Ranguel had been watching to see if the signals would come back but it was oddly quiet.

He looked up, again, at the images coming out of New Orleans. Pictures of the poor, the homeless and helpless crowded outside the big Superdome complex and outside of the Convention Center flashed across the big screen. There were pictures of angels interspersed within the crowds, black-winged Soul Reapers carrying off the souls of those who died waiting for help, blue-winged healers answering prayers for healing in the midst of the carnage. Occasionally, a flash of gold wings could be seen, counseling the population and gathering prayers. But no gray wings were visible. He had only a few Enforcers in the New Orleans area, mostly helping out with Soul Reaping or Messenger duties because of the high demand. He glanced at the assignment and tracking boards. Everyone in the field was highlighted and he could tell where they were at any moment.

All but Sullivan. Who had, seemingly, disappeared off the face of the Earth. He had been known to disappear before, usually when he was on a particularly tough assignment or, on a rare occasion, when he felt he needed a "vacation." He had explained that as a time to get away from all the duties and "unwind," but he couldn't really understand why anyone would need a break from their job. Angels worked. It was why they were created. But Sullivan had been around humans and paranormals for so long, he was taking on their characteristics, much to the annoyance of most of the Council. It was very unusual behavior and the Council did not really like anything unusual.

Could he be laying somewhere, harmed by one of the evil outlaws loose in the city since the hurricane? There had been reports of snipers and random violence against those who survived by humans who were more interested in their own and what they could take from others. Evil had been unleashed in the city since the hurricane, even above the normal range of sex, violence, and corruption; a height rarely seen in these more "civilized" years. The H.H.A.D. had been very busy working against the onslaught of death, dying, mayhem, and violence, every hand not occupied elsewhere were called in to answer prayers that were constantly going up from the suffering masses across the American South affected by the hurricane.

And somewhere in that morass was Sullivan. Unless he had taken leave of his senses and left the area.

Ranguel looked up toward Mikhail's office. The door was shut but he knew he was busy coordinating the actions of the world, he was always busy. He weighed his options about disturbing him about one wayward angel. On one hand he was not overly late, only a matter of hours. But at the same time, he could not shake the feeling something was wrong, very wrong.

He called over to his assistant, Kozimiel, who glided over, "Yes, sir?"

"I must speak with Mikhail. Sullivan has not contacted in over a day and a half and I fear something may have happened to him. You are in charge and need to watch for him in particular as you work. If you see his transponder, notify me immediately." he handed him the notes he had made and turned, furling his wings and gliding up to the terrace that held his superior. He reached his door and, before he could knock, it swung open. Mikhail was seated behind his desk, flashes of images on every screen in the area behind him, the entire weight of the worlds in this one room. He looked up at his entrance, calm reflecting in his eyes.

"Sir, it's about Sullivan." Ranguel started.

"He's not signed in yet, huh? You suspect something has happened?" no one could keep anything from Mikhail; he seemed to know everything at once. "You need guidance as to what to do." It wasn't a question.

"Yes, sir. I believe he may be in trouble and I believe we need to find him." he cast a gaze at the images from New Orleans behind the head angel. "I just cannot shake the feeling something has happened that he cannot contact us."

"Very well. A missing angel is very unusual indeed, even for that one." Mikhail tapped the board on his desk. Suddenly the room began filling with angels, the rest of the Operations Council responded quickly to his call.

Mikhail stood, his blood-red wings framing him. He took on the very air of authority, the room charging with the energy. "We have a missing Enforcer Angel. Sullivan was sent two days ago into New Orleans to find a couple of untuned vampires and has disappeared. With the chaos there, we are now of the opinion something may have happened to him. I am contemplating issuing an alert world-wide and in New Orleans and sending a Shadow Angel out to try to find him and assess the situation." He looked at everyone individually, assessing their thoughts. "Anyone have anything else to input?"

"Nothing has shown on any of the consoles of any of the areas, sir. We have enough angels in New Orleans that we surely would have seen him if he was there." Gabriel replied. He had been watching all actions since his messengers were needed everywhere, sometimes all at once it seemed.

"Ranguel tells me there is a chance he may have taken a 'vacation' without telling him about it. It has happened before but he always signed back on with the transponder when he arrived where he was going. That has not happened but we can always hope. So, we assume he's in New Orleans but we issue the alert world-wide, just in case." Mikhail said. "Any other comments?"

A shake of heads counted as a vote to do it. "Very well, we issue the alert. Make sure all of your angels are aware of what is going on. Uriel, I need one of your Shadows issued to Ranguel so he can send someone out who is especially looking for Sullivan, just in case." Uriel nodded. "Ok, out, I have work to do." Mikhail turned his back and walked to the desk as the assembled angels left. As he saw the last set of wings open and float down and away he shook his head, "Just what we need, a rogue." He liked Sullivan, admired his pluck and easy going ways. In some aspects, Mikhail wished he could trade places with the Enforcer and take some time for one of those "vacations" himself. That may be why he had never objected to some of the things the angel pulled against regulations. He shook his head and bent back to his work.

Ranguel went with Uriel to the Shadow's station. Uriel looked at the board and then tapped on one name. "I can let you have Sophiel. She's good, she knows the area, and I can spare her at the moment. A rustle of wings sounded behind them as Sophiel arrived. Small, dark headed with piercing green eyes, she wore the brown wings of the Shadow.

"Yes Uriel?"

"You are assigned to Ranguel for the moment. One of his Enforcers, Sullivan, has gone missing and needs to be found. How do you want this to be done, Rangu?" Uriel turned to the Enforcer chief.

"Search New Orleans. He may be hurt or something may have happened. Find out, find out the extent, and then come tell us. If you find him wounded, call for the Healers. But also be aware he may be off on his own and of his own volition. If you find him well, find out why he's not contacting before you report in." Ranguel did not want to think about what he may have to do in that case.

"Yes ma'am." Sophiel unfurled her wings and gently lifted up toward one of the nearest apertures and disappeared.

"Good luck." Ranguel thought as he turned back to his own busy board and yet another problem being handed to him by Kozimiel.

Chapter Nine

As DUSK CLOSED in on the soggy Louisiana city, another night of terror and fear was beginning. Sullivan and Lilly awoke still curled in each other's arms and Sullivan pulled out of bed first, knowing that if he waited, he wouldn't get out of bed at all that night.

"Hey." he smiled at Lilly, who was stretching, running her fingers through her hair. "Hey" she replied.

"I figure that I need to go to get you something to wear tonight. You can't wear your dress anymore and the stuff here isn't fitting either." Sullivan pulled on his jeans and shirt, then his boots.

"I want to go with you..." she started, standing, then looked down at herself, still wrapped in the sheet from the bed, lifting the remnants of her dress. "I guess I do need to let you go and bring something back, this will not work, certainly."

Sullivan handed her a dress shirt from the closet, left behind by the residents of the apartment they were staying in. "This covers, it will be better than the sheet until I get back. Is there anything else you want me to find and bring back?" He searched the apartment and found a small rope and an ink pen and turned back to her.

Her eyes got large and then she glared at him, "I am NOT going to remain tied up in here while you go off. I have done nothing for you to suspect me about."

He stepped toward her, stretching out the rope, "Calm down, I'm not going to tie you up, although that might be fun later." he smiled at her sustained agitation, a small surge of heat warming his crotch at the thought. "I am using this to get some measurements so I can get close to the right size for you." he ran the rope around her waist and then made a knot, writing *W* on it. Then he did her hips, with a *H*, her shoulders with an *S*, and finally from her waist to her ankles with *L*. "Now, let me do below your breasts." he reached up and did a final knot with *B* on it. He smiled and then said "One more," and grabbed her breast with his open hand. She slapped at it and he removed it with two words, "breast size." She frowned, not too sure what to believe for sure. But he had his measurements. He coiled the rope up and stuffed it in a pocket and headed to the door.

"I won't be gone too long, I hope. Keep Baron here inside the building, he can hunt the patio, but no one in or out while I'm gone. I've heard gunshots and we don't know how dangerous it still is here. I'm needing the key to get back in so I'll lock up behind me." he walked to the door of the room and looked back at her, "Don't get too lonely while I'm gone." He winked at her.

Her eyebrow shot up. He had to be joking, she was just fine, she had Baron and Marcus, a big room, and lots of time to figure out what to do. "I'll try." she walked over, picked up Marcus, and waved to him, "Go on." He took one last, long look at her, trying to drink her essence in, then turned and left. Baron followed him down the stairs, tossing a thought to her that he was going to go to the patio. She heard Sullivan lock the door below.

"Well, Marcus, it's just us again. Looks like we're going to be ok. I'm not sure about being out in the world now, things seem like they have changed a lot. But if Sully stays, we can learn about things and be all right." She stroked the dome of the skull gently, listening to the silence but hearing Marcus.

"You know I really wanted to stay where you might find me, but I get the feeling you were gone. Sometimes I think you are still around but other times I wonder why you haven't come back for me. Then I get mixed up and think you're with me and that I can hear you. Marcus. I love you. What's real? Are you still with me or are you gone?" She listened to the familiar voice of the skull, eyes brimming with tears. "I am trying, Marcus. I don't know what to do. Sullivan is nice, he's being so kind now and he seems to be serious and truthful with how he is treating me, but I really just want you. I'm not trying to be insincere with him but I'm not sure if I can be 'his' as I fear he may be thinking..."

"Excuse me, my lady. I wonder if you realize that you are conversing with an inanimate object there?" a male voice came from the area of the kitchen, sounding like it was in the wall. Then a tall man walked into the room, through the wall, medium build, dark hair with hazel eyes. He was dressed in early 19th century clothing. She looked up to see who was speaking and the sight surprised her, the man was almost there, but she could see through him. "I'm sorry, dear, I did not mean to startle you." he bowed, his eyes never leaving her face.

"Oh, hello. I'm sorry, I didn't hear you come in and we didn't think anyone else was here. I'm waiting on a friend to come back, then we can leave." she said, placing Marcus down on the bed table next to her and standing up.

"It is fine, lady. I did not want to disturb you but I did want to come and meet you. You are lovely." He smiled, almost a leering smile. Something about the man made her very uneasy and she tried to hide the feeling from him.

"Thank-you. I am Lilly Marchantel. I came with my friend, Sullivan. We were seeking safer quarters after the hurricane and some foul men hurt him. We are trying to find out where to go when we leave here. He went to get clothing and supplies." She knew she was babbling but his presence had surprised her and she was not used to talking to strangers.

"You are welcome to stay, Miss Lilly. I find you a beautiful woman, a very desirable woman, and I would like to get to know you better while you are here." He had traversed the area from the wall to the bed in very little time and he was standing right next to her. He was still non-corporeal and the room temperature had dropped considerably, making Lilly wish she had on a lot more than just a man's dress shirt to cover herself. She pulled the blanket from the bed and wrapped it around herself against the prying eyes of the leering ghost beside her.

"I am flattered you would like to talk to me, I am afraid my skills with others are not sharp any longer. Can you tell me about yourself and how you came to be here? We thought we were alone." She thought about getting up and going into the other room to the table but was afraid to move.

"My name is Joseph Wheaton. I used to come here to visit a lady friend who lived here. We had a, uh, disagreement and she fell out of the window there." He pointed to a shuttered window. "I was very unhappy that she fell..."

"And so that's why you, coward, killed yourself," a female voice sounded like it was just behind her and Lilly jumped and twirled to see another non-corporeal person, this time a woman with blonde hair hovering over the bed.

"And, I didn't fall, I was pushed, you bastard." Yet another female voice, this one walking through the wall from the outside, her clothing reminding Lilly of some of the boudoir paintings she had seen in Mahogany Hall, undergarments only. This woman had dark hair, whisps coming out of the bun piled up on her head and she appeared to have the smooth light chocolate skin of the other octaroons that Lilly had known, and Lilly herself possessed. She guessed that this "lady friend" was a courtesan, much like Lilly had been. The phantom drifted across the room to stand on the other side of the very confused vampire. "I'm not letting you get away with telling this woman a lie, Joe."

Lilly walked forward, almost through the ghost of Joseph, to the door of the room, turning as she went so she never lost sight of the three ghosts. "What do you want from me?" she asked.

"Us, nothing, my dear. I came to see you to meet you, to see who you were. You're not human, are you?" Joseph looked into Lilly's dark eyes, questioningly. Then he smiled and nodded.

Lilly ignored his question, turning to the women, "I do not believe we have met. My name is Lilly. Yours?"

The dark haired woman floated closer, not bothering to even try to feign walking on the floor, "My name is Angelique. I lived here. I died here, because of him." she pointed toward Joseph. "You would do well to be wary of him; he seems to have a mean streak where we are concerned. He's not a nice man."

"Now wait, bitch. I did not harm you..." Joseph protested, walking toward her. Angelique did not give ground; she stood, floating, just above the floor, a look of anger on her face.

"You did nothing more than throw me through a window. Do not call me that name, sir." she held her head high.

"Joseph, cannot you cease lying even for a

moment?" the blond woman tried walking but was missing the floor herself, her feet moved but did not touch the ground. "You know you killed her, afraid of me finding her." the woman turned to Lilly, "I am sorry he has come to cause trouble, Miss. He does not seem to have any compunction toward behaving himself, even in death. I am Mary Wheaton, the unfortunate wife of the man before you." She extended her hand. Lilly put hers out but it went right through the proffered hand, cold air embracing her fingers.

"No bother, Mary. He had just arrived when you and Angelique came. Marcus and I were having a private discussion and he barged into my room unbidden. He casts dispersions on my friend and then tries to woo me away, but you came in time." Lilly nodded her head toward the skull, still sitting on the bed table and pulled the blanket closer to her.

"Mary, please. Woman go away. You have dogged my every step for over 200 years and I am sorely tired of you. When we wed, it was 'until death do you part' but you have not left after death. I give you leave, once again; go away, find your bliss elsewhere." Joseph waved his hands up and down in agitation.

"Silence, bastard. You brought shame on our family and I will never give you peace. You should have gone to prison for what you did, not killed yourself in front of me!" Mary positively shrieked, her ghostly form getting larger than it was in life. "You should pay for what you have done to her," pointing to Angelique, "and to me! I could not live with the shame and took my own life because of you. Now we all three walk this forsaken hovel night after night as you try to assuage your own soul with lies. I should have been in heaven by now, but for you. Libertine! Debauchee! You could not keep your pants around your waist no matter how much you tried, if it was a trollop, you were on it. I used to beg you to stay home, to be a decent husband!" Mary screamed in anger and frustration, the room getting even colder than before.

"Woman, you overstep!" Joseph slid toward his dead wife, arm raised in a fist ready to strike her. They stood toe to toe in front of Lilly, and Joseph brought his arm down in a fearsome punch, only to go right straight through the apparition. Mary cackled as her form dissipated and then reformed, taunting him. Joseph shouted in anger, "Damn it, woman, damn you to hell!"

"You should be so lucky, bastard." she screamed back at him. "You will be there long before I, that is for sure, and in a lower pit as well, you and your whoring ways, your murder, and your lies. I have no doubt of it!"

Angelique, silent since the fight had started now floated up to the couple, "Whoring? You call me a whore, bitch? You, who could not keep your man satisfied so he had to come find love in another woman's arms? You, the shrew, have the gall to call me a whore?"

Mary whirled on the darker ghost, eyes blazing, "Yes, I call you whore! Slut! Trollop! You tempt married men away from their wedded wives and into debauchery. And it is because of you that he is now what he is and you caused my death as well. You are no innocent in this, madam."

Angelique flew toward the other woman, trying to grab her blond hair. But, once again, she turned to mist and reformed, the other ghostly woman passing right through her with a scream of angry frustration. She whirled around and went back again. And, once again, she passed straight through her target.

Lilly stood in the doorway, holding the blanket around herself and surveying this all-out catfight between the ghostly women. She was confused as to why they decided to pick tonight to show up and disturb her time alone with Marcus, but as Marcus didn't seem to mind the show, she stood silent and let the caterwauling continue unabated.

Mary continued to berate Joseph while hurling insults at Angelique who alternately hid behind Joseph and flew at Mary in an attempt to shut her up. Joseph hurled insults at both women and threatened bodily violence that he obviously was unable to achieve. The chaos continued for almost a half hour before Lilly tired enough of it to intervene.

"ENOUGH!" Lilly screamed into the fray. All three specters stopped in mid fight and turned enmass to her. She raised one finger and put it to her lips, "Shhhh, all of you. I am tired of listening to your fighting. If you came here to fight, you need to take it elsewhere because I am not going to put up with any more of it."

Mary's eyes narrowed, "And how do you propose to banish us should we choose not to listen to you, mortal."

"I have ways. I know ways of voodoo, spells from Marie Laveau herself that can banish ghosts such as you straight back to hell." She wasn't sure if the ghosts knew of the Voodoo Queen of New Orleans but she took that chance. Lilly had seen the daughter, the second Marie, when she was with Miss Lulu. Stories of the first Marie were still very popular and since the woman had been buried in St. Louis Cemetery, so close to Mahogany Hall, Lilly knew of the stories. She just hoped the phantoms would know the name.

"You lie!" Angelique was the one who spoke up. "I was at her ceremonies at the lake and I never saw you there! You try to intimidate us."

"Do I? Are you sure that I did not meet her after your death? You are much older than I am; you know I could know the Queen after you fell." Lilly hoped her information was correct; it had been a very long time since she had recalled the stories of the conjure woman and her life. "I know how to rid a house of shades and I will not hesitate to do it if you do not cease your fighting and leave here."

Mary started to speak up, "I do not think you..."

"Oh give it a rest already, Mary. She has told us to leave. We should give her the silence she craves and go, without telling her what we came here to tell." Joseph shook his head and started for the outer wall. The others turned to go with him, gliding silently.

"Wait! What were you going to tell me?" she called after them. "I did not know you had something to tell me. What was it?"

"Oh, now she wants us here." Mary whirled on her, "As long as we are here for you, strumpet, it is fine if we stay. Otherwise, we're banished from our own home." The ghosts began to come back toward her.

"That is not what I meant! I was trying to stop the fighting. It gives me a headache and I do not think it will solve anything. All of you are dead, you are stuck here, you should be trying to find a way out of this mess." Lilly tried hard to remain calm in the face of the advancing spooks. "What was it you wanted to tell me?"

Joseph stopped, the women stopping their advance as well. "Very well." he sighed, "Telling you what we came to was a try at that way out, maybe if we help you we can all move on to the afterlife and leave here forever." Joseph looked to each of the ghostly women and then back at her. "Lady Lilly, we know what you are. A vampire. You drink blood to survive, you are dead as we are but yet you have flesh that we do not."

"Well, yes. I guess that word fits my situation. You did not come here just to identify my condition, did you? You have something else you want to say." she cocked her head a bit, as if listening. "Marcus says you are hiding something. What?"

The ghosts looked back at the silent, dead skull on the bed side table and then back at her.

"You cannot be..." Mary started to say but Joseph held up his hand and she quieted.

"Marcus is correct. We are hiding something. We came to discuss the person you were here with last night. He is not what he appears to be." Joseph said. "We were checking you both out when you came. He appears to be a vampire, like you. But his being isn't completely vampire. There is something else there that we do not understand."

"He is vampire, true. I do not know what else you are talking about. I am the one who turned him into a vampire so I know he is." she shook her head, "That cannot be all you had to say."

Joseph shook his head, "No, it is not all. He is dangerous, Lady Lilly. Something dark is within him and he is not in control of it. We fear for you with him."

Lilly's eyebrows rose, "You do? But he is kind and loving. Marcus trusts him, I trust him. Surely you are mistaken in your analysis of him." She knew he had a temper, she had seen it firsthand. But he had had a good reason and he had apologized and seemed to be suitably contrite. She was wary of him but she wasn't going to tell these spooks that.

"No, we see what you cannot. He has a great capacity to love, true, but he is also dark and sinister and there is something very, very wrong with him. We came to warn you about him, tell you to beware of him and what he might do." Mary had come right up in front of her in her ardor. "You must beware!"

Lilly looked over to Marcus, trying to hear anything he had to say about the information she was getting. Then she looked back to the ghosts before her, "I will heed your warning. So far he has not shown me that he is dangerous but I will keep your words in mind. Thank you for letting me know."

"Well then, we will take our leave of you. We wish you well." Joseph turned again to leave, the women following him, across the room and then through the wall to the courtyard. The last words she heard as they passed outside were "Well, that appears not to have worked either. We're still stuck."

"That was interesting, Marcus. I wonder if they are right?" she said out loud in the silent room.

SULLIVAN APPROACHED THE shattered, unhinged main door of the River Walk Mall cautiously. His senses were on high alert because, as he had walked from the pub to the river and then across to the plaza, he had heard the gunshots and shouts from deeper in the city. Every shadow had the potential to hide someone out to do harm and Sully wasn't keen on having to fight anyone without his angelic abilities. He knew vampires were quicker and stronger than humans but he was not sure how different they were. He didn't want to have his first vampiric rumble to be with one with a drugged up thug with an attitude of superiority and that's what he was anxious about.

One thing he needed to do was try to catch any clues of the angels on assignment in New Orleans. He must to try to get their attention so they would know he was hurt, in trouble, and needing help getting back to heaven, to headquarters. Usually there were angelic contrails marking the movements of various angels in an area, each color coded to the wing codes of the different jobs. Any angel could recognize who else was in the area by these contrail signatures. It was something they could just see.

But Sullivan could not see them now he was alone and THAT feeling made him afraid. It was a feeling he had never experienced before, like all the other feelings he had recently experienced. Somehow the loss of his wings and his ring had severed the ability to communicate and even to see other angels. He looked into the sky, trying to will the contrails into sight but the darkness, with the stars shining bright with the lack of light pollution usually seen in New Orleans. The lack of electricity had at least one upside. He shook his head and breathed a prayer of help, hoping someone might hear it. The lack of communication with all he had known was disconcerting.

Of course, the doors to the mall had been torn open, a quick glance showed both the glass broken; the boards that had covered them were pulled off and thrown into the plaza. It was evident that looters had beat him to the mall and he hoped that the things he needed were still available, and that he didn't encounter any of the looters.

He ducked into the building and his eyesight adjusted to the difference in light immediately. He could see down the long, dark building, glass glittering on the floors where the windows of the various shops had been smashed. He strained to hear what was deeper into the building and he could hear a few heartbeats, some footsteps, but not large numbers. A random thug he would be able to take on without a problem.

He walked down the hallway, surveying each of the shops unnecessary. He was looking for a few, specific items and did not want to have to search everywhere for them. He found his first target soon after entering, a luggage store. He needed a couple of suitcases to carry items in. He stepped through the broken door and into the room. While it had been looted and things tossed, it held enough promise that he walked deeper, searching. He found a larger, wheeled red suitcase with a pull handle and then a backpack and a sports bag. Each item was tagged for sale and Sullivan pulled those off. On a notepad that he found in the back office, he wrote down each item and its price and then he wrapped the tags in a note promising payment for the items once things settled out. He did not want to be stealing from the stores but this was a situation where they needed things and he wasn't in a position to pay.

He carefully exited the store with his newly found items and walked further into the dark. He found a men's store and entered, gathering a couple of pairs of jeans and shirts for himself. He also found socks and another pair of shoes to replace the boots he wore; they were not comfortable enough for long hikes. He packed each item in the sports bag as he took the tags off, once again leaving the letter and tags for the owners when they were finally able to return. The list on his pad grew with items and costs dutifully noted for each store.

After finding the men's clothing, he went in search of the items he would need for Lilly. He found a store with clothing for women and went inside. He removed the rope from his pocket and started searching for the correct sizes. It was dark, complicate work; he had never had to dress a woman before. The stagnant air was stifling within the concrete building with no air conditioning. There were no open windows and, while the corridor outside was cooler because of the doors and windows being broken, the stores had no such breezes to cool them. He didn't, however, have a problem with the heat, the humidity just made the air feel close, like a second skin. Sully searched for just the right size. He finally found what he thought would work and began to gather items. Three pairs of jeans, three t-shirts, a pair of sneakers and a pair of high heels began to pile up on a table he had cleared. Then he saw it: a magnificent green cocktail dress still mounted on a mannequin. He carefully measured the dress and, finding it the size he needed, he removed it from the dummy and placed it on the pile. He found undergarments and socks to complete the stack and then began to list each item, pull the tags. He noted that this store had an additional bulky plastic clip attached to each item and he had to search to find the tool to remove them. Once that was accomplished, he taped the tags into the letter, left it on the desk in the back room, packed his finds carefully in the red suitcase and left.

As he traversed the corridor, he caught a shadow moving along one of the walls. He stopped and listened but could not identify any heartbeat or footsteps. He scented the air revealing nothing but the stench of wet, mildewing and rotting things, not pleasant. Whatever the shadow was, it didn't seem to be anything to worry about so he dismissed it and continued his quest.

His final stop was a small pharmacy. He could hear voices in this store but he needed items from it. He heard four males in the pharmacy area, obviously ferreting around for drugs added by red tinted flashlights. Stashing the bags in an out of the way corner, he steeled himself for the upcoming confrontation and stepped into the store. He silently moved toward the red glow.

"Damn it, Dark, can't you even read, idiot? We're looking for cough syrup, codeine, pain killers. Not fucking vitamins, man. Pull yo head outta yo ass!" the voice drifting from the back sounded familiar.

Very familiar.

Sullivan's thoughts ran through the beating he took when he first came to New Orleans and the voices matched. He had stumbled upon the four guys who had given him that beating. He smiled a very grim yet pleased smile; he would get a chance to pay them back for the beating, for frightening Lilly, and for taking his wings. He had a score to settle and he was more than happy to do so.

The one called Lips walked out of the pharmacy area, carrying a sack with bottles in it. He collided with the large angel-turned-vampire and he looked up. Then he shrieked, dropping the sacks and scrambling back to his friends.

"Shut the fuck up...dumbass!" Chewie fiercely whispered. "We gotta be quiet! Or some dickhead is gonna hunt us 'n find our shit. It's bad enough we got secon' pickin's."

"Eeek." Mockingly squealed Dark, "A Mouse!" He nudged Razor and both men laughed.

"Chewie, th... that guy, f...from the cemetery that w...we beat? He ain't dead, he's s...standin' out th...th...there in the d...dark w...wa...waitin' f...for us." Lips could barely get the words out.

"You dumbass. He's dead. Razor killed him dead when he cut those fancy wings off. You are imaginin' things." Chewie whispered as he punched the scared man in the shoulder. "Go on and get out, we're right behin' ya."

Lips shook his head and stepped aside, motioning for the other guys to go out of the pharmacy door before him. He knew what he saw and he was not looking forward to stepping out there again. Razor stepped out first, Dark following. Chewie grabbed him by the shirt and almost threw him through the door in front of him.

"God DAMN!" Razor yelled as he encountered the big, dark shape that began to seem to grow out of the tile toward him. He fumbled for his blade and whipped it open, holding it in front of him. "You's dead, dude. We killed you!"

"It obviously didn't work, did it? Hello gentlemen, long time, no see." Sullivan tried very hard to reflect the calm he wasn't feeling. "Fancy meeting up with you again, doing more stealing." He shook his head.

"W...well, you's not d...dead right now b...but we b...be killin' yo ass now." Dark pulled out a kitchen knife from his belt.

"Hey dummies, you don't want to take me on. Remember, who was it who got you to go back into that graveyard in the beginning? Who stood by while you got your hands dirty with my blood? And who keeps making you do all the hard work." Sullivan looked straight at Chewie. "Why don't ya'll just let the big guy here take me on, mano-a-mano, and ya'll step back this time." Sullivan pointed at Chewie. He smiled and chuckled deeply when he noticed the nasty scratches and bite marks on his face. Glancing down, he saw Chewie's bandaged arm, all courtesy of Baron.

"Man, I ain't fightin' you. That's what I have a gang for, I don't have to fight." Chewie puffed up. "Razor, go cut that guy, and make it good this time."

Razor started toward Sullivan, who anticipated the charge, grabbed Razor's wrist, twisted, and the pop of the broken bones as the knife clattered to the floor was just audible under the scream of pain coming out of Razor's mouth. Sully dropped him and the younger man scrambled out of reach, holding his wrist, tears flowing down his face.

Chewie gestured to Lips who shook his head, then he turned to Dark, "Dude, kill that sonofabitch." Dark took three steps toward Sullivan who took one step forward, meeting him eye to eye.

Dark glanced at Razor and then backed off, "Hell no, m...man. You kick his ass. I'm outta it."

Sullivan kept staring at Chewie. The thug stood very nervously despite his bravado. Then Sully noticed the black top hat with the gray feather. HIS feather, stolen from the wings the gang had beaten him and taken. Sully wanted that feather and he wanted this particular man dead. A fleeting thought of knowing he should not kill floated through his brain and evaporated. He knew he had the short guy rattled but he also knew guys like him didn't back down it was now a matter of pride for the gang leader. He had to prove himself to the others or lose them. Sullivan gestured, opening his hands, palms up, inviting the thug to rush him, mimicking the same gesture Chewie had directed at him in the cemetery.

Chewie stood his ground for a moment, trying to get a read on what the man was doing. He wasn't sure that the guy didn't have brain damage from the beating that he took at their hands. But he wasn't going to move without a little more idea what he was up against.

"Afraid Chewie?" Sullivan taunted. "I see, you're the big man, you hide behind the other guys so you don't have to do the hard stuff. You're just a big old coward, aren't you?"

Coward. That word was the one thing Chewie would never let anyone use against him. His old man had called him that when he used to come home drunk and beat him and his mother. It was the one word he loathed more than anything and the use of it by the man standing in front of him would not happen a second time. With a shout, Chewie charged the man, the baseball bat Lips usually carried held high in his hands.

As he rushed Sullivan, the vampire reached out and plucked the bat out of his hands like taking a lollypop from a child. Chewie flew past him and crashed into a shelving unit, head first, the top hat falling to the floor in the process.

"Hey dude. That was clumsy. You trying to hurt me or are we dancin' here?" Sullivan taunted. Chewie shook off the effects of the fall and scrambled to his feet, He doubled up both fists and that was when Sullivan saw it: the angel-wing ring. His ring. The link to the heavens. The bastard was still wearing it after he had him beaten and torn up in the cemetery. His vision flashed red. Then it narrowed until the room only contained the offending hand with the ring and he snapped.

Sullivan reached out, punched the cocky kid in the face once, twice, then grabbed him and held him while he punched him over and over. He dangled the hapless thug by the one bandaged arm as he punched his punctured face, midsection, and even his crotch with brutal blows, over and over again as the others watched in horror. It was vicious and it was fast.

Then he smelled the blood. The coppery tang hit Sullivan's nose as he pounded the man, enticing him to further violence. Somewhere in the back of his mind, something called "stop" but he ignored it as the sound of the pounding heart in the body in his hand beckoned him. He felt his fangs descend and the pull of the smell of blood became overwhelming. Sullivan grabbed the man, holding his head over with one hand as the other clutched the struggling body to him. He looked, briefly at the shocked faces of the other men and then plunged his fangs into the jugular vein, blood spurting up into his mouth.

He drank deeply, not bothering to worry about what he was doing. As he drank, his hand slid from the head of the aggressor to the hand that wore the winged ring. He tugged and ended up pulling off the finger with the ring. The feeling of the wet, bloody finger on his hand jolted him back into reality and he dropped the body. The heart still beat...barely. Sullivan looked up and into the faces of the shocked and stunned, frightened men who had called Chewie boss. They were pale and Lips had pissed his pants in fear. Sullivan closed his eyes and felt his fangs retract. He took his hand and wiped the blood from his lips. Then he removed the finger from the ring, flinging the offending digit to the floor next to the now dead body. He placed the ring on his finger and looked at them.

"Anyone want to go next?" Sully worked to

keep his voice steady. He was beginning to shake at what he had just done but he could not let the others know just how much this had affected him. The remaining men shook their heads and took off at a run, Razor still cradling his broken wrist.

Sullivan looked down at the cooling body, a little blood still leaking from the puncture wounds in his neck and from the missing space on his hand. He wanted to be upset about having killed someone, his first kill, but he just could not muster the emotion. This man had tried to kill him twice and he couldn't find it in his heart to be emotional about it. All he could feel was the blood energy flowing through him, filled with electricity. He could take on anything at this point, he was invincible. Picking up the battered top hat, Sullivan plucked the feather from it and dropped the hat on the dead body. The precious feather was the last vestige of his former life, a life he was sure was over. He knelt down and put the feather into the red suitcase, laying it carefully among the t-shirts to protect it.

He turned his back and walked across the drugstore to the makeup. He carefully picked out some eye shadow to match the dress and the blouses that he had picked up. He found some powder and then a hairbrush. Then he went to the perfume cabinet. He smashed the glass case and started pulling out bottles, smelling the contents of several bottles. Then he found the right scent, one that had floral tones that he thought would complement Lilly's own scent. He looked at the label and smiled. Channel No. 5. He laid that into the basket on his arm and went looking for a few other items. He found some cheap jewelry, a hand mirror, shampoo and soap, two pairs of sunglasses, a large brimmed hat. Each item went into the basket.

Then he went to find the last things he thought Lilly might like. He picked up some magazines, a news magazine, a fashion magazine, an automobile magazine. He found a travel magazine with many pictures and he smiled. She thought automobiles were strange, wait until she got a look at an airplane. He went to the office and began, once again, to catalogue the items and take tags off of them. He wrote the note and then he caught sight of a laptop computer laying between the wall and the desk where it had fallen. He picked it up, opened it, and pushed the power button. It came up and, surprisingly, there was no power-on password or lock. He added the information about the laptop to the letter and his list, found the power cord, and then shut down the machine and tucked it into the red suitcase. The other things went into the backpack. On his way out he grabbed some chips and cookies and slipped out of the store and down the corridor to the exit. He had what he had come for but also left something he never counted on.

He walked down the corridor and slipped through the door and back out into the hot, New Orleans night.

THE DEATH BOTHERED him, but not as much as he thought he would. Sullivan knew he should be remorseful but somehow, as he walked through the night back toward the pub, he found he couldn't really round up the necessary feelings. Had the change to vampire changed his conscience somehow?

His finger rubbed the ring and he looked down. He had the key to being able to contact heaven, the ring acted as a transmitter to allow angels to communicate. He looked up, seeking the contrails once again.

The stars winked back at him, bright as ever. Not one colored streak of condensation was visible.

The ring did not work. His ability to communicate with other angels was severed, possibly with his wings. He wasn't sure if that was what happened but the resultant inability to contact was dismissed quickly as he caught the shadow once again. It was sliding around the top of one of the buildings about a block down the street. He could not tell if it was a bird or animal shadow or whether it was something more sinister. He set his shoulders and walked purposefully down the street, putting out an air of calm, cautious "don't fuck with me" attitude, something rather hard to do when you were wearing a backpack and carrying luggage. He hoped he didn't make too much of an opportunistic target.

Shadows played on the tops of the building, catching light from who knew where. Sullivan felt like he was being watched but he could not find the source. Probably his mind playing tricks on him after the fight and near blood-lust. He didn't believe that the other guys were going to follow him, after what he did to their leader; they were probably half-way to Baton Rouge by now.

He debated which direction to take back. Canal was still heavily flooded, but now it was Looter Central. He really didn't want to be closer to the river even though it was high ground, not sure that there wasn't trouble along the trolley tracks lying in wait either. He finally just took off running across Canal, heading as straight as he could between buildings heading for Iberville. All along the way he heard gunshots off in the distance. His hearing had changed and he wasn't sure just how far away the voices he could hear occasionally but he didn't want to stick around to find out. He went just as fast as he dared to St. Peters and then hugged the buildings all the way back to Toulouse. He could swear there was something following him and he ducked into the doorway of the restaurant on the corner to listen for footsteps. He could hear one lone set of footsteps approaching from the next block. He grabbed the luggage and walked, carefully trying to appear normal to whomever was out there. He didn't want cops asking questions, especially with blood splattered on him like it was. He could feel the night fleeting and knew he had to get in and settled before the dawn. He could see the building just ahead and began to ease his walk a little more.

He slipped his hand into his pocket and withdrew the key to the pub. Just a bit more and he would be...

"Halt. Stop and turn around where I can see your hands." a male voice called from a few feet away. Great, just what he wanted, a cop trying to figure out who he was and why he was here and covered with blood. He lifted his hands, dropping the handles to the luggage and turned. What he saw wasn't police, the tall, beefy kid in his mid-20's wearing a naval uniform, holding a flashlight in one hand and a pistol in the other.

"Hey! Glad to see another sane face! I thought I was getting jumped again before I could get into the building." Sully smiled and tried to turn on the charm, hoping to cause the guy to leave him alone.

"You're pretty bloody. What have you been doing and where's the other guy?" The name tag on the uniform read "Deere". The stripes had him pegged as a second-class Petty Officer and the little symbol in the stripes looked like a medical symbol. Not Shore Patrol, thankfully. Maybe he could talk this guy out of making a scene.

"Man, I was on my way over here from a friend's place that got flooded. Damned asshole looter tried to grab my gear. I had to beat the hell out of him to get him to leave me alone." Sullivan shrugged. At least that wasn't a lie, mostly.

"You walked all the way over here to the Quarter?" the kid was sharp, skeptical of the story Sully was trying to weave. "What's here that you can get into?"

Sully jingled the keys in his hand, "Buddy of

mine owns this place. I have keys. He told me we…I…could stay here if things got bad. So, I'm going to bunk here until I figure out what I'm going to do." He hoped the story would ring true enough, and he hoped the Corpsman didn't flash onto the mistake he made about another person being involved.

"We? I don't see anyone else with you." No such luck, the kid was sharp.

"My girlfriend is upstairs. I went to get our things and come back. She's expecting me to be here." Sully could feel the darkness waning, he didn't have much time to waste trying to get this guy to leave. "We're fine, just hanging out and trying to figure what we are going to do next."

"You know there is a mandatory evacuation coming, right? Everyone is evacuating the city because of the devastation. You would be best to move on to the Convention Center since that is where everyone is going to leave from." The guy gestured with the flashlight toward downtown. "It's not safe any longer in the city and they want everyone out."

"I really don't want to leave the city. We've got stuff here, food, drink. A decent roof and lockable doors. We should be safe here until the city gets back up and running." Sullivan was talking fast, trying to figure out what he needed to do to get this guy to go away.

"I can't just leave you here, there's no water, no sanitation, little food and no help. There's a lot of looting, well, you know that one already." Corpsman Deere was not letting this go, that was obvious.

Sullivan closed his eyes for a second, gathering the energy to try one more time to talk this guy out of having them leave O'Flaherty's. "Look, Mr. Deere. I need you to understand, we are not going to evacuate. You need to just note we're here and then go on your way. We are safe, we are fine, and we will be fine. Just listen to what I'm telling you and go on your way, leave us alone." Sullivan looked the sailor right in the eyes, trying to show that he would not back down on the question.

Corpsman Deere's eyes seemed to glaze over and his demeanor changed. "I really should be just notating this and then leaving you here. You are fine, you are safe. I will leave you alone."

Sullivan raised an eyebrow. Did he just hear what he thought he did? He tried something, "You will leave. Just notate a man was going to check on his business and then left. Nothing was wrong and the gentleman was fine, not bloody, just wet with flood water. He was leaving town."

The Corpsman took out a pad from his pocket and a pen. He wrote down the address and then a few notes. Then he pocketed the items. "I guess I will report to the hospital. You be safe, ok?"

"I will be. Be careful. Goodbye, Corpsman Deere." Sullivan was amazed as the young sailor put his pistol away and walked on down Toulouse Street toward Bourbon Street. He never even looked back.

He looked up and saw the beginning streaks of dawn above the buildings. Turning, he unlocked the door, pulled the luggage in, and locked it again. Carrying the pieces on one arm, he opened the door to the pub inside and started in. Baron, done with his night's hunt, ran under his legs and streaked up the stairs toward the apartment they were staying in. Sullivan followed and opened the door to the room for them both.

Baron sauntered in and went to the couch, jumping up and curling into a ball. He ignored the couple, closing his eyes.

Lilly sat on the bed, still wrapped in the blanket. "I didn't think you were going to make it back." She looked concerned.

"I didn't think I would be this late. I ran into some difficulties." he pushed the suitcases into the bedroom and smiled at her. "But I made it."

"You're bloody. Did you have to fight someone?"

"Yes. Those thugs who jumped me the first night were in the building. I had to convince them to leave me alone. I managed to get my ring,..." he held up his hand, "...back again. They won't be bothering us, or probably anyone else, for a while." he sat down next to her. "I'll explain when we wake up. I don't know about you but I feel the dawn coming and I'm getting pretty heavy-eyed." He yawned, even though he didn't need the oxygen any longer. He said nothing about the feather.

Lilly smiled at him, stood, and laid the blanket back on the bed, straightening it out. Then she took off the shirt she was wearing and crawled into the bed, naked. Sullivan stripped down and slid in next to her, taking her in his arms and kissing her deeply. He wanted to go further but the pull of the rising sun took over and pulled them both into their deep, deathlike sleep for the day, still wrapped around each other.

Chapter Ten

RANGUEL WAS CHECKING his boards when the flashing caught his attention. The communication was coming from New Orleans by the information. He punched the board "Ranguel"

The voice coming through the speaker was female but not one he immediately recognized. "Sir, this is Sophiel. I think I have a sighting on Sullivan but his energy signature isn't right. I was not sure because he's been moving in closed buildings where I had trouble tracking him but the signature I got was vampire, sir."

Ranguel's eyebrows narrowed and his wings darkened. "Are you sure? Could a vampire be nearby and that was what you are picking up?"

"I'm not sure. I was close enough to him while he was talking to another man but I was getting defined vampire signals. I am not sure of which man had the signature and I was getting overlap from another couple of places that confused it. But I wanted to check in and let you know that I have found someone I believe may be him but I will be checking further and report back." Sophiel closed the communication, leaving Ranguel to think about what might have happened to his angel and what, if anything could be done about it if Sophiel was correct.

He decided to be quiet and not go to the Archangel Council until he heard more definite information. He knew one thing, this wasn't good, didn't sound good at all. He shook his head and turned back to his boards.

Chapter Eleven

THE SUN SET and Lilly opened her eyes to see Sullivan looking at her, a smile on his face. "Good morning sunshine!" he said, then screwed up his face and re-smiled, "Or should I say 'Good Evening'?" He pronounced the two words with a very bad Bela Lugosi accent.

"Why did you say it like that? It sounded strange." she asked him and he groaned.

"Movie reference, sorry." He was still surprised when she didn't understand a modern reference. "Moving picture. I think you had these back in your human days but they weren't called that." He struggled to remember just what was going on in 1900 in the film industry. "They put things in a little box; you would pay money and put your face on a viewer on the top. The box would light up and there would be pictures shown that looked like they moved. They told stories…"

"Oh! Vitascopes!" she blossomed into a big smile. "We would down to Canal Street early in the morning. There was a place, Vitascope Hall, that showed moving pictures on a big screen, outside the boxes. The boxes were called

Kenescopes, but those were old by the time I was here in New Orleans. The Vitascope Hall was brand new. I think I remember it opening in either April or May before I moved to the little house. They would not let us, the ladies of Storyville, come during the evenings or when the 'decent people' were there. The ladies of Storyville were very restricted in what we could do, even more than the other Negroes in the city." Lilly looked into the distance, her smile fading. "We were 'soiled' and shunned, even by our own. Oh, they would come for sex but we were hidden, like their sin." Lilly forced her smile back on and the lightness back into her voice. "We would be, however, allowed to go to some of the special things when they were not being used otherwise. I do not know how Miss Lulu managed it but one day she gathered all of us up and took us down to Canal Street to this place, a former store that had seats in it. It was dark. The man who was there stood in the back and worked a machine. The room lit up and there were these pictures on the wall. People were dancing in a garden in the sunshine. It was not very long but it was magical." she sighed, smiling so. "Was that the thing you are talking about?"

"Yes, those were very early motion pictures, movies. They have gotten so much better since then, you will love it." He wondered what her reaction to Star Wars Episode III or Batman Begins would be, or if she would like an animated film like Madagascar.

"There is something though, you used a word,

Negroes, in your description. You will want to take that out of your vocabulary. It was right in your era but it is now considered a bad name, a slur." Sullivan made a mental note to take her to a movie just as soon as they left New Orleans. He wanted to watch her face as she saw her first one.

"Really? It's not used anymore? What do they call people like me now?" The change in language was strange and she wanted to know more.

Sullivan hesitated, wondering how to compress over a hundred years of civil rights history into a mere few sentences. "Most call themselves African-Americans. Or Black. And they are part of the entire world now, not kept away from others. They are in government; the mayor of New Orleans is a black man. The police force, the fire department, the city council all have blacks in prominent positions. There are blacks on the Supreme Court and there's hope that soon there will either be a black or a woman, or a black woman, as President of the United States. You can live where you want, be what you want now Lilly. A lot of good people gave their lives to get that achieved but it's now a reality." Sullivan had to admit; civil rights was one of the most important changes since she was living.

"Indeed? Well that sounds wonderful. So, I can go anywhere, be anything I want now?" She asked almost skeptically, Sullivan nodded. "Wow." she sat up in the bed, pulling the blanket up in front of her. "So tell me, what new thing we do tonight?" her smile was back. Sullivan loved to see her smile and he would do almost anything to keep it there.

"Well, why don't you go look in the red suit-case I brought for you then?" he pointed to the bags he had dropped in the room just before dawn. She looked at him, smiled, and climbed out of the bed and pulled the cases over.

Then she began to turn it over and around, looking for a lock to open the red one. It had a strange handle with little wheels on it, she noticed. The handle was something that she hadn't seen before, it wasn't wood or metal, it was smooth and felt lightweight. But she could not find the lock anywhere. "Ok, I think it opens but I cannot find the lock."

He swung his feet over the edge of the bed and laughed, "You have never seen a zipper either. Look, take that little tab right there..." he pointed at the edge of one side, "...and pull it toward you, down the line."

She grasped the little tab, noticing the strange line around the suitcase. She pulled and the two parts of the line parted and she could tell that the lid would come up once it was separated. She couldn't help herself, she smiled, giggled, and then pulled the tab the other way and the line closed again. "What did you call this?"

"A zipper. It's very common now. Made of plastic..."

"Plastic? What is that?" She was sure she would eventually figure out all this strange new world she found herself in.

"It's something they use a lot to make almost everything. It is lightweight, not metal or wood, and is less costly." He was so amused by her enthusiasm, her willingness to learn. Something as simple as a zipper was a wonder and he loved watching her discover it.

"Ok, pull this and...oh, yes, that opens it! So much better than locks and keys." she tossed the lid open and looked into the case. "Now, what do we have here?" She dug out one blouse and held it up. She cocked her head at it, trying to figure it out, "It looks like a blouse but it has no buttons. The color is so bright." She frowned, obviously disappointed, "It is far too small for me.".

"Oh no, it's not. That is something called a T-shirt. It's made of cotton with a blend of a type of plastic. It stretches. You pull it over your head and put your arms in it, like the one I am wearing. It's supposed to fit you. There are three of them in there, that blue one, a green one, and a purple one with a design on it." He pointed into the case. She pulled out the green one and held it up, folded it, and then pulled out the purple one. It was like the others but it had writing on it. A masquerade mask, some beads, and the words 'New Orleans Mardi Gras' were all on the shirt but it wasn't woven into the fabric. It looked like paint but it didn't flake off. "I know, another new something. But I like it. It's pretty. I always loved Mardi Gras; it was always so much fun."

As she pulled out the t-shirts, the gray feather fell out and floated to the floor.

"What's that?" Lilly asked as Sully reached out and plucked it up.

"It's a feather. They are supposed to be good

luck so I kept it. We could use some luck."

"Oh, okay." She pulled out something that looked like men's trousers, made of the material that looked somewhat like dungarees that was common with the workers, much like the ones Sullivan wore. It had a button at the top, a...zipper, and they were blue. "I think you got your clothing in with mine." She tried to hand the jeans to him but he laughed and pushed them back at her.

"They are blue jeans. Very popular now, everyone wears them, men and women." The look of shock on her face was priceless.

"No. Women wear men's clothing in public now?" she was really shocked, from the tone of her voice. "I don't know that I could do that. It doesn't seem proper. Even a Storyville girl has some dignity."

He leaned over and pulled over the backpack. Lilly watched him unzip it and he pulled out some books. "Here, let's look at these." He laid the magazines next to her and she picked them up gently, almost afraid of what they contained.

She took the first one and whispered, "L'oh mon!" The pictures on the front of the fashion magazine looked like they could step off the page. The girl in the red clothing looked less dressed than she did in her clothing in the brothel; it was tight around her body, no sleeves, and very low cut. And this was out on the cover; she was curious and opened up the pages. Sullivan was right; women were wearing trousers, in public. Tight ones. And the dresses were all short, above the knee and much more form-fitting. She kept turning the pages, looking at each incredible picture of women. The stories talked about jobs, makeup, hairstyles, and clothing. And sex. Openly published in a magazine.

"I think things have changed much more than I ever thought! This is so, incredible." she waved the magazine, "I have so much to learn! What else did you bring?" She picked up the travel magazine and started to leaf through it.

"Hey! We can look at those later. You were going to get dressed and we were going out, remember?" Sullivan chuckled. He lifted the magazines out of her lap and took the one in her hands. "Check out the rest of it," he encouraged.

She dug out the other jeans, one in black, then she lifted out a black bra with a very confused look on her face. "What's this?" she asked.

"A bra." He was confused too, that had been such a normal part of women's clothing for so many years. "You don't know bras?"

"No. what is it used for?" The 'bra' had two rounded parts connected by several straps. She turned it over in her hands trying to figure it out. It looked like nothing she had ever seen. He had it with the clothing, was it made to wear?

"Ok, ok. Bras are coverings for the breasts. That's why I measured you breasts yesterday. The two cloth pieces go over them and it has shoulder straps and hooks in back." he took the garment and held it by the straps to show her how it looked. "They consider these very sexy these days."

"Looks odd." she put it aside and grabbed another silky item. It looked a bit like a silky pair of drawers but much smaller. "And this?" She was very amused by this point at all the changes and giggled.

"Panties. They go on the bottom. And yes, they stretch." She put her hands on her hips and looked askance at Sullivan. "No, really, look." He grabbed a ladies magazine and flipped to a Victoria's Secret ad. He handed it to Lilly, "See!" Her smile twinkled in the darkness. Sullivan hadn't realized just how beautiful she was, how much he was loving the chance to be with her and show her the world he knew. Her laughter was contagious and sounded like the happiest bells he had ever heard, even in Heaven. He was fascinated with her, everything about her.

She lifted the laptop out of the suitcase with a puzzled look, "Not clothing. Right?"

He burst into raucous laughter, "No, no, not clothing. It is a computer. I will show you what it does later; it's like a book with pictures. We need electricity for it, though."

"Ok, good. I could not figure out how to wear a box." She dived into the suitcase and lifted out the green dress. "OOH, this is very pretty. It looks like a dress but where is the rest of it?"

"It is a dress, just a short one. The fashion now."

She thought for a second and then asked "Can I wear this tonight?" she realized she had no idea what they had planned and what she should wear. She did not want to start her new life being thought of as a jaded trollop. The man beside her smiled again but shook his head.

"I would love to see you in that dress but I think we can hold off until we know what is out there now. There's a lot of unknown out there, some serious bad things, and I don't think you want to run in heels, and the dress would look silly with sneakers." he held up both types of shoes. The heels did look like they would be hard to walk/run in, there wasn't much to them and the back was angled high. The 'sneakers' looked like men's shoes but made out of something other than leather, white with a pink and blue emblem on the side.

"Ok. I will wear what you suggest, then. But, before I do, I would like to take a real bath. I saw a tub in the other room that looks like it would be good for a bath." She gestured toward the small bathroom.

While it had occurred to him that she would want a bath, he didn't expect it to be now. But it made sense, then he had to ask, "Lilly, in all your time in the cemetery, how did you bathe?"

"Oh, I did not actually have a bath after I left Miss Lulu's. At first I did not do anything. Then I would set out a small bowl to catch the rain and use that to wash. But then Marcus gave me an idea. I could move the door stone so I would wait until very late at night whenever it rained and step out and let the rain wash me. I did not have soap but the water did feel so good. And, sometimes there were roses dropped outside my door and I used to use those to lighten my smell a bit, rubbing them on some of the spots like my neck, wrists, and such." she looked at the room again. "I think a bath, a real bath, would feel wonderful."

"Well, let's do that." Sullivan stood up and went to the bathroom with her. They turned the water taps and nothing came out but a dribble and it was cold. Sully sighed. He was going to have to do this the hard way to give her a real bath.

"I'll be right back, I need to go down to the kitchen for a few minutes. Stay right there and keep looking gorgeous." He winked at her and she smiled.

As he bounded down the stairs, he caught that familiar feeling in his groin starting all over again. Every time he looked at her it seemed to happen. She was sexy and beautiful and he wanted to spend all his time in bed with her. And that concerned him because it was such a departure from the time he had spent as an angel.

He pulled out a large soup cauldron and filled it with hot water from the kitchen, which still worked, for the moment. Then he carried it up to the apartment. He quietly thanked God that the water heater seemed to be operated by gas instead of electricity.

"You aren't going to carry water like that and fill the whole tub, that is too much work." She remarked when he stepped back into the bedroom.

"Why not? I want you to have your first real bath in ages, it makes me happy to see you happy. And I would carry water from the river and heat it with a fire in the patio if I had to, just to see you smile." He slipped out and made a couple of trips down and back up carrying the hot water and filled the tub.

He helped her step in. As she sank down into the water, she moaned, sounding all the world like a sexual satisfied moan and his cock let him know it heard it very clearly.

"I think I am in heaven." she smiled, closing her eyes. Sullivan retrieved the backpack and came back into the room, sitting down beside her on the closed toilet. He began to remove items from the bag and show her each, the make-up items going onto the cabinet by the sink for later use. "You got me a brush!" she was obviously happy with that one.

"Ah, here's what I was looking for." Sully said, pulling out a bottle. "I picked up some shampoo, conditioner, and soap for you." He set the bottles on the side of the tub. She looked at them curiously. "Ah, ok, shampoo is liquid soap for your hair. Conditioner gets put on and then rinsed out next to make it easy to comb/brush out. The other bottle is a liquid soap for your body." He looked in the cabinet and pulled out a washcloth for her and one for himself. He rinsed and washed at the sink with a little of the water that he had saved back in the last cauldron, not wanting to use up any more of the hot water than he had to, saving it so that Lilly could enjoy another bath soon.

After drying, he sat by her side and chatted as

Lilly washed, helping her with the shampoo and washing her back. Once she was finished, he held out a large bath towel for her and helped her dry her hair. They walked into the bedroom; she grabbed a few items, and returned to the bathroom, shutting the door after her, leaving him staring at the door in anticipation. He removed the jewelry he had picked up, grabbed the perfume, and set those items on the bed where she would find them. Then he dressed himself in the things he had picked up.

She soon emerged, dressed in the black jeans and purple Mardi Gras shirt. Her hair was down and she was wearing makeup. She looked like a modern woman, a very beautiful, desirable modern woman. His cock stiffened in his own jeans with the look and he growled appreciatively, something in the back of his mind dismissing the question of why he was acting so sexually all the time. He was beginning not to care, at least when she was actually in the room with him, filling his senses.

"Does this meet your approval, Sullivan?" she turned slowly in front of him. Everything was in place, she looked luscious, and he grew harder and more uncomfortable in his jeans.

"Oh yes, you look ravishing, which is what I will be doing if you do not get yourself finished and we get out of here—we'll be spending the entire night in bed." he turned his back, adjusting the bulge, trying to will his cock to go down.

She walked over to the bed and picked up the jewelry, a necklace, a few bangle bracelets. "Oh, this is lovely! Thank you." Then she picked up the perfume bottle. "Channel No. 5? I've never heard of this one." She opened it and sniffed, then put a little drop on her wrist. "Oh, that is wonderful! It smells somewhat like the old perfumes I wore in my life."

He turned back and smiled. "Oh, yes, that is one of the expensive and coveted perfumes out there. Very popular." The smell on her, with the shampoo, soap, and now perfume just made his head spin. It was all he could do to keep from grabbing her and keeping her in the room for the night. "You ready?"

She nodded her head. She turned and reached out for the skull that was sitting on the bedside table. "I'm ready."

Sullivan let out a snort, trying to cover the annoyance about the seemingly single-mindedness Lilly showed about that skull and it being a real person. First it was her wanting that thing with her all the time, next it was the talking to it, but worst of all it was that it represented another man to her, someone she was obviously infatuated with. Sullivan disliked the guy and had never met him, probably never would either.

"Sweetie, I think Marcus needs to stay here." He hoped that didn't sound like he was feeling.

"Really? Why?"

Sullivan started to tell her he wasn't real and it was kind of creepy that she wanted to carry it around all the time but he figured that it would just upset her and that was the last thing he wanted to do. "I think he needs to be the one to guard our stuff and make sure no one breaks in and takes it." It sounded plausible, at least.

"Oh, ok, that makes sense." She turned the skull back toward her. "Marcus, we're going to go out for a while." She said as she gazed into the empty eye sockets. "Yes, I trust Sullivan to keep me safe for you while I'm gone. I promise I will be careful." She listened to the voice in her head for a moment and laughed, "Yes, yes, I'll be home before dawn, it will be ok." She gave a kiss to the forehead of the dead bone and laid it back on the table, facing out into the apartment. She smiled and patted it on the top. "See you later, dear one."

Sullivan stifled a shake of his head, sometimes he thought she really must be insane after the time in the crypt. But then she smiled at him and he took her hand and led her down the stairs to the bar, out the door to the breezeway, Marcus out of the way. Baron, of course, had followed them down, running past them on the stairs, waiting by the door and slipping out with them.

"Baron, you go have a good time too. We will be back in time for bed." Lilly stopped to pet the cat before he stepped out the main door to the street. He purred loudly and rubbed her legs a few times, then stepped out and disappeared into the night at a run.

SULLIVAN AND LILLY walked the quiet streets of the French Quarter. The stars shined bright in the absence of the lights usually there, being a new moon there was no shining orb in the sky to dim them further. They talked about how the city had changed, Lilly asking questions about things she would see that were new to her. They walked to Jackson Square and checked the cathedral doors.

"Locked." her tone of voice was unhappy. "I wanted to go in and light a candle for Marcus. As much as I feel him with me, I know he's probably dead after all these years. But I still love him."

Marcus. The ghost between them. Sullivan bristled at his name, jealousy rising in his veins. He was beginning to really hate this Marcus she always thought of, always talked of, always missed. And it was hate, that strong emotion coming to the surface for the first time.

"I know." He tried to call up the sound of empathetic concern in his voice when he really did not give a shit about the little, missing man. "I think you are probably right, he's probably passed on a long while ago" He managed a little more emphasis on long. "A candle is a nice gesture. I'm sure we can come back again later and do it."

They walked on, winding their way down streets with closed businesses, most shuttered or boarded against the hurricane. Sullivan could hear some loud music playing in the distance and steered their walk in that direction, curious to see what could be going on.

They turned the corner and walked down St. Ann's back toward Bourbon. As they walked, the music grew louder and festive voices. "Sounds like a party." Sullivan noted aloud.

"I thought you said everyone left before the storm."

Sully knew there were a lot of people left in town; the chaos of the first days after the hurricane had been the topic of conversation in the Angel headquarters as assignments were being handed out. People had been trapped in rising water; there were dying people all over the city. But, as they walked, he could see nothing of that. The venerable French Quarter, having been built on higher ground, had escaped the flooding and most of the wind damage of the storm. "Not everyone left, some stayed because they wanted to, others could not get out. There is death here right now; the city has some bad problems with trapped people. Other people are taking things, looting the stores. In some places, it is very dangerous to be out. But it appears the Quarter is quiet."

As they reached Bourbon, the music was louder. There were very colorful flags hanging from a balcony. About two dozen people danced in the street. Lilly noticed that they were not wearing much in the way of clothing. One person wore some pink wings and a frilly thing around the waist, her long hair coming down her back. But, as she turned, the "she" turned into a "he", a man with a beard. She had absolutely no idea what she was looking at but she knew that she had never, ever seen anything quite like it.

"Hey, we have more company, welcome!" A man wearing what looked like pants full enough to almost be a skirt with slits up the sides to the waist and tied at the ankles, no shirt, and a big smile came walking up to them, "Welcome to Southern Decadence 2005. Come join us, we're going to parade Bourbon Street." he gestured to the others in the street. "I'm Mike Stephens, the unofficial organizer of this little party."

Sullivan was uncomfortable with the situation. He wasn't too sure what was going on but he knew these people were not only inebriated, but also there was something else going on, something odd, but he couldn't quite put his finger on it. "Southern Decadence?"

Mike smiled "Yeah, some people call it the Gay Mardi Gras. We were supposed to have over one hundred thousand people here this weekend for the biggest party on the planet but that damned old hurricane tried to rain on our parade. We were all here for it and most of us were either stuck because of flight cancellations or didn't want to leave and are now stuck. So, we're going to have the party anyway!" he smiled and waved at a young man walking up the street, "Hey Shawn, come meet the new folks!"

Shawn was wearing a pair of leather chaps, a vest with a white star on one side and a red and white stripe on the other side, Sullivan recognized it as a flag from the state of Texas. Both he and Mike were wearing something that made their skin glisten with little colored flakes, he searched his memory and came up with the word for it, glitter. The new guy was smiling from ear to ear. "Hi y'all. Welcome to Decadence." He turned and kissed Mike deeply.

Lilly's eyes grew wide at this. She knew there were men who did this but it was never talked about and never, ever done in public. But the two men acted like lovers right here in the middle of the street! She looked at Sullivan, who was looking anywhere but at the two men. She looked back as the men finished the kiss. "I have a question. I know Mardi Gras. But why 'Gay' Mardi Gras? Gay just means 'happy' or 'light-hearted', doesn't it?"

The two men looked at each other, trying to figure out what she meant by that question, but the look on her face showed nothing more than confusion so they decided she might be honestly asking. Shawn smiled answering, "Well, yes, But now 'gay' also means homosexual. Love between two guys, or two girls. You don't recognize the word, really? Have you been living on the moon or something?"

As Lilly thought about the question, Sullivan stepped in, "Lilly here has been away in boarding school for several years. It was a very strict boarding school and she was really, really sheltered. Oh, by the way, I'm Sully." The lies came so easily now, he thought. They nodded as he turned to her, "Lilly, gay is a common phase, really the accepted phrase for male homosexuals."

Lilly looked shocked, "Sullivan! You mustn't speak of such things in public! My word, do you not have any decorum at all?" She had turned a blush red and was trying to cover her face in shame.

The men laughed and Sullivan took her hands

down, "Sweetheart, it's ok. Really. Sexuality is an open subject now. We don't hide it in the bedroom anymore."

"Obviously, that." She was still rather shocked, "So now homosexuals can go out into the street and sodomize each other without fear of being arrested?" The thought totally confused her.

All three men looked at her, then Shawn spoke up, "Not really. We still have laws against that. But, especially here in New Orleans, we can be open about our love and celebrate it, which is what Decadence is all about."

She didn't seem to be much comforted but she forced a smile. "Ok, that is good. So, you are having a celebration now? Even without everyone else?"

The men looked at each other, trying to figure out if she was kidding, As the official-unofficial, Mike responded, "Yes, everyone who could got out, we either couldn't or wouldn't so we're making the best of it."

"Why is that man in a skirt and wings? Is he someone specific, a character?" She also looked at the clothing Shawn was wearing with questions in her eyes. Sullivan knew that this was going to have to be a conversation best done in private where he could answer the multitude of questions she obviously had about sexuality changes in the 21st century.

"No, it's just a fun costume. We like to be, shall we say, a little crazy on this weekend." Chortled Shawn.

"Are there any other festivities going on tonight? I don't know that we quite fit in." Sully was hoping there was, not that he had a problem but it was very obvious that Lilly was going to have a lot of questions that he wasn't really prepared to answer now. And he needed time to puzzle out how to deal with it and that panic had him concerned, yet another odd and new feeling.

The two partiers exchanged a glance and then Mike pointed down Bourbon Street toward Canal. "Down there, Johnny White's is open, there's a little action down there. Of course, you could just hang out here for a few; we're all going to process down there. You can join us!"

Lilly and Sullivan looked at each other. Shawn sensed their hesitation. "We don't bite." Their heads jerked in his direction. He paused for effect, then added quickly, "Unless you want us to!" He grinned, winked. Lilly and Sullivan explosively laughed, for Shawn had no idea of the inside joke. All awkwardness disappeared they were being included in the party. "I think that sounds like fun!" Lilly exclaimed and clapped her hands. "What do we do?"

"Well, just hang on and let me run back to headquarters. I think I've got just what you need." Shawn grinned, squeezed Mike's hand and shouted "Yee-haa!" He took off galloping into the group. Mike led them to the knot of people and introduced them around to the oddly costumed people. Everyone was hugging them and welcoming into the group like old friends. Shawn came back with his hands clutching a bag. He put it down and started pulling out items. He had several strands of Mardi Gras beads he place over Lilly and Sullivan's necks. He handed Lilly a big purple hat, a stick with a star on top that lit up, and sprinkled glitter on her.

She laughed and spun around. "I love it! And this star lights up magically! I don't know how but it is so pretty. What are you doing for Sully?" she grasped his hand and smiled such an electric smile that Sullivan couldn't help but feel another sexual pull. She was so cute, so excited over the littlest thing and it made him want to show her the world.

Shawn brought out a folded set of white feathered angel wings and stepped behind Sullivan, putting the straps across his broad shoulders and across his chest, buckling it on the sides. Sullivan looked at Lilly with in distress. Suddenly his grey eyes darkened as he remembered when he had the real thing and the responsibility it entailed, Shawn was having so much fun decorating them he didn't notice. Then the man threw glitter on Sully, who started to brush it off, "Sorry, I'm just not a glitter sort of angel."

They thought he was joking.

"Ready everyone?" Mike called to the assembled group. Everyone cheered and one guy was holding a drum, pounding on it. "Ok, let's roll this ball on down the road!"

The drummer played a dance beat and everyone started dancing, walking, and singing on the way down the street. They were having a great time, even grabbing Lilly and Sullivan and swinging them around in dance. They got separated some but managed to dance their way back. Sullivan was more walking than dancing but Lilly was obviously having a great time. She lavished attention on each dance partner, even the winged and bearded fairy, smiling broadly the entire time.

But Sullivan was also watching something else, a shadow that played on the tops of the darkened buildings, seeming to follow along with the parading group. It wasn't a defined shape but almost a mist, semi-transparent. Sullivan had noticed it back at the cathedral and he had seen it off and on all the way down Bourbon. It was a "something" and not a shadow, he was certain, but without his angelic powers, he was unable to discern what exactly. He resolved to just watch it, keeping an eye on it in case it made a move toward them. He had no idea what he would do if it did, but he had to protect Lilly.

Then, suddenly there was a shout of "Halt!" in front of them. Six New Orleans police officers stood in the road, guns drawn, blocking their way. Everyone raised their hands, stopping all frivolity.

Mike took a step up, "What is the problem officer?" He kept his hands where they could be seen.

The ranking officer stepped up, "You can't do this. The festivities were cancelled due to the crisis. You need to stop and go back into your homes." There were grumbles around the group.

Mike waved his hand toward his friends to try to quiet them. "Sir, the main festivities were, indeed, cancelled and we are planning to keep low. However, we do have a parade permit for tonight and we intend to parade down Bourbon Street just as the permit allows." He pulled a piece of paper out of his pouch at his waist and unfolded it, handing it to the officer.

Obviously annoyed, the officer read the paper and then shook his head, "You're right, it's a permit. I don't like it and I'm not really sure I have to let you do it anyway, given the situation in the city..." his voice started to trail off as Lilly stepped up, smiling at the officer.

"Sir, I know it's irregular for us to want to have a party after such a tragedy, however, we have survived and we would like to celebrate this fact. It really would not harm anything to let us have our parade; in fact, it will probably raise the spirits of those who are still here in the Quarter to have some normalcy." She was looking straight into the officer's eyes, trying to convince them to let them go. Mike, Shawn, and Sullivan watched her charm the officer.

The officer nodded his head, his eyes slightly glazed over, "You are right, it won't hurt anything to let you go on. Have fun and be safe." He turned to the astonished officers next to him and led them to the sidewalk, clearing the way.

"You heard him, boys, we can continue the party!" Lilly smiled, looking to the group of celebrants. Mike signaled the drummer, who resumed the beat and the parade continued to roll on down Bourbon Street.

Shawn danced up to Lilly and gave her a great big hug, "Lilly, I don't know how you convinced that cop so easily but I'm damned glad you're with us!" He spun away, heading for Mike and slipping his arm around his back, put his hand on the man's ass.

Lilly shook her head, smiling and thinking, "What a strange world I've stepped into," as she danced back to Sullivan.

THE PARTY STOPPED outside Johnny White's Sports bar on the corner of Bourbon and Orleans. Everyone in the group gave great hugs to both Lilly and Sullivan, wished them luck, and the parade continued down Bourbon as rowdy as ever.

"That was fun." Lilly's face was lit so brightly by her smile that the darkness seemed to retreat from her. Sullivan hugged her, gave her a kiss, and then led her into the bar through the side door, which was open. Unlike the rest of New Orleans, Johnny White's was lit up, the televisions on the wall turned to the news, which was reporting on the situation in the city, the room lights bright in contrast to the street outside. There were several people in the bar, an interesting cross-section of the residents of the city.

"Hi y'all" the woman behind the bar called out. Like everyone else, she looked a bit "worse for wear" after the storm but she was cheerfully refilling glasses and wiping down the bar. "Welcome to Johnny White's!"

Lilly and Sullivan stopped inside and took in

the scene. It was a typical bar, the room itself and the bar and back shelves looked like most bars she had seen back in Storyville. Pictures on the wall, an old cash register on the back bar, a couple of video poker machines that were not working, a couple of neon beer signs were on the wall but unplugged. A scattering of kitschy knick-knacks were scattered around the bar area. Lilly was understanding some of what she was seeing but most things still looked odd to her.

Then she caught sight of the bright, moving screen on the wall. It showed pictures of people crowded together in front of a building and words on the screen said "New Orleans-Live". She stared, open mouthed, watching. Everyone else in the bar stopped talking and turned to watch her with a mix of amusement and pity. It was obvious to them that she was seeing the situation in the city for the first time; they had no idea that it was the first time she had ever seen a television.

Sullivan nudged her, "Honey, why don't we sit down over here at this table and have a drink while you watch the television coverage, okay?" He was trying to get her to move while trying not to get more questions about why she didn't know about something like television. She let him guide her over to the table and got her seated and then went to the bar.

"You are open for business, and with electrici-ty, I'm surprised." he said to the bartender.

"Yep, Johnny White's has never closed, even during the worst of that hurricane. And we have a generator." She was very proud of that fact. "We had the State Troopers by here earlier, trying to close us down but, as I told him, no-can-do because we don't even have locks for the doors. We shut the main one but left the side door open so anyone who wants to drop by for a drink or just to see other people could come on in. My name is Marsha. What can I get for you and your lady?"

"I think a couple of glasses of Jamisons if you have it." He smiled, glancing back to check on Lilly. She hadn't moved a muscle, not even sitting down, she was still staring at the television with an expression of awe.

"Ya'll aren't from around here, are ya?" Marsha said, pouring the whiskey into a couple of small glasses. "Sorry, it's going to be neat, we're out of ice and the water may not be safe. We've got bottled water, though, if you want, but it's extra. We also have Coke and other pops." She pointed at the forgotten fake wings, "Nice wings."

"Thanks. Nah, that's good, we like it neat. Yeah, we just got into town just before the hurricane hit," he was hoping to forestall too much of an explanation.

"Ah, picked a bad time to visit. But your accent, you're not originally from the U.S., let me guess, Scottish?" Marsha turned on the charm.

"No ma'am, Irish. But you were close." Sully smiled at her as she handed him the drinks. He walked back over to the table and sat down, putting the drink in front of Lilly who didn't even notice. "Hey sweetie, I have your drink."

Lilly turned to him, looking down, confusion

on her face, "I am trying to understand what I'm seeing. They are talking about New Orleans being destroyed, thousands of people are dead or missing, and those who are alive are together somewhere in the city without water or food."

"The hurricane broke the levees that were supposed to keep the city from flooding. There is water in a lot of places. The television coverage has been non-stop and the situation is getting to be very desperate." A lady sitting near them, nursing a drink and holding a white Lasso Apso dog answered. "Me and Apollo, we rode the storm out in our apartment a few blocks away. We have a tree down in the courtyard, some tiles are off the roof, but it held together."

Lilly started, turning toward the people at the bar, "I am really..." but Sullivan spoke over her, "I hear there was a lot of that. We've been staying at a friend's place across the way and while we got the blow, nothing seems damaged there." He turned to Lilly and said under his breath, "Don't let on you don't know what that is, explaining it is going to be hard enough without trying to come up with a story to tell these good folks." He nodded toward the television.

"Are those pictures of New Orleans?" Lilly asked, still staring at the images. She knew he would explain what magic made those happen as soon as they got out so she could focus on what it was saying now.

"Yes, that's from here. It's strange, the reporters could get here but we can't get outside help fast enough to keep people from dying." A man sitting at the end of the bar said. He was wearing a Greek fishing cap and nursing a warm beer. "The bridges are messed up and the roads have been flooded, it's hard to get the trucks in with the supplies. We thought about bringing them into the city by boat but so many of the vessels are piled up and broken in the marinas. We couldn't get through and I was lucky that my boat didn't get destroyed."

Marsha smiled at the old seaman as she re-filled his glass, "Capt'n Griff Mott has been around here for a long time, off and on. I think he probably considers this bar home."

"Marsha, darlin', it's you that keeps me coming back." His eyes twinkled as he smiled at the bartender.

Lilly was watching the broadcast intently, really ignoring most of what going on around her. The pictures, while horrible, interested her. Some of the pictures were of a New Orleans she knew but so many of them had pictures of shiny big buildings and other things she couldn't identify. People were dressed strangely; they held things she didn't recognize. This was all so confusing to her and she had lots of questions.

A sound from the door caught her attention and pulled it from the broadcast. Two men had come in, one of them holding a strange looking box. They were greeted by everyone and Marsha passed each of them a drink.

"Hey, aren't you the KBQ network reporter we've been seeing on the TV?" the lady with the dog asked the newcomers.

"Yes ma'am. I'm David Jones; this is my cameraman, Ryan Casey." The dark-haired man smiled. "Who is in charge here?"

Marsha waved to him, "I am. The owner hasn't been in yet so I'm it."

"Well, I was wondering if I could do a news report from here. You seem to be about the only thing open in the whole town, which is interesting. We would be doing a live cast, so everyone here would be on the TV." David swung his hand to include everyone in the room.

"I guess so. I think we probably are the only ones open, but we didn't close, even during the worst of the storm." Marsha told him. "I don't see any problem with you doing the broadcast." She turned to the rest of the people in the room, "If ya'll are ok with it, that is? I'm not speaking for everyone here."

There was a chorus of "Ok", "sure," and "whatever" from the people in the room. Sullivan looked at Lilly and thought it over. If he was seen on the TV, maybe someone would see it and he might have the chance to get word back to H.H.A.D. that he was in trouble. He nodded his head in agreement, "That would be fine."

"Good, Ryan, if you would set us up over there" David pointed to a point in a corner of the room that would give him the widest shot of the interior of the bar. The cameraman walked to the area, placed the camera on the table, then walked through the bar with a square box in his hand, periodically holding it up and then looking at it. Then he walked back to the camera, picked it up, and lifted it to his eye.

"We're ready. Whenever you want to start." the man said.

"Ok, on my mark, three, two, one...This is David Jones, KBQ Network News reporting from New Orleans, Louisiana. We're in the French Quarter at Johnny White's Sports Bar, the only open business in the city as far as we can tell." As he spoke, the camera was slowly turned to show the interior of the room and the people gathered there. "This is Marsha Reynolds, bartender. Miss Reynolds, could you explain why you are open and how you fared during the storm?"

As Marsha talked, the camera panned around through the room, Sullivan stood up and made sure to stay facing it, in hopes of being seen. Lilly was turned, her side facing the camera, the big purple hat still on her head, the wand forgotten on the table, still glowing. She was watching the broadcast signal coming over the television as it was being made, just a standard 7-second delay making it run just behind the action in the room. She stood, turning to look at the camera and then back to the television, amazed at what she was seeing.

"That is me? I'm in that box!" She said to Sullivan, patting him on the shoulder in her excitement. "I can see you too!"

"Shh, yes, we're on TV. The thing that Ryan is holding is a camera, like the old photographs were made from, but it's able to capture movement and sound and send it to the truck outside. The truck sends the pictures to...well, I'll explain it later.

But yes, we're being seen by everyone on the planet who has a TV turned to KBQ's broadcast." He tried to explain and decided against the technical explanation.

"The whole world can see this? Everyone?" She was caught between fear and excitement, not understanding how that could be. Sullivan took her hand and held it, caressing it with his thumb.

"Yes, KBQ has an international audience." Sullivan explained quietly, hoping that what he was saying wasn't being picked up by the microphone. Lilly, still staring at the television, watched the coverage being done in the bar with intense fascination. She would raise her hand to her hair and the picture of her in the box would do the same thing. She turned around in a circle and so did the picture of her. She was amazed at what she was seeing.

"...and we will be reporting from downtown New Orleans tomorrow. This has been David Jones, KBQ News Network reporting." Then the picture from the bar stopped and someone was singing.

Lilly drank the last of her drink and laid the glass down on the table. She glanced around the room and then said, "I think we need to probably start back."

Sullivan glanced up at the clock behind the bar. It appeared to be battery driven and read 4:14 a.m. "I think you're right." He turned to Marsha, "Thank-you for the drinks. We've got to head back to our place. Nice to meet all of you."

They left the bar to calls of "good night" and

CHARLAYNE ELIZABETH DENNEY

"take care," and started walking back up Bourbon Street toward Toulouse, Lilly still in her hat and beads with her wand and Sullivan's fake wings fluttering as he stepped.

Chapter Twelve

THE ROOM ALWAYS had a subsonic hum to it. With that many monitors and receivers working all the time, the sound was just part of the ambience. The light was kept low so the monitors would be easier on the eyes. Everyone had headphones on their heads, both the video and radio monitors.

The Media Monitoring Center, or MMC, of the H.H.A.D. was its own building in the heavenly compound. Each angel working there had dark purple wings and were assigned to monitor either the video or audio/radio feeds from a particular area.

It was Hariel, or Harry, as he was known; who was monitoring the United States national media broadcast feeds that particular night. With everything going on in the United States, especially with the hurricane that struck on the Gulf Coast, there was a lot of news being broadcast, especially from New Orleans. It sometimes got boring seeing the same images and stories played over and over again. Harry kept having to move in his chair to keep from finding himself just glossing over the scenes.

He was watching the KBQ Network feed when something caught his attention. He hit the pause button and quickly typed on his terminal. A picture of an angel came up on the monitor. He pulled in tight on the face and then, with a few clicks of the keyboard, he isolated the picture in the background of the news feed and pulled up the couple that had caught his attention.

He was sure he was correct, and if he was, he had just found the missing angel everyone was looking for, standing next to a raven-haired woman.

"Hey, Farael, can you come here a moment?" He called out. A short, brown-haired angel glided across the room to stand behind Harry, his dark-purple wings barely moving with the effort.

"What is it, Harry? You're supposed to be monitoring the U.S. feed..." Farael was in a dark mood tonight, it seemed. Harry rarely saw him in any other mood.

"Look at this. I think I found the missing angel." He motioned toward the frozen feed with the enlargement in a separate window. Farael moved closer to study the picture and then the picture from H.H.A.D.

"You may be right. Pull this off and give it to me and I'll take it over to the Operations Center and show it to Ranguel." he watched while Harry pulled the information into a key and handed it to him.

Farael floated out of the room's aperture and across to the H.H.A.D central building. Gliding through the nearest aperture, he flew directly to Ranguel, who turned to watch him approach.

"Sir, one of my angels found something, you will want to take a look at this." he handed the key to Ranguel who put it into the monitor and looked. There, in the center of the screen was his missing angel, Sullivan. He was with a woman, dark hair and brown eyes but light mocha skinned. They appeared to be talking and both looked very comfortable in each other's presence, Sullivan was holding her hand and, he was wearing white fake wings. There was no doubt that he was seeing his missing angel. He shook his head and stabbed his finger at the monitor, opening up a communications link.

"Sophiel, we've confirmed that Sullivan is in New Orleans, in the French Quarter bar. Have you kept up with him?"

"Yes sir, he just left the bar, walking with a woman down the street. I've been following him all night."

"Go ahead and bring him back." Ranguel wasn't sure why his angel had gone off without communicating but he was going to get some answers.

"Sir, something is still not right here. I want to follow him just a while longer and confirm a couple of things I am suspecting." Sophie was carefully watching Sullivan from the tops of the buildings as he walked back toward O'Flaherty's Pub with Lilly.

"What are you suspecting?"

"I keep getting vampire signatures on this

couple. I cannot tell why the signature is so strong. She must be an ancient to have such a strong signature or something is very wrong. And I don't know why Sullivan isn't picking up on the communications, he has his ring. And I didn't see his wings, the ones he is wearing are fake and the wrong color for an Enforcer."

Ranguel ran a hand through his hair. This was not what he wanted to do but he had to trust Sophiel to find out everything before he jumped to conclusions. "Ok, follow him until you are sure, but I want you to let me know the moment you are certain about things, understand?"

"Yes sir, I will."

Ranguel pulled the key out and put it in a pocket. He would have to wait a little bit longer to find out just what was up with his wayward angel.

Chapter Thirteen

"**...a**ND THAT'S HOW television works." Sullivan concluded as they walked along. He had tried to explain it as easily as he could, it was a hard concept to grasp, pictures going through the air to a box on the wall.

"Seems like magic to me." She smiled. There was so much of this new world she didn't understand and she had decided that she would not worry too much about the "hows" but rather learn what she needed to know to just make things work. "I know that Marcus would be fascinated with this. Everything would really pique his curiosity."

Marcus, the thorn in Sullivan's side, the ghost in their relationship. He was getting so tired of hearing about Marcus in every conversation they had. Damn the man! Sullivan let loose on Lilly, "God damn it, why do you have to bring that bastard's name up every time we're having fun? Can't you just forget him and pay attention to the one person who is here with you, for once?"

As the darkness seemed to deepen around the top of the buildings, Lilly looked like she had been slapped, her mouth hung open in shock. Red tears welled up in her eyes and spilled over. "I don't know that you have the right to make demands on me like that. Marcus has been with me for a very long time, he…"

"He's a fucking GHOST!" Sullivan screamed at her, "If anything, he's dead, he has been dead, and he remains dead after all these years. Damn, Lilly, you had, what, one night with the guy and you've built this fantasy world around the bastard!"

She balled up both fists, holding them down by her side, "I knew him even before we had that night; he was frequently at Mahogany Hall and had always taken time to talk with me, even while being with the other girls." She felt the tears and got angry all over again at Sullivan for making her cry.

"So what, Lilly, he's been dead probably at least 20 years! And if he's not, he's over 100 years old! An old codger who can't get it up, even in the presence of a pretty lady! You went bat-shit crazy in that tomb, woman. You built a fantasy lover out of a dead skull and you've lost your mind talking to it! All I wanted was for you to pay attention to me the way you talk to that damned skull, want me the way you want your dead lover. But you, you…" Sullivan was red-faced with rage.

"I what? WHAT, Sullivan? I didn't stroke your ego enough? I've not forgotten where I came from and just swooned at your feet and whined like a little smitten girl? You're jealous. Stupid and jealous." She ripped the hat off her head and threw it, and the wand, onto the street.

"You're damned right I'm jealous! Wouldn't you be if I was paying attention to another woman, pining away for some mythical broad that was the hottest thing I'd ever fucked and compared you every second to her, and you came up SHORT!" He was standing toe-to-toe with her, yelling in her face.

She took a step back and then tried to walk past him, "I'm not listening to this! I am not going to stand here and...get your hands OFF me!" She screamed as he grabbed her arm to keep her from walking away. "You overstep, you have no right, sir!"

"I do! You and I have a relationship here and you are damned well going to come down off your high-horse and fucking listen to me! You're MINE!" He pulled her into him, clutching at her as she struggled against him.

"I am no ones! I am no longer owned by anyone, nor do I owe you, or any man, my life and body. You will remove your hands from my body right now or I will begin to scream and you will get unwanted attention!" She struggled against him and was able to pull away as he wound up for his next volley.

"You are the most ungrateful, self-centered little bitch! I'm here because YOU killed me. I lost my wings," he pulled off the fake ones and threw them down with her hat and stomped them, breaking them and shattering the discarded wand. "My *real* fucking wings because you wanted to save me. But, you didn't save me, you damned me and I fucking forgave you for it. It's YOUR fault, you made me and all you can think about is that stupid piece of bone!" He grabbed for her again and she slapped him with every bit of the strength she had, considerable force since she was a vampire. His head twisted around as the sound of the slap echoed off the dark shadow on surrounding buildings. When he opened his eyes, she had walked half a block away and was determinedly storming down the street toward the pub, wiping away the tears with her hand. Out of nowhere, Baron bounded from the darkness and took up step with her, looking over his shoulder with a glare at Sullivan.

"Lilly! Stop!" He yelled, trying to get her attention as he ran to catch up with her. "Hey, slow down, stop!"

She was ignoring him; she kept walking even when he made a grab for her hand. She pulled it away, not even looking at him as she walked the last of the block to the pub. He stepped in front of her, putting both hands out to stop her. She walked around him, not even looking up into his face. He turned to watch her go, shaking his head. "You are the most pig-headed, stubborn, infuriating slut I have ever had the chance to..."

She stopped and then whirled on him, "Slut? You dare call me a slut? I will not tolerate that type of slur against me, sir! I worked hard, yes, I was a prostitute in a brothel but I was not one of the Crib Girls, selling it cheaply when I wasn't giving it away for booze. I was in a reputable house, the best in the city. I may have been a whore, but I was never, ever, a slut." She had walked up to him, standing toe-to-toe to him and trying to pull herself up to his height, even though she came up to the middle of his chest.

He reached around her and unlocked the pub door, opening it. He started, "I wasn't..." Then he felt something poke him in the back. He heard Baron growl and hiss.

"You will turn around slowly and put your hands up." A male voice said sternly. Sullivan turned, trying to push Lilly behind him as he did. A medium-sized man stood in front of him holding a large gun, pointed at him.

"That's better. I want everything you have, money, jewelry, watches, everything. Now!" the man pulled back the slide on the gun, an action Sullivan knew put a bullet in the firing chamber.

"Hey there, mister." Lilly stepped out from behind Sullivan. He made a grab for her but she pushed his hand away, her demeanor changing from the angry wild-cat to the seductress in the span of a couple of seconds. "I think I have a couple of things here for you." She looked him right in the eye, holding his gaze. "You are looking for valuables. The most valuable things I have are upstairs in our room. If you put the gun down, I will take you up there and you can get everything you want..."

The robber's eyes glazed over and he stopped talking. Lilly continued, "You really don't want to rob us, we don't look like we have anything you might want. You are wanting to go away, go to the church closest to your home, and confess to the priest about your crimes. You need to confess, you need to stop and you will do what the priest tells you to do." She kept talking to him, looking deeply into his eyes.

"I'm sorry, ma'am. I did not mean to stop you." The man said woodenly.

Lilly smiled and looked up at Sullivan, who had begun to shake his head at the power she seemed to wield so effortlessly. "What is your name?" She asked.

"Andrew James. Andy, ma'am." His tone of voice was flat like he was answering by rote.

"Well, Andy, you can do us a favor. Stand right here and don't move for a minute." She turned to Sullivan. "He's calmed now. I think we need to take our sustenance before we let him go. If we only take a little, he will be tired but none the worse for wear. From trial and error I learned that when you drink, only take 10 sips, this is half what I would do by myself. I will take 10 sips as well. Then rub your tongue over the holes to close them. Do not take more than 10 or we risk his life."

"This does not stop the conversation, Lilly. Once this is handled..." he growled. He was not going to let her continue to treat him like a cast-off.

"We can talk afterward. This needs to be done now, then we can talk until we sleep." She kept her voice level, in control of both the situation and the man standing before them. "I will go first."

She stepped up to the man, trying to find a way to his neck. He was taller than she could reach and the gun was in the way as well. "Hand the gun to my friend and then lean down here to me." She never wavered in her tone of voice.

Andy James never realized what had hold of him. One moment he was stalking his prey, the next minute he was the prey. He handed the gun to Sullivan and bent down to Lilly. She took his head in her hands, turned it away from her and bent it where she could get a good look at his neck. Then she opened her mouth and bit down, fastening her lips to his skin.

Sullivan watched her with a growing sense of need of his own. He wanted the blood, but he also wanted the woman as well. His head spun as the need rose in him, the residual anger still burning inside of him about that damned skull. The jealousy blazed to white hot as the robber was kissed so intimately by Lilly. She finished after a moment, licking the wounds shut and stepping back. It was all he could do to keep from grabbing her right there and dragging her up to the bed.

"Your turn. Remember, 10 sips only!" she stepped back and motioned for Sullivan to step up. He put the pistol in his belt and grabbed the man, pushing his head aside and fastening onto the other side of his neck with his fangs. As he drank, he started to count but the taste, the need overwhelmed him and he began to pull the blood harder and faster into his mouth. The roar in his ears as the blood entered his system grew, he could hear Lilly saying something and pulling at him but there was no way he was letting go of the man. She hit him once, twice and he broke contact, only to grab her by the arm and fling her away, down the corridor in the pub, all the way to the patio, stunning her as her head hit the well-worn bricks. He then bent his head back to the man and once again bit him, drinking deeply.

As he drank, he could hear the blood rushing in his body and he could hear a steady heartbeat, one that began to slow as he took more of the blood, finally to stop as the blood slowed to a trickle and then stopped. Angered that the blood was gone, Sullivan lifted the lifeless body of Andy James into the air, walked around the side of the pub, and threw the body over the six-foot wrought-iron fence and across the parking lot toward the buildings lining St. Louis Street to the south. The body hit the pavement and slid the last few feet to come to rest under a tree by a building.

He pulled the gun out, popped the magazine and bent it almost in half with one hand. Then he pulled the slide back and dumped the bullet from the chamber. He pitched the gun in the same direction as its former owner and the broken magazine the other direction.

Sullivan did not wait to see where the gun landed, he turned and walked into the door, the shadows seeming to follow him, and locking it on the way through. Then he stalked down the corridor to the patio where Lilly lay, still trying to clear her head. He grabbed her and dragged her by the arm into the pub, up the stairs, and into the apartment. Baron was running between them as if to slow him down and he kicked the cat across the room. He pulled her to the bed, stripping the clothing off of her as he went. He threw her on the bed and pulled his own jeans off with one tug, then jumped on top of her, holding her down.

Lilly's head spun, still dizzy from smacking her head on the paving stones of the patio. She remembered the few times a customer had gotten rough at Mahogany Hall. She had fought off the first one, screaming, crying, and finally kicking him in the balls. The customer was thrown out and prohibited from returning but Miss Lulu had also punished her for retaliating. Abe had been the girl's protector and they were supposed to yell out a code word if they feared for their life and Abe would come in and put a stop to the problem. A merely rough session of sex or trying something the woman didn't want to do wasn't enough to interfere in the session. Miss Lulu didn't want to lose a well-paying customer.

All this training came roaring back as Lilly tried to fight Sullivan but his hold on her was way too tight. She began to scream and he slapped her as he roughly grabbed her breasts and bit her nipple. She plead with him to stop but nothing she said got his attention.

Suddenly he rose up and screamed, both hands reaching toward his back. Baron had recovered from the kick and had launched himself onto Sullivan's back, landing with all claws extended and biting down on the big man's shoulder. His fangs punctured the skin and Baron began to suck, digging his claws in deeper.

Sully rose up off of Lilly, backed off of the bed, and ran backward, slamming himself into the wall, squashing Baron between his back and the wall as he had in the little crypt days ago. The cat let go long enough for him to grab it by the neck. Sullivan opened the door to the closet and threw the squirming vampire cat into the darkness, slamming the door shut and locking it. Furious screams and the sound of the cat hitting and clawing the door continued for many minutes while Sullivan went back to Lilly. She had crawled into the corner of the bed, holding the blanket over her in an attempt to shield herself. He jerked it from her, grabbed her ankle and pulled her down and across the bed. He continued the violent attack, replete with many fangings and beating her when she would not cooperate. She screamed out for Marcus and cried. The very mention of this name only served to enflame the angel-turned-vampire further and he slapped her to make her stop. Finally the beginnings of dawn took the fight out of him. He collapsed beside her, closed his eyes, and surrendered to the sleep of the undead.

Lilly fought the need for sleep. Survival pressed her from all sides and she slowly got up from the bed and went into the bathroom. She couldn't get the water to come on, so she just wiped down her skin and then went to the suitcase Sullivan had brought back. She took out underwear, a pair of jeans, and another of the t-shirts and the wide-brimmed hat, putting them on. She laid the sunglasses next to her and then she carefully repacked the other things. She found the gray feather in between the t-shirts and picked it up. "Some luck this turned out to be." She crushed the delicate thing and dropped it to the floor, then reached over and picked up Marcus. She held the skull up and looked into the vacant eyes, stroking the head. Then she placed it with the clothing in the suitcase and zipped it closed. She took the handle and carried the suitcase down the stairs, putting it by the door.

On the way back up to get Baron, she stopped in the kitchen. Very sharp knives were attached to the wall somehow. She took one of the larger ones and pulled, it came off the wall into her hand with ease. She turned it round in her hand, getting used to the weight, and then smiled a very grim smile. She laid the knife back on the counter, turning back to the staircase, ascended it. She walked up the stairs and over to the bed where Sullivan slept, unaware of everything around him in his newly-turned vampiric sleep. She had learned by experience that a young vampires couldn't manage to stay awake like she was doing so she didn't fear Sullivan's return to consciousness. She thought she saw a movement in the top of the room, near the ceiling, but nothing was there. She reached into the old satin pillowcase that contained the last of her worldly goods and retrieved the bone knife she had made and used for decades. It just felt better in her hand, familiar. She turned back to the man on the bed and held the knife in both hands, directly over his heart. She closed her eyes and steeled herself to drive the bone into him.

She stopped the motion just at his chest, nicking him. As the blood welled up, she let the knife drop down into one hand at her side. She shook all over in shock, tears flooding her eyes and spilling down her cheeks. "Why?" She asked to empty room. She had been angry with him, now she was afraid of him and furious that he had not only violated her body but her trust in him. She had saved his life and he had beaten her.

"No, you will not die so easily. I want you to suffer instead." She said, bending down over him again. She used the knife to slash his throat deep enough for him to slowly bleed out but not enough to make the blood spurt all over the room. Then she took the handle in both hands and pushed the blade into the mattress, tight under his left arm and against his torso, all the way to the hilt. Inches from his heart, and final death.

She then dipped her hands into the blood he was losing on his neck and walked to the wall facing the bed. Slowly she wrote on the wall in big letters with the blood, she had to make three trips to make everything thick enough to stand out. Then she wiped her hands on his chest and then the remains of her purple t-shirt he had ripped off of her, dropping it on his face.

She opened the door to the closet and Baron slowly stumbled out, the dawn trying to knock him out as well. "Hey boy, come here." She bent and picked up the cat, who relaxed into her arms. She noticed the inside of the door was shredded, long and deep claw marks indicating just how hard the vampire cat had tried to get out of the closet and to her. "You're my hero," she whispered to the cat.

Then wearily resisting the urge to take one last look around the room, she picked up the pillowcase, pulled out the rosary and dropped the rest, abandoned, onto the floor. She walked out, down the stairs, took hold of the handle of the suitcase and pulled it out, then walked out the door of the pub, locking it and then sliding the key under the door, back inside. Then, putting on the sunglasses against the light, the door behind her. She saw the shadow receding down the street behind her as she turned and walked down Toulouse Street back toward the only home she knew.

Chapter Fourteen

S OPHIEL TOOK OFF into the heavens like she was shot out of a cannon. She was having trouble with what she had observed even with seeing it with her own eyes. She had known Sullivan forever. What she saw him do, what he had become, wasn't anything like the Sullivan she knew. But, there was no doubt, it WAS Sullivan and he was a vampire. And he was out of control.

She hit the aperture to H.H.A.D. at full speed and had to widen her wingspan to slow down before she crashed directly into Ranguel, she barely managed it. Pulling them in, she stood waiting while the Archangel finished with another angel and then turned to her.

"Ranguel, I've found him. And he should be stripped of any further angelic power he has and sent straight to the demons in Hell. Sir." She was obviously furious with what she had found, Rangel observed.

"Slow down, take a breath Sophie. What has happened that has you calling hellfire and brimstone down on one of our own?" He laid his hand on her shoulder in an attempt to calm her.

She was having none of it.

"Sullivan has fallen. I spent the better part of two days observing him. He is no longer an angel and he is no longer following the codes. I demand he be sent to Hell for what he has done!" Forgetting her training and in defiance of the codes of conduct for the heavenly host that demanded complete control of emotions, her anger got the better of her and she slammed her fist down on the console, denting it. As she raised it a second time, Ranguel took hold of it and held it firmly but gently.

"Steady, Sophie. Calm yourself and then start explaining from the beginning, please." Ranguel's touch had a calming effect on the young angel. She slowed her breathing and then closed, then opened her eyes and looked straight at the head Enforcer.

"Sullivan has been turned. I don't know how it happened but Sullivan is a vampire. He is with a female vampire, quite probably the one he was sent to talk to in the beginning and a vampire cat. Somehow she turned Sullivan into a vampire as well. He has lost all control of himself. The list of transgressions is long and progressive. He has blasphemed, became drunken, fornicated, stolen, murdered twice, and finally he beat and raped the woman who turned him. She escaped him with the cat but he is still in the place he's been staying in the French Quarter. She disabled him after the sun rose."

Ranguel frowned, "You are sure of these charges? Be very sure of how you answer because what I must do if you affirm them will be serious." His eyes blazed, holding her transfixed as he delved into the shadow's mind for the answers. He closed his eyes and they returned to normal and he turned away.

"I have seen what you have. You are correct, something has happened to turn Sullivan into a vampire. He still has his ring but there are no wings, no way for him to communicate. He has fallen, the first of the angels to ever do so since the war and this may be the very first angel changed into a vampire." Ranguel turned back to her. "Stay here, you may be called to report again. I will go to Mikhail and inform him. What he does from there..." The words trailed off as he touched the screen and cancelled the All Points Bulletin for his missing angel. The message of cancellation also carried a warning to not approach Sullivan if spotted. He knew it would be obeyed without question. "At least he's been found...." His words trailed off as he rose into the air and flew to Mikhail's office. The door opened without his touch, obviously the High Archangel was aware of a problem. He entered and the door shut behind him.

Chapter Fifteen

LILLY AWOKE THE next evening and promptly hit her head on the top of the crypt. Baron was curled up next to her and he opened his eyes and looked at her, lazily yawning. She yawned too and stretched, petting him. "Hi there, Baron. I hope you slept well enough." The cat answered with a deep meow and jumped off the platform. Lilly crawled down and looked around the little room.

She picked up the skull and sat down on the floor. Little bits of glitter, a reminder of the fun she had had the night before...before.... She shook her head and more little bits of glitter floated out of her hair and fell onto Marcus. Baron walked over and laid down in her lap, beginning to bathe his face. She looked at the makeshift door to the crypt, worried when Sullivan would figure out where she went and came storming back to her to resume what he obviously thought was their relationship.

"Marcus, I don't know how I didn't see what kind of man he was when he first yelled at me. I must be the stupidest woman in the world." She talked to the skull, holding it at face level.

"Somehow, I seem to be less of a judge of character than I was back with Miss Lulu."

Suddenly she heard a sound just outside the crypt. Baron stopped grooming himself but did not move from her lap. The makeshift door slid aside but, instead of Sullivan, Lilly saw a woman kneeling at the door, looking in at her.

"Well, hello there. I heard you talking and thought I would peak in and see who was inside." The lady was pale, with big green eyes and full lips that smiled at the surprised woman inside the crypt. "What's your name, dear? Mine is Arianne Campbell."

Lilly looked at Marcus, then at Baron, thinking about what to do. Marcus was silent and Baron did not seem to be very alarmed at the appearance of the woman at their door so she answered, "Lilly Lenora Marchantel. And this is Marcus, and Baron Bast von Samedi." She indicated the skull and the cat in her lap.

Arianne's interest was piqued, her eyebrows rising at Lilly's name, and then again at Marcus'. "Really. Well, you are just who I have been looking after all this time."

Lilly's face clouded with confusion, "Excuse me? You have been looking after me? Could you please explain?"

"I have been coming to this crypt for years, once a week, bringing fresh flowers so you would not be forgotten. A friend of mine knew of you and asked that I take care of the duties since I live in the city. The storm delayed my regular visit and when I reached this crypt, I saw the door had been broken and a wooden one put over the opening. I had no idea you were alive and living in there. Everything looked locked up and solid, quiet until this moment." Arianne reached into the tomb and held out her hand, "Why don't you come out of there and come home with me. You can stay there, I have plenty of room, and we can talk about you and figure out what to do."

Lilly looked again to Baron and to Marcus. Neither of them indicated trouble. It was up to her to make the decision. She could stay here and have to face Sullivan the minute he found her or she could escape with Arianne to another part of the city where he could not find her and start her life over again. "I would want to bring Baron and Marcus with me..." she ventured.

"Of course, dear. I would not want them left behind. Gather them and your things and let's get out of here." Arianne dropped her hand and backed away from the opening.

Lilly took a last look around, hoping that this would, indeed, be the last time she would see the little crypt, and gathered the few possessions she had, zipped the suitcase, and crawled out. Baron followed her.

"Let's go to my car. I know Old Roy will be waiting to lock up, he's always been so nice to wait for me on the days I come to the cemetery, I wouldn't want to keep him much longer." Arianne took the suitcase from her and walked through the cemetery to the gate, which was open. An old man stood by the opening, next to a door to the gate keeper's shed. Arianne smiled when she caught his gaze and he smiled back. "Roy Hebert, this is Lilly Marchantel and Baron. They've been living in your cemetery for a while and I just found them. I will be taking them home with me."

Roy did not seem surprised at her revelation. "I'm glad to meet you, Miss Lilly. I know that Arianne will take good care of you and your cat." He didn't even seem to notice the skull she carried tucked into her right arm.

"Roy, I will stop coming to the cemetery for a while, other activities intrude. You will still get your checks sent to your home and if there is trouble, please send a letter to the address you have. I will handle it." She hugged the old man. "You take care."

The old man returned the hug, "I hope you will be well and we will see each other again." Then he turned to Lilly, "Little lady, you have a good life," and he hugged her.

Arianne led Lilly to a large car parked on the curb. It was larger than the ones Lilly had seen in the French Quarter with Sullivan. A very large man in a dark suit and hat stood by and when they approached, he took the bag from Arianne and opened the door, helping first Arianne, then Lilly in. Baron leapt in after Lilly and the door was closed. The man put the bag in the back and went around, getting into the front. The window between the front and back was down.

Lilly looked around, there were lights around the area, tiny ones that put out a lot of light. There was music playing but she couldn't see any musicians.

Arianne turned to her and said, "You need to buckle your seatbelt, even in a limo." Lilly gave her a puzzled look and the lady indicated the belt she was wearing around her hips. Lilly looked down and found two ends of the belt, one flat and one that looked like a box. Arianne pulled up on the top of her belt buckle and the thing came apart into two pieces like the one Lilly held. Then she inserted the flat part into the slot on the side of the box and there was a click and the belt was locked again. Lilly followed suit and locked the belt around her. Arianne then reached over and pulled the loose end, snugging the belt down around her.

"Mitch, take us home." Arianne called out. The window moved up and shut the sound out between the two compartments. The car started to move and Lilly looked out the tinted windows into the night. The speed made the buildings pass very quickly and this scared Lilly. She had never been in something so fast. And the temperature in it was cool; a nice, cooling breeze came out of a grate along the top of the car. It was delightful.

"I wish I could see better." she remarked. Arianne smiled and pushed a button and the window next to her lowered. The hot, muggy New Orleans air, rife with smells of rotting and mold funneled into the compartment. Lilly wrinkled her nose but leaned closer to the window, watching the large buildings of downtown New Orleans, some still boarded up against the storm, passing. They wound their way carefully back into the Garden District, dodging debris in the road many times.

"This is your first ride in an automobile, then?" her hostess remarked, observing the way Lilly was transfixed on the passing sights.

Lilly reached over and petted the very anxious and growling Baron, trying to relieve his anxiety. "Yes, I had never even seen such a thing before a couple of days ago." This surprised Arianne, while Lilly had not ridden in a car, she had thought surely she would have seen the progression of automobiles since they had been created after Lilly's turning in 1900.

"You did not see them prior to this? How is this possible? You should have at least seen them over the years."

"No, I did not. I was living in the little house," she corrected herself, "the crypt, and I did not leave it except to let the rain wash me in very late night storms, until the door was broken by Sullivan." She shivered with the last memory of him. Baron let out a snarling growl at the name and Lilly hugged him a little closer to her with the hand that was not clutching the skull she had not let go of since leaving the crypt.

Arianne wondered who this "Sullivan" was and why Lilly and the cat reacted that way with the mere mention of him but the question would have to wait; they had arrived at her house on Prytania. Lilly stepped out with Marcus in hand and Baron following behind her. She looked up at a huge, white house with Greek revival columns and a big porch. There were lights blazing in the downstairs rooms, a big change from everything else she had seen, except the bar, which was dark from the electricity being out after the hurricane. Lilly looked to Arianne who just said, "We have a generator, thankfully."

She could tell the trees were old, but the hurricane had broken many of the majestic branches, depositing them into the lawn and patio. Wooden boards were laid next to the windows, obviously having just been removed and awaiting storage. While the smell of rot and mildew was less here, there was a scent of it on the air still, mixed with the scent of the garden. As they walked up to the door, it was opened by an older black woman in a gray dress with an apron. She stepped back to allow them inside, but she started to shut the door on Baron, crying out "Shoo, cat!"

"No Eloise, the cat belongs to Miss Lilly here, he can come inside." Arianne smiled back at Lilly, who had begun to react to the affront to her friend and had opened her mouth to object. "Please get us some wine and a bit of food, please." The servant exited to the left and out of sight.

"Thank you, Miss Arianne. I could not bear it if he was made to stay outside, especially in the daylight."

The difference in temperature between the hot, smelly outside air and the cool air in the mansion was considerable. Lilly didn't know how this could be and she made a mental note to ask later as Arianne led the way into the front parlor and indicated a seat for her. "Why would that be troubling to the cat?"

Lilly thought about how to explain it. "Because he is like me, he cannot be out in the sunlight."

She hedged her comment, not knowing how much the woman knew about Lilly or her 'condition.' "We've been inside the little house, uh, crypt for many years and…"

"You are a vampire, Lilly. As am I. I know exactly what you are and it is ok. You are saying the cat is a vampire as well?" She wasn't sure what this would mean, even as old as she was, Arianne had never heard of an animal vampire, unless it was a bat.

"Yes, he is. I was hungry when he came into the crypt and I bit him. I am afraid I took too much and so I did what I could remember Marcus doing to me and I bit my wrist and put blood in his mouth, making him swallow it. He died and I planned on taking him to another crypt to lay him to rest when he awoke the next night and was good as ever. He grew much larger than other cats, and he would trap nutria and rats, bringing them back and sharing his catch for me to take blood from." She reached down and ran her hand down the back of the cat who was sitting by her leg, staring at the woman.

"Oh my, you lived on nutria and rats? How long were you in that crypt, Lilly?" The thought of biting or taking blood from either animal made her stomach roll.

"I died and was buried in late August, 1900." Lilly said, matter of factly.

"And you never came out except to wash, you said." she shook her head, "I ought to beat Marcus Lancaster within an inch of his eternal life for not coming back to check, not making sure you were truly dead!"

"Marcus?" Lilly looked down to the skull she held in her hands and then back to Arianne, a very puzzled look on her face. "Marcus, the man that I knew so many years ago?"

"Yes, that Marcus. Your maker. The lout."

"But how...my...maker?" She rolled the thought around in her mind, trying to meld the memories with the dreams and fantasies that had become so much a part of her reality.

"You remember him biting you, right? And then feeding you blood? That was how you turn someone. You figured that out by yourself with the cat." Arianne shook her head, "I still can't get over that one, a vampire cat. Anyway, he went to your funeral, watched you buried. But you didn't come awake when he thought you should and he left you in the cemetery and ran to Texas. He contacted me and asked me to lay flowers on your grave, light candles, and make sure it was tended properly. I came there tonight to check to see how the cemetery faired after the flooding. I've been doing it for most of the one hundred and five years now. When I couldn't, I paid a servant to make sure it was done, the things I do for that man, I swear!" Arianne had stood and was pacing as she talked.

"So, Marcus is..." she looked down at the skull again, "...alive?" The dawning truth was coming across her face.

"Oh my heavens, yes! It's very hard to kill a vampire, unless you are a damned angel." She turned back and sat down again, reaching out to grasp Lilly's hand, "I had never known you were in there, living like you were, or I would have taken you out of there years and years ago."

"Where is Marcus now?" Lilly clutched the skull even as she realized that Sullivan spoke the truth, she had built a history with someone who never knew she existed.

"I think he's somewhere in the states, I'm not sure exactly where." Arianne hedged her answer. She knew full well where he was but she didn't think he deserved to have such a lovely vampire at his side. Arianne was angry at him for his mistake in not checking back on Lilly, and she was lonely. She had her servants who had been with her for several years, especially Mitch Mercer, who had become her assistant, her chauffer, and, at times, her lover and blood doll. She fed him just enough blood back to keep him living as human, not fully turning him. She had done this for over two hundred years; Mitch was now a ghoul, living on uncooked meats between blood feedings from her. He handled her daytime activities, kept the house running, and guarded her undead sleep. Theirs was an easy relationship but they had become stale over the years, there was no excitement and very few new experiences.

Lilly sat in her parlor, fresh faced, new to the world, needing Arianne to teach her how to be a proper vampire, requiring education on all the things that had passed since she went into the crypt. She offered new experiences, new challenges, and a friendly, female companionship that Arianne had missed over the years. So, Arianne, at that moment, made the decision to keep Lilly living with her for as long as she could. She just would not let Lilly know where Marcus was and she would not tell Marcus that Lilly was alive. "Screw him." She thought.

"I would like to contact him, if you could find him. I would like to see him." Lilly said, absently stroking the top of the skull and looking into the distance before bringing her attention back to Arianne.

"I can try dear, but the last time I talked to him, he was travelling," Arianna added, "...with his lover, a woman named Eadwina." Lilly's face fell. She had finally found the man she had fallen in love with in her mind and heart and now she heard that he loved someone else. Her dreams were breaking along with her heart.

Lilly began to cry. Baron looked to Lilly and then to Arianne and hissed at the older vampire, fangs extended. He had been with Lilly for many, many years and seeing her cry, so shortly after the attack by Sullivan upset him. He twitched his tail violently, turning his back to the other woman.

Eloise came into the room bearing a tray with wine. Behind her was another woman carrying a large tray with an assortment of small sandwiches, cheeses, and fruit. As they placed them on the table next to the two vampires, Eloise asked, "Will there be anything further, ma'am?" They seemed not to notice the blood falling down the visitor's face.

"This looks good, thank you Eloise, Sarah."

Arianne nodded to each. The women left the room and Arianne continued, "I suppose you have so many questions about being a vampire since you've never had anyone train you. Anything you want to ask?"

Lilly managed to calm herself, thinking that she would have time later to mourn her dreams that had just exploded. She wiped her face with her hands and then on her jeans, smearing the blood.

Arianne stepped across the room to the crystal water set on a nearby table. She took a linen napkin from a drawer and wet it, bringing it back to the still bloody vampire. Lilly took the napkin with a word of thanks and wiped her face and then her hands and held the napkin out to her hostess.

Arianne grasp the cloth and then reached out, wiping the missed remnants of Lilly's tears from her face and smiled. "Have some wine, my dear."

Lilly picked up the wine glass and took a sip; it was thicker than she thought it would be. She rolled it around in her mouth to taste it, then swallowed. She looked over at her hostess "This is...interesting."

"Oh, that is the house wine. I have it mixed special. A mixture of moscado, spices, and blood. Do you like it?" Arianne sipped from her own glass, smiling.

"Surprisingly, yes, I do. It's interesting." Lilly then sampled the sandwich and smiled. "I love these too."

"Those are very rare roast beef with cucumber

spread. Another house favorite." Arianne was enjoying watching Lilly's exploration of food. "Didn't you have regular food during your time in St. Louis Cemetery?"

Lilly shook her head and swallowed the bite she was chewing. "No, not really. I tried eating some of the meat from the things Baron brought to me but found it to be rather nasty tasting so I just existed on the blood. I didn't think it hurt anything not to eat."

"Not too much, maybe depleted a bit of vitamins and minerals you need. We mostly survive on blood. Food can be consumed but other than a little bit of minerals, we don't get anything from it. If you eat, you have human bodily functions, if you subsist on blood only, you don't. It's personal choice." Arianne ate a few grapes.

"How long have you been a vampire?" Lilly asked.

"Longer than I care to remember. I was born in the northeast of Inverness, Scotland in a small fishing village called Baile an Todhair, or Balintor as it is called now. It was 1387 and I had turned 24. I was married to a fisherman who was out at sea. A boat foundered on the rocks and a man washed up on shore. At first they thought he was dead, he was very cold, but then he was warmed and woke up. He said his name was Viktor Alexandru and he had sailed from France and the ship was lost in a storm. He was taken in by the community and given assistance. None of us knew why he didn't come out in the day but worked at night. I was out gathering extra wood for my fire when Viktor came over to me. He wanted me to have sex with him but I refused. He then glamoured me that I was his lover and while we made love, he bit me. He turned me at that time."

"Glamoury? What is that?"

"We are able to convince people to do things, forget them, or other things by having them look into our eyes and holding them in our gaze and planting the information in their head without them being aware." Arianne explained, "It comes in quite handy at times."

"Oh, that's what it's called. I think I've used that a few times but never understood that it was a 'power' or anything special. I just thought I was really good at talking people into things." Lilly thought back to the policeman at the parade. "So this Viktor...glamoured you into thinking he was your lover?"

"Yes, and when I awoke, he told me that I was now his and we were leaving Balintor forever. He took me away in the night, I never saw my family, my husband, or my home again. He taught me about being a vampire, he was a good maker. We travelled throughout Britain and Scotland until we ran into a problem in 1440 and he was taken from me. From there, I was on my own, working where I could, and trying to stay one step ahead of the damned angels."

"Angels?" Lilly swallowed her wine and asked.

"Yes, the damned meddling angels. They keep us 'in line' by watching us after they do their infernal tuning. They tell you the rules and then do something to you so they can tell if they've given you the rules and they can track you to see what you do." her face flushed in anger, "I lost Viktor to them. They came to us one night and said he had killed someone, that it was his last chance, and they grabbed him, two huge male angels, one with red wings and one with brown. A third angel was there, a woman with brown wings, and she told me that I knew the rules and that they would be watching me. They are just waiting for me to screw up enough so they can drag me to Hell where they took Viktor. That's what they do when you misbehave, you get dragged to Hell." At the memory, Arianne rubbed the back of her lace glove covered right hand.

Lilly didn't quite know what to believe about this. She knew one angel, Sullivan said that he was one and he had been furious when he found that he was a vampire, but she had never been talked to by any other angels. She didn't know the rules Arianne was talking about. "I have never learned these rules. What are they?"

Arianne looked at her as if to see something on her. "I guess they never found you so you haven't met them yet. Once they find you, they let you know all of them. They are things like don't make a vampire but every 100 years, don't turn people who don't want to be turned, don't turn children, and don't feed off children, the disabled, or the insane. There are more but those are the ones that get used against us all the time."

"So Viktor disobeyed these rules and he was taken to Hell?" Lilly was trying to mentally check to see if she was in danger. She wanted to ask about Sullivan outright but she wasn't sure she trusted Arianne totally yet. And, speaking of him was like giving him power and all she wanted to do was forget he ever existed and get far away from him.

"They said he did. They gave a list of things he had done and one of those was turning me without my permission but I didn't mind after it happened, I rather liked it. They never asked me what I wanted; they never asked if I was okay with becoming a vampire, they just blamed him for it. They had other things they said he did, I didn't know about any of them. I just wanted them to leave Viktor alone and leave him with me. But they refused and I heard him scream all the way, until I couldn't hear him any longer. He was terrified of what they were doing, damn them to their own Hell!" One single bloody tear slid out of her left eye and down her face, falling into her wine.

Lilly sat, silently munching on an apple and thinking about what Arianne had said. The angels had not caught up with her, yet. And she had turned Sullivan without his permission. Was she in danger of going to Hell for that? Her mind raced through all the teaching she had gone through in the Church over the years she was alive and she wondered if there was a way to get absolution for something like that if she went to confession. Cataclysm never covered vampire sins.

"So I should expect the angels soon?" Lilly ventured, hoping not to hear the answer.

"I suspect so. They can find me anytime and if they find an untuned vampire, they swoop in and make sure that the vampire knows the rules. I don't know why they didn't find you all these years but..." Arianne looked around as if to try to see if there was an angel lurking. She continued running her fingers over the back of her right hand.

"How will they deal with Baron? He's a vampire too but I doubt he will understand their rules. And do they have rules for cats anyway?" While she didn't worry at all about Sullivan, she was terrified that the angels might take her friend because he wasn't human. How would a cat defend himself from being taken to Hell?

Arianne shook her head, "I have no idea what they might do. My experience is that they are not forgiving about anything, they have their rules and nothing will stop them if they think they have been broken. We can only hope they don't figure out that he is a vampire and leave him alone."

Lilly started to try to think about what she would do if she had to defend Baron from the angels. She would fight for him, no matter how it ended up because he had taken such care of her over the years. He was her friend and companion and was closer to her than any human had ever been. She reached down to pet him and scratch him between the ears the way he liked it. He looked up at her, his gold eyes twinkling. She knew he was hearing her thoughts, he seemed to be able to do so, even doing things she had thought of without her saying it out loud. She started to think about how she would protect him, how she wouldn't allow the angels to take him away from her, trying to reassure him.

They talked more through the night, about Arianne's past, about the history since Lilly became a vampire. Then Arianne heard the large grandfather clock in the hall chime three a.m. She was wrung out from the excitement of the night and wanted to have a chance to feed before she retired. She stood and held out her hand, "Come dear, let me show you to your room. Mitch has placed your bag in there; you will find everything you need in the attached bath. I figure you will want a bath and such before you retire for the day. Do not worry; the windows are made of a glass that does not allow the sun's harmful rays through, just the light. You will not be harmed."

"Thank you." Lilly tried to stifle the tears falling down her face. She did not want to seem ungrateful to her hostess for the kindness she was showing. She and Arianne walked through the massive house, passing through several rooms decorated with many old pieces of furniture, large beautiful paintings, and figurines of dancers. They finally arrived upstairs at a very cozy room with a large bed that had dark green velvet framing gold curtains hanging at the head, gold chairs, light mint green paint on the walls. Beyond the bed, through an open door, was a salmon colored room with a slipper-shaped bathtub.

Lilly stared around her. This was even grander than anything that Mahogany Hall had. Her little red suitcase was laid on the bed. She turned to Arianne, "This is my room? Are you sure you aren't giving up your room? I can sleep in the parlor if need be..."

Arianne threw back her head and laughed loudly, "Oh no dear, this is your room for as long as you live here, unless you want to choose from the other six bedrooms, other than mine or Mitch's." She indicated a couple of doors a few feet down the hallway.

"And you and your servants only live here?" Lilly could not conceive of a house this size, larger than Mahogany Hall, being occupied by so few.

"No, not all the servants. Eloise and her sister live in a house a few blocks away and come here to work in the evenings for me. It's just me and Mitch most of the time. That is why it is so wonderful to have you here." Arianne walked to the door. "If you need anything, pick up the phone next to the bed," she stopped, pointed to an object on the side table, and then continued, "You do know what a phone is, right?"

Lilly looked at the place where she pointed and walked over, picking up the handset with a questioning glance at her hostess.

"Put the top to your ear and speak into the bottom where the cord is. This is only connected within the house so Mitch will answer if you pick it up. Lilly held it up to her ear and spoke into the mouthpiece. Mitch did, indeed answer. After thanking him and saying goodbye, she placed the handset back on the rest.

"We had a telephone in Mahogany Hall but it did not look like that." Then she pointed at the dark window on the wall. "Is that a television?"

"Oh, you know about those?"

"Oh yes, I saw one at a bar in the French

Quarter when we were," she stopped and corrected herself, hoping Arianne wouldn't pursue the mistake, "I was out just after the storm and went to look for food. I found a place open and they had one."

"Well, here's the remote, the control for the television." Arianne had noticed the change but didn't feel like following it up right at that moment. "You turn it on and off here and the volume is controlled with this button. You can change channels with this button, up goes one way, down the other." she indicated the buttons as she described them, "there isn't much on this time of night but you might see something new."

Lilly smiled, "I bet I will, I think the world has changed."

"Well dear, things have changed beyond your wildest imagination and I look forward to helping you explore your new world." Arianne hugged her and then went out the door with a "good day" and shut the door behind her.

Lilly went into the bath, washed and then went to the bed and curled up under the covers. She played with the buttons on the remote and looked at some of the things on the television. Everything was so confusing. Baron jumped up on the bed and curled up next to her, purring for the first time in several nights. Lilly pet him while she watched the strange things on the screen. When she felt the pull of the impending dawn, she gave him a last pat and then pulled the skull over to her. "Oh Marcus!" she sighed, then closed her eyes and let the dawning day whisk her away into sleep, leaving the television on talking to the quiet room.

Chapter Sixteen

THEY HAD BEEN making love in the back of the stable, up high in the loft away from prying eyes. While Eadwina Ferguson didn't mind having her moans and cries of passion heard, she drew the line at being watched.

As Viktor Alexandru pumped into his lover and she clutched at him, his fangs dropped and he bent to her neck, biting down. She shouted his name and returned the bite. As they each shared the other's blood, their bodies hit their climax.

Viktor raised his head as their fangs retracted and said, "I love you. I never cease to be amazed at you, your beauty, your strength, and the depth of your passions." He smiled at her, pushing at her hair with his right hand. A burn scar, in the shape of a circle with three parts was on the back of it. Two of the parts had a small symbol in it.

Eadwina kissed him lazily, still feeling the effects of his passion, "I love you too, beloved. You are my world."

As they parted, a very strong, bright light filled the entire barn, making the two lovers shield their eyes against it.

The light faded and when they could get their eyes to focus, they could see three figures standing beside them. Viktor leapt to his feet, pulling Eadwina up and behind him, trying to shield her obvious lack of clothing as well as protect her from the unexpected.

Then he noticed their visitors were wearing very large wings, two gray and one blood red.

"Damn it! Fucking Angels!" Viktor swore in recognition. "What the Hell do you want?"

The large male angel with the blood-red wings was holding a flaming sword and he leveled the sword at Viktor and then moved a few inches to the side. "Female, move away from him." It was not a request.

"No!" Eadwina stepped to Viktor's side in defiance. Viktor gripped her hand, hoping the angels wouldn't hurt her.

"Move away." The angel said again and lifted his left hand, index finger extended. Eadwina was forced, against her will, to walk backwards a few steps, far enough to have to drop her hold on her lover. "Stay." The angel dropped his hand.

Try as she might, Eadwina could not move.

Then the angel lifted his hand again and pointed at Viktor and with the same monotone voice commanded, "Kneel, vampire." Viktor unwillingly sunk to his knees. "Stretch out your right hand." Viktor's hand shot out and stayed, palm down.

The small female angel with the gray wings spoke up. "I am Nida, Voice of God's angel, Mikhail. You are Viktor Alexandru, vampire."

"I am." Viktor answered, he knew it was no use to deny it.

"You are given a chance to speak. Do you have a defense for your actions?" she asked.

Viktor began to rapidly go over his memories of the last few decades. While he had not been pure, he couldn't seem to find anything that would have called down judgment on him.

"I have not..." he began. Then he stopped.

The child. The image of a very scared and very sick child swam to the surface of his mind.

"I had to do it. He had been brutalized and starved. He had no relatives to take him. What I did was save him from a crippled life of misery! I would not have wanted to live like that!"

He spoke the truth of his heart. He had killed the boy's father as the man was in the middle of beating the sick child. He drained the miserable sadist and left his body in the village square. The child was so sick, Viktor had wrestled with what to do.

But, in the end he had chosen to place the child into a deep trance and then quickly kill him with the sword he carried, piercing his heart. The child didn't feel a thing and died fast, a matter of seconds.

The woman angel, Nida, stood silent for a moment, then nodded. "Viktor Alexandru, you have been judged and will be marked for your sin."

"No!" Viktor screamed out. The woman pointed her finger at the top of his hand and a burning pain seared through the place where the mark was made, a small symbol made into the circle that had already resided. Viktor screamed in pain.

"Please, don't hurt him..." Eadwina screamed out. "Help us, someone!"

The other gray winged angel, a male, said, "No one will hear you. Everyone who is within hearing is in slumber and cannot hear you."

Eadwina screamed Viktor's name, bloody tears coursing down her face.

"Silence, woman." The red-winged angel snapped and pointed and she found herself unable to speak.

Viktor's screams ended, He was crying in pain but silent.

"Are you ready for your punishment?" Nida asked.

Viktor looked to his hand. This newest mark completed the judgment sigil.

He was damned. As this fact dawned on him, he began to screamed and kept screaming. Over the din, Nida spoke. "Viktor Alexandru, you have been judged three times. You are hereby condemned to eternity in Hell."

The male angel with the red wings grabbed the distraught vampire from his knees and the light grew. They rose into the air and as they did, Eadwina could hear Viktor scream her name and what she thought was "I love you."

The two remaining angels stood before her. Nida spoke. "Eadwina Ferguson, born Urquhart, you were not involved in the incident. Let this serve as a warning to you. Do nothing against the laws set down for vampires. You are watched and will be judged."

Arianne jerked up with a shout, thick blood tears falling down her face.

Mitch came into the room without a knock, shutting the door behind him and crossing to her quickly. He gathered his mistress up into his arms and let her cry against his shoulder. He stroked her hair as she sobbed. This was familiar territory, he knew exactly what she had been dreaming about, she had the dream often, waking in screams and tears. It was her past, it never let her have a moment's peace in the hoped-for peace of the day. And he hated the angels for what they had done to her to cause them.

She finally calmed and looked up into his eyes. She mumbled, "It was a dream. Just a dream."

No, more than a dream, a nightmare, the memory of her beloved maker's fate...five hundred and sixty five years ago tonight.

Chapter Seventeen

T HE SETTING SUN triggered Sullivan's need to awaken and he opened his eyes and groaned. There was something covering his face and he grabbed it and pulled it off, throwing it. Everything hurt, like he had been fighting all day. He especially hurt on his neck and chest. He reached up, touched his neck and felt an open wound and when he pulled back his hand, it was bloody.

"What the hell?" he exclaimed and sat up, brushing his arm against the hilt of the buried knife in the mattress next to his armpit. He grabbed it and pulled it out, looking at it. It was Lilly's bone knife. He looked down and saw a large nick on his chest, over where his heart was. He turned to where Lilly slept beside him... He dropped the knife and it clattered as it hit the floor.

She was gone, no indication that she had slept next to him, no indention in the pillow. He jumped up roaring her name, looking in fear around the room.

Then he spotted it, the blood on the wall. It had the form of words. He looked at them, totally aghast at what they said, "Leave me the Hell alone!" He reeled as he remembered what had happened, the memories flooding back in all horrifying detail. The man he drank to death, throwing the body away, dragging Lilly up to the room, kicking the cat and then locking him in the closet.

Raping Lilly.

"Oh God!" he cried aloud, the sound of his voice hitting the silence of the room. "Lilly!" he called out, stumbling to the closet and opening the door. The cat was gone but there was considerable evidence he had tried to get out of the door by clawing it deeply. Sullivan closed his eyes, his stomach rolling in nausea. He walked through the rest of the apartment, knowing he wouldn't find Lilly there. He checked the luggage; her little red suitcase was gone.

He turned back and looked at the bed which was bloody with little bits of glitter stuck on the drying goo, then the wall. "Leave me the Hell alone!" The words were written in blood. His blood, he realized. She must have been terrified of him, of what he did to her and cut his throat in his sleep. She just didn't do it enough to kill him.

She should have killed him, he thought.

He looked down and found the gray feather laying on the floor, crushed and broken as he felt his heart was. He picked it up and stuffed into the pocket of his jeans.

He had to find her. He had to apologize to her, make it up, let her know he really wasn't in control when he did it and he would have never,

ever harmed her if he was in his right mind. He stepped into the bathroom and looked at his neck, the gash was open, not bleeding much but very noticeable. He looked in the medicine cabinet but there was no gauze or anything to cover it with. He couldn't go out looking for her looking like the victim in a horror movie. He went back to the bed and pulled off her pillowcase, smelling it as he did. Her scent, the scent of the shampoo she had used was still on it and it sent a fresh wave of regret and nausea through him.

"Lilly, I'm so sorry." He moaned as he pulled the pillowcase apart and then into a long strip. He carefully wound it around his neck and tucked the end into the top to hold it. Then he grabbed a clean t-shirt and jeans and dressed. Pulling on his shoes, he took a last look around the room, his eyes sweeping over the open wrecked door to the closet, stopping and absorbing the look of the words on the wall.

"Leave me the Hell alone!"

Those words seared into his soul, cutting deeper than any knife she could have used.

He had to find her.

He stepped out the door, ran down the stairs and to the door of the building. He pushed on the door to the outside but it was locked. He caught the glimmer of metal, bent to look, and found the key. He picked it up and slipped it into the lock, and opened the door. He stepped through and relocked it, depositing the key in his jeans pocket. Then he stood there on the sidewalk and looked around, trying to figure out where she would have gone.

He started walking the streets, trying to find any sign she had been there. Shaking his head miserably, if he still had his angelic powers, he could have found her, a vampire, easily. He played with the ring on his finger, useless since he lost his wings. And he had lost his power when he was turned. Now he was head-blind, unable to sense anything, nothing he could use to find her in this city. As he walked, his mind kept going over and over the events of the night before, from the walk, to the parade, to the bar, and then the walk home. Each time he saw her face in his mind, first laughing and then screaming in terror and his gut twisted.

How in heaven was he going to get her to trust him again?

His steps took him to Jackson Square, right up to the cathedral. She might have come here seeking asylum and the comfort of the church she loved. It sat quiet and locked up, no sign that anyone had been there. He pounded on the door in frustration, growling at the emptiness both in the church and his heart. Then he started walking again, back down toward Bourbon Street.

On the way, he encountered a man walking down the street. His stomach growled and he noticed, for the first time, he was ravenously thirsty. He needed blood and needed it soon. He waved at him, putting on a smile he did not feel. "Hey, I'm glad to see someone else out. How are you doing?" He asked, trying to make the man stop for a moment.

"I'm doing ok; the house came through the storm ok. How about you?" The man smiled back at him.

"I did fine, kept safe and everything is fine. You and I need to step back into this doorway a moment; I need to talk with you privately." Sullivan looked into the man's eyes as he tried to convince the man. He noticed the man's eyes glazed over and his body seemed to relax so Sullivan took him by the arm and pulled him into the shadows. Then he laid the man's head over to one side and his fangs lowered. He bent to the neck and bit down.

"When you drink, only take 10 sips, this is half what I would do by myself.... Then rub your tongue over the holes to close them. Do not take more than 10 or we risk his life." He heard Lilly's words echoing in his head. The words he hadn't heeded because he was already angry from the argument he had caused. He closed his eyes and counted very carefully to 12, swallowing after each number. Not quite what she said she would do herself but he didn't want to chance having to change the man or harming him. Once he thought the last number, he rubbed his tongue over the holes and they closed up.

He lifted his head and looked at the man standing next to him; he seemed to be okay, not harmed much by the action. "You want to go home and eat and drink well. You never saw me, go down the street and turn the corner, not looking back." Sullivan instructed him. The man walked away, never looking back, and disappeared.

Sullivan let out a sigh of relief; he had fed and not harmed someone. He hoped Lilly would be proud of him once she forgave him. He wished he had paid more attention when he had learned of the vampire's abilities when he moved into Enforcer. He had learned only what he had to, the things he had to tell them to keep from going to Hell. The rest of it had come and gone in his memory without another thought and he now regretted that.

Then he noticed his neck was itching. He reached up under the makeshift bandage and touched. The wound was closed and rapidly healing. The blood intake must have triggered some sort of vampire healing effect, he thought. He unwound the bandage and dropped it to the sidewalk. He pulled the neckline out peering at his chest; the nick was gone as well. He didn't know if these developments were a good thing or not, he really deserved to carry those scars forever for what he had done to her.

He walked on, finding the place where they had encountered the parade participants. The street held a few people, the rainbow flags still flapping in the light, hot September breeze. He walked down to the building that Shawn had run to find the beads they were given, the door was open and people were inside talking in the night's darkness. Multiple candles illuminated the room to a soft brightness. Sully looked around until he found Shawn and Mike sitting together, arms around each other, talking to others. He walked up to them and said, "Hi guys."

"Oh, Hi Sullivan. Where's Lilly?" Shawn asked, smiling and looking around. Sullivan's grim face took the smile off the other man's. "What's happened?"

Sullivan shook his head, trying to think of what to say that wouldn't make him appear to be the overwhelming asshole he felt like. "We argued. She left while I slept, I need to find her to apologize. I'm worried about her; it's not really safe in the city to be alone."

"She's not been here, man." Mike shook his head. "We would have welcomed her in and helped her out, and kept her safe. She's one very nice lady."

"You need us to help search? Do you think something has happened to her?" Shawn asked. He nodded to the group of guys hanging out in the room, everyone nodded back to him, confirming their willingness to assist Sullivan.

"Thanks, just keep your eyes open. If you find her, try to keep her here, I'll check back. I tend to be rather...nocturnal and a night owl" If they found Lilly and she told him about the rape, he would be arrested. Which would be a problem... angels didn't have fingerprints and...

"You ok?" Shawn interrupted his train of thought by laying his hand on Sully's arm. He hadn't been aware of just stopping talking but obviously he had.

"Nah, I'm worried. Feeling like a real jerk." He owned up to at least that much openly, the worst of it still very much in front of him. "Thanks guys,

I appreciate it." He nodded, shook Shawn and Mike's hand and walked out of the room to the calls of "take care man" and "be safe" from the other guys. He walked out of the building and back up Bourbon Street.

The streets were a bit busier than the previous night but nothing like a normal evening. Those who were out in the Quarter were either living there or had businesses there and were coming to check on them. Nothing was open for business, except for Johnny White's. It was to the bar that Sullivan headed next. As he neared, he could tell that this bar was the center of life for the area at the moment. He was greeted warmly by those who he had met the night before, back again to drink away whatever was going on in their lives. Captain Mott waved at him and Sully walked over and took the stool next to him.

"Hey Sully, how's your night going? Where's Lilly?" He asked between sips of warm beer. He gestured with his bottle, "Get this thirsty man a beer, will ya?"

As Marsha got the beer, Sullivan frowned and answered, "I had hoped she was here. She got up before me and left and I can't find her."

"You think she's in trouble?" The seaman passed the beer to him.

"No, well—maybe." Sullivan shook his head. "We quarreled. I was an idiot and caused it."

"Yes, we men always do!" said Capt. Mott, nodding. "That's why I ain't married!" He winked at Marsha.

"Ah! Who'd have ya?" chided Marsha with a

laugh, this was obviously friendly, well-rehearsed banter.

"How 'bout you, darlin'?" he looked hopeful.

"You're too late!" She held up her left hand and waggled her simply adorned ring finger. Smiling she danced off to serve another patron.

The seaman returned his attention to the troubled man. "Then what?"

Sully stared forlornly at his warm beer as he picked at the label. "After I...uh, fell asleep, she left...took all her stuff, her dumb cat, and left."

"Man, that sucks ass, seriously." Patty said from the other side of the captain. She still held her dog in her lap and fed him peanuts from time to time as she drank. "Must'a been a bad fight. Didn't hit her, did ya?"

Sullivan really didn't want to answer that, much of what he had done was so horrible and none of these good people would really understand. He looked down at the bottle for a minute and then said, "No. We argued over her ex-boyfriend. I was jealous as hell of him and she didn't think I should be."

"Did you have a reason to be jealous?" Teddy asked from her stool on the end.

"No. Not really. He's been gone a very long time but she still has a lot of feelings for him. She talks about him a lot and I finally got mad about it and let my mouth overload my ass." He looked down again, flushing a bit at the thought of just how far out of line he had been.

"Well, if it helps, she's not been here." Marsha said. "I've been here pretty much since you saw me last."

Sullivan took a long drink of the beer in his hand, draining it. He slammed the bottle down on the bar, a bit harder than he intended.

"Hey man, one thing the authorities who keep coming in here trying to shut me down are saying is that they are trying to get everyone to go to the Convention Center down behind the River Walk on Convention Center Blvd." Marsha told him, "Someone may have found her and taken her there, you might check."

Sullivan stood up and hugged her across the bar. "Thank you, Marsha. Everyone. I appreciate your help. If you do find her, please help her and keep her here, I will come back and check." He walked toward the door.

"Good luck, man, hope you find her." Captain Mott called as Sullivan slipped out the door.

Head down, hands shoved into the pockets of his jeans and caressing the feather, he headed straight down Bourbon, waded across still flooded Canal Street, walking toward the Convention Center. Constantly looking from side-to-side and squinting down every alley and every shadowed doorway, he cut across the business district, watching for people who might not have the best of intentions, hiding in the shadows. He intended to avoid them, the police, and the military who were patrolling the area. The stench of the city got worse as he crossed it, the smells of mold, rot, and other things in the standing water, along with the humid and almost still air. Even with the sun down, the city sweltered under 77 degree heat. No breeze relieved the stench that was growing just as foul as his mood. Sully knew that, if angels and vampires could perspire, he would be soaked in sweat by now.

He smelled and heard the area of the Convention Center blocks before he arrived there. Voices carried down the streets, crying, talking, screaming, moaning. What he walked into was as bad as anything he had seen in his lifetime as an angel. Inside and out of the Convention Center the noise was deafening, a roar of humanity punctuated by the wailing and crying of old women and children. The smell was a putrid mixture of sweat, human waste, rot and filth, all made worse by the stifling heat and humidity. Thousands of people sitting, sleeping, and walking around. Most clutched desperately onto the few meager belongings they were able to gather before they evacuated or were rescued from their ruined homes. This was all that remained of a life that would never be again. Each face wore a haunted expression of desperation, fear, anger, sorrow, and above all hopelessness. At one end, there was a long line queued up to get onto buses that were standing, running, to take them out of the city to parts unknown. People were boarding the busses and helping each other.

Sullivan walked through the sea of young and old, black and white, men and women, all in shock, looking for Lilly. He called her name out occasionally but was met with the sounds of the throng, never hearing her voice. He walked through the outside of the center, then through the inside and back out. None of the faces were hers. He felt his heart sink. Hopefully she had not left the city before he arrived.

He looked across the throng. He knew there

had to be many angels in the area with all the suffering and misery apparent. But none of them approached him. If they were looking for him, he would be approached and they would alert HHAD. The truth dawned on him.

They weren't looking for him.

He was wondering why when a small child came up to him and tugged on his shirt. Sullivan stopped and looked down into the dark tear-stained face of a little girl about eight desperately clutching a yellowish teddy bear with only one black button eye, a torn ear, and almost loved bald. "Mister, I can't find my mom," she said. He shook his head and looked around him. He spotted an army soldier with stripes, someone with authority.

He crouched down to her eye level and smiled at her. "I don't know where she is but I know someone who can help you find her." He stood and scooped her into his arms, walking over to the soldier.

"Sir, I have someone here who needs your help." he touched the man on the shoulder and he turned to face Sullivan and then looked at the little girl. "This is...what is your name, sweetie?"

"Keisha Johnson." She said it like she had memorized it. "My mom is LaDonna Thomas." She smiled brightly at Sullivan; a smile that looked so much like Lilly's that his heart lurched.

"Sergeant..." he looked at the man's name tag, "Barthelemy, this is Keisha Johnson. She's lost and looking for her mother. Can you take her to find her Mom?"

The sergeant looked at Sullivan and then at the little girl, "She's not yours?" he asked.

Sullivan and Keisha looked at one another with amused grins. "He's not my Daddy!" giggled Keisha.

"Nope, sorry about that. I am a total stranger looking for my...wife" he didn't know why he said it, It just sounded better than "I lost my girl-friend," he guessed.

"Ok, I'll take her to the registration area. Good luck in finding your wife, sir." Sergeant Berthele-my took the little girl's in his arms and turned to walk away. As Sully looked after them, the little girl turned and looked at him over the man's shoulder, smiling again, and waving goodbye, still clinging to her one-eyed teddy bear, once again making his heart skip.

Sully turned back to the sea of humanity and took one last look, hoping to see Lilly. Sighing in defeat, he turned away and started walking back toward the French Quarter. He didn't have any idea where to go now, he had struck out every-where and there was not a lot of night left to search. Then something occurred to him, he had not checked the cemetery. He hadn't thought about her going back there, he couldn't imagine anyone wanting to go back into a crypt after getting to come out into the city again, to a bed and people. But, she might have gone there. He had no idea why he didn't check there first, now it made sense to go there. He began to run, finding that his speed was much faster.

He dodged patrols and gangs, splashing his way up Canal and then across to Basin Street. He ran the few blocks to the cemetery, which was locked. He hit the bars of the gate in frustration and one bent. Then he decided to try to jump up and grab the top of the gate and try to climb over. He was able to easily jump the height, grab the wrought iron gate and vaulted over, hitting the ground gently. Then he ran through the tombs, homing in on the one in the back that he remembered.

Reaching it, he found the door wide open, the wood pushed back. A bouquet of red roses were laying discarded on the walkway in front of it, a jar candle lying next to it. He ducked into the crypt and looked around. It was empty, no sign of Lilly having been there.

Then he saw them, laying on the sleeping platform. The sunglasses he had grabbed in the River Walk. And, in the small amount of light, specks of the glitter she had been wearing. She had been there, at least for a time. He sunk to his knees and began to rock back and forth, holding the glasses against his chest. He began to cry, blood tears falling down his face. "Lilly. Darling where are you? Where have you gone? I want to find you, I need to find you. I am so very sorry for what I have done. Oh God, please help me find her." He found himself praying for the first time since he had come to New Orleans. "Please, God, I'll do anything, just let me find her and get her to listen to me. I'm so very sorry for what I've done." He prayed over and over again, begging.

Then he felt it, the pull of the sleep of the undead. He would not be able to find her tonight, his time was up. He pulled the door closed and climbed up onto the platform he had shared with her just a couple of nights before. Holding the glasses, he thought of her as his eyes closed and he fell asleep.

Chapter Eighteen

LILLY AWOKE WITH Baron still curled up with her and Marcus sitting next to her pillow. The television was still on, playing images of a rabbit being chased by a man in a hat with a gun. A black duck came into sight and the characters started trying to confuse the hunter about what season it was, duck season or rabbit season. Somehow the gray rabbit was able to get the duck to say "Duck season!" and the hunter shot the duck in the face.

Lilly didn't know why but this was very funny. She giggled as she watched the continuing hijinks between the characters. A knock on the door threatened to interrupt the fight between the rabbit, who was dressed up as a duck and the duck dressed up as a rabbit and Lilly ignored it to continue watching. The hunter shot the duck again after seeing a "Rabbit Season" sign on the tree, then the duck walked up to the rabbit and said "You're desthpicable!" Lilly rolled with laughter.

A knock sounded again and Arianne stuck her head inside to see Lilly laughing so hard that bloody tears were beginning to fall from her eyes. The girl pointed at the television and said, "I love this!"

Arianne just shook her head. "Bugs Bunny and Daffy Duck, classic Warner Brothers cartoons. I like those too." She stepped inside the room, "I know you're enjoying this but maybe you want to come down and have a bit of breakfast before the night gets started?"

Lilly pried her eyes off the screen as an elephant walked up to the hunter and knocked him to the ground. She couldn't stop smiling. "Yes. Please excuse me. I will dress and come down to..." she stopped.

Arianne finished, "... the kitchen, there's a small table there we can sit and watch the night from the window and talk." Arianne snuck another look at the screen as the characters continued to taunt and get each other shot. "I know where I can get DVDs of these cartoons and you can watch them whenever you wish."

Lilly didn't know what a DVD was but the idea she could watch these 'cartoons' as much as she wanted sounded fun so she agreed. Arianne shut the door and Lilly rose, going to the little suitcase and pulling out another pair of jeans and the last of the clean t-shirts. She would have to think about finding a way to either wash what she had or get more. Maybe it would rain tonight and she could leave her clothes outside, she thought. After washing her face in the trickle of water from the faucet in the big, beautiful bathroom and dressing, she used the brush on her hair and put on the sneakers again. Then she gathered up the dirty clothes and Marcus and walked down the stairs. She wandered about, looking into many of the beautifully decorated rooms until she found the kitchen. Baron followed at her heels.

Arianne looked up and smiled at her as she entered. Lilly was very pretty but Arianne could tell she needed more than just jeans and t-shirts to wear. Lilly placed Marcus on the table and then indicated the clothing in her hand, "I need to go out for a moment and lay these on the tree branches so if we get rain tonight, they will be washed. Or, if you have a washtub I may borrow..." She remembered the way the laundry was done back at Mahogany Hall.

Arianne tried not to laugh. She was becoming aware of just how much Lilly didn't know about how things had changed. "Lilly, dear, you do not have to do that, we have machines to do that now."

Lilly stopped, her hand on the door to the outside. "Machines? You are wealthy enough to have a machine? Those are huge and only affordable to the businesses that do a lot of laundry." The thought of a steam-powered commercial washer like the one down in Treme came to her mind.

Arianne didn't manage to stifle the laughter any longer, "Oh no child, they aren't huge and they are quite affordable by most people now. Let me show you." Arianne walked the confused girl into a small room off the kitchen. Two red machines with round glass windows on the front stood side by side. Her hostess opened one of the rounded windows like a cupboard. She took the clothing from Lilly, placed it in the machine and shut the door. "Now, we add soap, some softener, and push this button." She added the ingredients from bottles sitting on top of the machines, the scent of them strong to Lilly. The machine clicked and the sound of water started and then stopped. The machine beeped hysterically with flashing numbers on the little television screen. Alarmed by the noise, Lilly stumbled backwards into the wall.

"Oh damn, what have I done wrong? Sarah!" she called out loudly. Lilly could hear footsteps hurrying toward them and then Sarah appeared,

"Yes, Miss Campbell?"

"Sarah, I have started Lilly's laundry but the machine made this horrible noise and just went crazy. What did I not do?" Arianne didn't want to admit to Lilly that she very rarely touched the machine, allowing Eloise and Sarah to take care of most of the domestic work in the house.

Sarah checked the machine's indicator and then pushed a button to make the machine go dark. She turned around and opened the spigot on the wash sink behind her. The water trickled out of the faucet and then stopped altogether. Sarah shook her head, a frown coming across her dark face. "I'm sorry, Miss Campbell, it looks like we're out of water. There have been fires around town, a house caught fire a couple of blocks from our house and the firemen had to let it burn because there was no water in the hydrants."

"Well, I guess we'll have to pull Lilly's clothing out and do them by hand." Arianna looked at the girl. She was smaller by several inches so Arianne could not loan her any clothing. They would have to make due until the water came back on. "Sarah, if you could see to that, please. You can use the dryer after they are clean."

Arianne turned and walked back into the kitchen and heard Lilly thank Sarah for her help behind her. Then she came out to join her hostess at the table. Eloise brought wine, cheese, and fruit to them.

"So, Lilly, did you sleep well?" Arianne asked.

Lilly smiled, "Oh yes. The bed was wonderful and once I finally went to sleep, I rested." she sipped a bit of the wine from her glass.

"Good! So, tell me, last night you mentioned someone named Sullivan. Who is that, dear?" Arianne's curiosity got the best of her.

Lilly closed her eyes and sighed. He was the last thing she wanted to think or talk about. She had hoped that Arianne had forgotten her slips about him during their talk the night before. She shook her head and then answered, "He is someone that I met recently. He is not a nice person and is out of my life." She hoped that the statement would put her off any further questioning.

No such luck. "Recently? But you said you were in the crypt. How did you manage to meet a man while living there?" Arianne was not going to give up on the information; something in the back of her mind told her that this was something more important than Lilly was trying to let on.

Lilly laid her head back and then forward again. She casually and thoughtlessly rubbed the top of the skull beside her and Baron ran in and jumped up on her lap, his big body threatening to dwarf her in the chair and knock her out of it. She pulled the cat to her and rubbed her hand through the multicolored fur. It was obvious to Arianne that her guest was very unhappy with the thought of this Sullivan and that made her very curious.

"Ok" She took a deep breath and launched into the story she really didn't want to tell. "He was attacked and left for dead outside of my crypt a couple of days ago, the day the storm blew through. Once it was quiet and I thought it was safe, I opened the door and looked out. He was lying in a pool of blood, cut and broken, on my doorstep. I didn't think it would hurt for me to help him so I pulled him inside, sent Baron for a nutria to help replenish my own blood supply, then I bit the man, drained him and then gave him my blood like I remembered Marcus doing to help me. Once I refed, on the nutria that Baron brought back, and shared with him, I curled up on the sleeping platform with him and slept. He came awake and was, at first, very angry with me for turning him. But then he calmed down and we talked. The bad men who hurt him came again and we tricked them, and Baron frightened them away." Lilly looked down at Baron, smiling. She continued to stroke his soft fur and he purred loudly in response. "Then Sullivan took me out of the cemetery to a place in the French Quarter that a friend of his owns."

Lilly hoped that the little bit of information would mollify her and they could move on to other, less stressful subjects but Arianne pressed her for more. "So this man saved you and then what happened?"

"He went out and found these clothes for me, mine had fallen apart. Then we went out and explored the Quarter, finding a parade and a bar open. We met some interesting people and the bar was where I discovered television. They were showing the destruction of the city by the storm, it looks horrible!"

"The storm has been very bad for the city and the levees have burst in several places, flooding everything that wasn't blown down. We've had a lot of people hurt and killed, many have lost their homes. So that is where you saw the television, this bar? Where is this Sullivan now?"

Lilly sighed. She would be able to manage to get out of telling Arianne about the fight and the rape. "I don't know. We separated and I went back to the crypt shortly before you found me."

Then they heard a hard pounding on the door to the front yard. It sounded as if whoever was doing it was trying to beat down the door. Arianne rose and walked to the door of the kitchen and spotted Mitch walking quickly through the house. "Mitch, find out what is going on and get rid of them, please." she instructed.

"Yes, Eadwina, uh, Arianne. Right away." Mitch fumbled with the name, never missing a step as he continued through the house. They heard the front door open, close, and then open again a few minutes later.

"Arianne, I think you better come here." he called from the entry.

Chapter Nineteen

S ULLIVAN FORCED HIMSELF awake before the sun completely set. He had to get moving, he had to find Lilly and apologize and she had been here, in the crypt, the night before. He sat up and immediately bumped his head on the ceiling.

"God damn it!" he let fly. He rolled and dropped off the sleeping shelf onto the floor and opened the door. He stepped out into the approaching twilight, squinting against the sun's rays that were reflecting off of the concrete crypts around him. His skin began to itch where it was touched by the light.

He picked up a rose from the bunch discarded in front of the crypt and cursed again as one of the thorns pricked his finger. He instinctively stuck the finger in his mouth and licked off the blood, which made his stomach immediately clutch in hunger. He sighed and started walking toward the gate; he would have to get something to eat later.

As he approached the gate, he saw the old man who he surmised must be the caretaker. His uniform was dark blue and contrasted with his gray hair, cut short and left natural. His medium skin had skin tags and some age spots dotted across his broad nose. He was shutting the gate.

"Hello there!" Sullivan called out to get his attention.

The man turned and gave him a dark look. "What are you doing here? I walked the cemetery and didn't see you. I'm closing now." He indicated the gate in his right hand.

"I'm sorry, I didn't see you, I was looking at the crypts. Say, I have a question, who came by and left flowers and a candle by the McCall/Jones crypt back in alley number nine?" Sullivan smiled at the man, trying to reassure him that he wasn't some threat.

"I don't give that information out, mister. I just keep an eye on the cemetery so things don't get vandalized and I sometimes tell some of the history. Who comes to decorate the graves ain't any of my business." The man pulled the gate open and indicated that Sullivan should walk on through.

But Sully held back, not taking the hint. "I have a friend who comes to the cemetery occasionally to put flowers on a grave and I have lost his address. He told me it was one back in that area and I think he may have been the one that left these." He waved the rose.

The guard wasn't impressed, obviously. He shook his head. "Look, I have several people who come here to leave flowers. I don't keep up with who they are so I can't help you. Now, if you don't mind, my wife is home alone and I want to get there to make sure she is safe."

Sullivan rolled his eyes in frustration and stepped like he was going to go through the gate, then he stepped sideways, stopping very close to the man, and put both hands on his shoulders. He looked deep into the man's eyes and said, "I need you to give me the name and any other information you have on the person who brings flowers to that particular grave. You are going to do so because I'm asking nice and I don't want to hit an elder."

He watched the man's eyes glaze over and he opened and shut his mouth a couple of times like his brain and lips were disconnected. Then he slowly nodded his head. "Her name is Arianne Campbell and I have her address on a card in the office." His voice had dropped to a monotone.

Sullivan stepped into the little building by the gate and found a card box. He pulled the cards out and quickly went through them, dropping each on the desk as he looked at it, rejecting every one until he ran across one with the name of Arianne Campbell on it. He pocketed the card and went back out. He stepped up to the man again and said, "You never saw me. You lock up as usual and you go home to your wife. It's been a good day and you are hungry and tired. You won't remember anything about me, about the woman, about all of it. You've never seen anyone at that crypt, ever. Nod your head if you understand."

The old man nodded slowly and Sullivan added, "Now, count to twenty slowly and when you get to that number, you will wake up from this and not remember." Then he slipped out the gate and walked quickly back toward Canal.

It was going to be a long walk to wherever Arianne Campbell lived, he thought. He stopped and looked down at the card once he reached Canal. He stepped up on an overturned metal box to get out of the knee-deep water. The address was on Prytania but he had no idea where that was in the city. He walked off toward the central business district, angling toward the higher land and away from the water. The further into the city he got, the less the water became until he was back on dry pavement again. The city was not quiet but it didn't sound like the New Orleans of just a week prior. There was intermittent traffic, mainly large military vehicles with several people, which he managed to avoid by ducking into alleys and doorways.

Then he spotted what he needed, a New Orleans police cruiser. After making sure there was only one person inside, he stepped out and into the lights where the officer could see him and waved. The cruiser stopped and the officer rolled down his window.

"Boy, you shouldn't be out here, there's a curfew and it's dangerous." The big man inside said.

"I am lost, sir. We came in before the storm and were staying with a friend. I got separated when I went out to get some water and food and am trying to find my way back there. Can you direct me to Prytania Street?" Sullivan hoped the excuse didn't sound too flimsy.

The officer frowned. "You are a couple of miles

away from it; it's over the other side of the Ponchatrain Expressway, in the Garden District. That's a very long and dangerous walk from here."

Sullivan leaned down and caught the cop's attention, "I don't suppose you could give me a ride down there, then, could you, sir?" Once again he was finding the ability to glamour the people he came in contact with very handy.

The officer slowly nodded, "I think I can take you there. You won't get into trouble that way. Get in."

Sullivan ran around the front of the patrol car and jumped into the front passenger seat. "Ok, here's the address." He passed the card with the information over to the man who looked at it and then handed it back. Then he started driving down the street, trying to avoid the glass, tree branches and other debris in the road.

Sully watched the scenery pass and tried to think of how he was going to get Lilly to listen to him so he could convince her that he was sorry for going out of his mind. She was so sweet and nice, she had to be terrified to cut his throat and write in blood on the wall. He still couldn't understand why she would even let him live after what he did. How in the universe was he going to get her to hear him out? The car passed under the freeway and then turned left, then right again. The street sign read Prytania Street and he knew he was close. They dodged many tree limbs and various debris. Then the car slowed and pulled up to the curb in front of a huge house set back from the street with a wrought-iron fence.

Sullivan started to get out but stopped. There might not be another chance, he thought. He reached across the seat and pulled the officer toward him. Then he sunk his fangs into his neck, carefully counting to 10 as he swallowed the blood. As he ran his tongue over the holes, he thought he tasted something odd, something that tasted like kerosene smelled. He frowned; hoping that the taste didn't mean the blood was tainted with something. Then he pulled back and leaned to open the door. "Thank-you for bringing me home. You will remember me as a little old lady you helped but you won't remember where you took her but you know she's safe. Now you are on your way back to Canal Street, there is an emergency call." Then he slipped from the car and shut the door. The patrol car began to move and then turned quickly around the corner and Sullivan heard the sirens come on.

He turned toward the house, found and opened the gate, and then walked across the lawn, dodging the downed branches from the old trees in the yard.

Sullivan paced out in the yard for a few minutes, trying to figure out what to do, his thoughts raced a mile a minute, it seemed. All he wanted to do was barge into the house and grab her and drag her out with him. She was HIS; everything in his body screamed the fact. And, despite the depression he felt at his actions the previous night, he found himself growing hard with desire. The woman just held so much power...

He came up closer to the house. It was strange; there were lights on in there, something he had not seen except for the bar. He took a deep breath and walked up the stairs to the porch. He could hear voices inside, louder than he should have been able to hear. And one of those voices was Lilly's. His heart seemed to pound in his chest as he pounded on the door.

The door opened and a man emerged from the house, closing the door behind him and stood on the porch. "Who are you and what are you wanting?" The man was larger than Sullivan and did not sound like he was going to be willing to talk without a problem. Sullivan walked up closer. He looked up at the man and tried to pull his attention to his eyes.

"That's not going to work on me, vampire. What do you want here?" The big man growled, literally growled, like a wolf. Sullivan backed up a step.

"I have heard my girlfriend is here and I've come to talk to her." He just laid it out straight. He wasn't going to leave until he talked to Lilly, no matter what else happened.

"Let me talk to Miss Campbell and see if she is receiving visitors. Wait here." The man went back into the house and shut the door, leaving Sullivan standing on the porch, angry and more than a little horny, pacing in frustration.

Chapter Twenty

ARIANNE WALKED THROUGH the house to the front entry; Lilly cradled Marcus and followed with Baron trailing behind her,

"What is it, Mitch?" Arianne stopped about halfway through the entry. "What is going on?"

"There's a man outside who is looking for our house guest. He calls her his 'girlfriend,' and," he shook his head, "He is a vampire. He tried to glamour me to gain entry to the house."

Arianne turned and looked at Lilly. The color had drained from the girl's face and she was clutching the skull tightly. The cat was walking circles around her knees, rubbing her legs and growling.

"A vampire, huh? Did this vampire give his name?" Arianne could not shake the feeling that it was Sullivan and he had come to try to get Lilly back.

"No, he didn't. Should I send him away?" Mitch didn't like the vampire outside, that much was very obvious to Arianne.

She was thinking about her answer when, from behind her, Lilly said, "Please! I do not want to talk to him, see him, or anything. Please send him away."

But Arianne was curious about the man. "Lilly, you are his maker. You have to be able to work with him. Just because you had a disagreement with him is no reason to abjure him." She lectured the young vampire.

About that time, the door exploded inward and Sullivan came storming in. "Lilly! You are not sending me away. I came here to apologize to you, to tell you that I didn't mean to hurt you, I was out of my mind at the time!" He shouted. He knew he should be calm but he couldn't seem to pull it together.

"Was something in that cop's blood?" the thought flashed through his mind until Mitch grabbed him, holding him back from coming further into the room until Sullivan pushed him away forcefully. The ghoul hit the wall but did not go down. He stood his ground, growling again.

A tall, red-headed woman caught his notice when she exploded, shouting "How DARE you enter MY house unbidden and push my houseman around?" Arianne seethed as she charged forward. Her temper boiling just beneath her regal exterior. Cold fury burned in her green eyes "You have no right to force entrance and demand to speak with my house guest. Get OUT!" She pointed to the destroyed doorway.

"Listen lady, I didn't want to upset you or hurt anyone. I came here because my girlfriend misunderstood what I said and did a day ago and left and I think she should hear me out before making any decisions." Sullivan started to push past Arianne. She placed her right hand onto the center of his chest and easily held him motionless. She was an Elder vampire of great power. He could feel the wave of energy holding him immobile.

"Misunderstood? Misunderstood?" Lilly cried out, "How the hell could I have misunderstood being raped? Beaten? Called a slut?" she shook with fury, "I misunderstood NOTHING, Sullivan. YOU" indicating the great difference in their heights, "Attacked me! Because you are insane...jealous of someone you have NEVER met! Losing control is no excuse for what you did!" She straightened to her full diminutive height. "I meant what I said. LEAVE...ME...ALONE!" Pausing to put extra emphasis on the last three words. Then, quite calmly, "Go Away."

Sullivan relaxed, taking half a step backwards. Arianne dropped her hand but still stood between them. Sullivan looked past her at Lilly. He opened his mouth to utter more excuses but saw the fury and pain. He shut his mouth and hung his head, shaking it ruefully.

"You never listen to me, Sully." Frustration and fury tinting every word. "You never have. I have told you many things you just dismiss. You just don't listen." She repeated for emphasis, hoping this time he would hear. "And then you KILLED that man. You drained him after I cautioned you not to and you threw his body away like so much trash! And then...and then," she Paused and shaking her head slowly in disbelief, she said very quietly, "You raped me. You hurt me!" Blood tears flowed down her face. "You hurt me over and over again. Please...Please...Please, just go away and leave me alone," she pleaded.

The sight of her, crying and undone stopped him cold. The pain rolling off of her was worse than any knife she could have used. He reached toward her, trying to will her to step to him. When she did not move, he dropped his arms and pleaded. "I'm so sorry, Lilly. I never meant to kill that guy. I lost my mind somehow. I never meant to hurt you, either." He stopped and winced in pain, feeling the breaking of his heart. "Lilly, I love you."

Lilly stopped sobbing and looked at him. The look in her eyes was not what he expected to see at those words. Arianne felt the energy shift and backed aside in order to watch the interchange. "You. What?" She said quietly, barely a whisper but it had the impact of a bomb. The look in her eyes was pure, fire-fed hatred. "What did you say? You love me? That would be laughable if it wasn't so pathetic. You cannot love, you are not capable."

At that moment, his soul died. His head spun as the words hit him and continued to ring in his ears. He hung his head, unable to argue with her. His mind wouldn't work, he couldn't come up with anything to answer that wouldn't sound...pathetic, as she had said.

"Just go away. Leave me alone." Lilly said quietly, the fire having left just as fast as it had flashed, leaving her feeling empty and wrung out.

He looked up at her, all the fight washed out of him. "You are right. I should never have come here. I was wrong in what I did and I have no right to ask you to forgive me or to take me back. I should go now. I'm so sorry I hurt you." Then he turned to Mitch, "I'm sorry for my behavior toward you, you were not involved." The man nodded his head in acknowledgement. Finally, he looked at the woman standing to the side. "Ma'am, I am sorry for the damages to your home. I don't have the money to fix it right now, but I will send it just as soon as I am able. I'm sorry I barged in." He turned toward the open and destroyed door, taking a step to leave.

"Just...a moment." Sullivan stopped and turned. Arianne stepped slowly, thoughtfully forward to the center of the entry. She had watched in fascination as this man had fought for Lilly, tried to reason with her, and tried to get her to take him back. She had to admit, she liked a man who would fight like that. He reminded her of Marcus and of Viktor as well. She was drawn to him, to his type of male; she had to know more about him than just the little that Lilly had disclosed. The girl was probably hysterical, or they had an argument and she was using rape as an accusation to keep the man away. She reached out and laid a lace-gloved hand on him, touching his arm, stopping him. "Please come in and let's talk this over. It seems there may have been things said and done that need examination."

Lilly looked at her in horror. What was the

reason for this sudden change Arianne doing, inviting Sullivan to stay and talk after he had said he would leave? She didn't know whether to scream or just sink to the floor and cry in frustration.

Arianne crossed to the large double mahogany doors, opened them revealing an elegantly appointed parlor. Turning, nodding to each in turn, "Lilly...Sullivan...Please join me." It was worded like a pleasant invitation but both of them knew it to be a command. Arianne turned and glided into the room and took position by a beautiful wingback chair on the opposite side of the fireplace.

Lilly entered the room with Baron carefully placing himself between her and Sullivan, his tail twitching fiercely and his eyes sparkling. "Lilly," Arianne indicated another wingback chair directly across from the fireplace. Baron jumped into the next chair, defiantly preventing it from being occupied by Sullivan.

"Sullivan." Arianne indicated that he should occupy the chair opposite her...

"No ma'am, I will stand." he said, shaking his head. "I don't expect this to take long enough to get comfortable."

Arianne looked at him sternly, "I asked you nicely to sit. We will not proceed with the discussion until you do so. I will not be denied this courtesy." Sullivan sat down. "Thank-you. Mitch, would you ask Eloise to bring some wine for us, please?" the ghoul nodded his head and backed out of the room, closing the doors behind him.

Baron rearranged himself so that he could keep an eye on Sullivan, his tail not slowing its twitching. Lilly knew her feline friend was guarding her. She sat, the skull in her lap, mindlessly stroking the top of its head, her eyes down, not meeting his. She was not fond of the idea that Sullivan was going to get a chance to charm her hostess and get a chance to hurt her, or Lilly. But, it was Arianne's home and Lilly did not think she had any other choice, just as it had been Miss Lulu's house and what she said was law. Lilly could not find it within herself to argue about it, the habit was deeply ingrained in her.

"Now that everyone is settled," Arianne said as Eloise brought a tray with a crystal bowl and a carafe of wine. Eloise poured, served and she placed the filled crystal saucer next to Baron. Strategically place so he could drink and watch Sullivan at the same time. "Thank you Eloise. That's all."

"Yes, welcome Madam." She curtsied and exited the parlor, closing the doors behind her.

"I have some questions." Arianne took a sip and then looked at Sullivan, who was cautiously sniffing the substance in the glass. "It's blood wine, Sullivan. It won't harm you." She took another sip, then turned to address her other guest, "Lilly, you are his maker so, ultimately, you are responsible for him. You may want him to go, but if he does anything, the damned angels will come looking for you."

"But how can I be responsible for him if he's not around me? Isn't he his own man, with his own set of morals and actions?" Lilly spoke out. The last thing she wanted was to be saddled with this man.

"You are only responsible for me in the aspects of what you have or have not taught me. We won't count the actions of a progeny vampire against the maker in most cases. You are mostly responsible for your own actions." Sullivan explained.

Arianne, alarmed, stared at the man. "You say 'we' like you speak for the angels. What interactions have you had with them and when? You are just made, they should not have had time to search you out and tune you. Lilly hasn't even seen them yet." She looked at the gloved hand holding the glass of wine.

Then Sullivan shocked his hostess beyond anything she had ever had with the words, "I was an Enforcer angel before Lilly turned me." The look on her face was one of total surprise.

"Really? I see no wings under that t-shirt. And I've never heard of an angel being turned. Do you think you can lie to me and I won't know any better?" Arianne began to get annoyed. To claim to be one of the infernal angels in a lie was toying with destruction.

"I may be many things, ma'am, but about this, I am not lying. I had been dispatched to give the rules to Lilly and tune her, and find the other vampire with her."

Baron stopped drinking and fixed his gaze on Sullivan. He growled, flipped his tail, and went back to drinking. We had reports there were two together. I reached the cemetery where she had been reported to be in on the day the hurricane hit. I was accosted and beaten by some thugs who were robbing graves. They were able to get behind me and one took my wings, which left me defenseless and unable to summon help from heaven. Lilly found me and, trying to help me, turned me into a vampire. And I've never heard of it happening either, ever. I have no idea what will happen from here, I hope we can reverse it, but, for the moment, I'm a vampire." He played with his ring as he spoke and Arianne noticed it. She had seen ones like it before, on the hands of the angels who tuned her and the ones that had taken Viktor.

Could it be true? Could she have, in her home, an angel who was turned? What an interesting pawn against the hosts that attacked vampires for the most minor of things, she thought. She had to keep him with her, that much was very clear. She drank more of her wine and thought about what to do to keep him with her. She looked at the young woman seated next to her, holding that stupid skull.

The skull. Marcus.

"I have a solution that may work out for all parties." She was taking a chance on this but it was too tempting not to try to accomplish what might be the impossible. "I know where Lilly's Marcus is living, he is my progeny and we communicate frequently. I will send her to him and let them continue whatever relationship they can work out if you, Sullivan, will agree to stay with me as my friend and companion. I will assume responsibility for your teaching and actions, in effect letting Lilly renounce her claim as maker, freeing her." She turned and looked at Lilly, who stared at her, shaking her head in disbelief. "You can be free of him, dear. That is what you desire, isn't it?"

"But Marcus doesn't want me, he has this other woman, you said her name was Eadwina, who is his lover. I cannot break up a couple like that." Lilly didn't want to mess up yet another life.

"Sweetie, I have an admission. I lied to you about that. Marcus isn't involved with anyone else; he's refused to do so since you went to the grave. He's resisted every attempt of every woman, and man who has come to him with the intention of catching his attention and his heart. It's pathetic, really." Arianne was smiling.

Lilly was struck with the words. Arianne lied to her. Marcus didn't have another lover; he was waiting and mourning her! A smile spread across her face and her hand stilled on the skull in her lap. "You are telling truth this time? There is no other woman. And he is waiting for me?" She could not stop the rising joy within her.

Arianne smiled slyly. One part of her plan was working. "Yes, I am telling you the truth. He would be waiting if he knew you walked still. Unfortunately, I have no way of contacting him right now, the hurricane has severed most of the phone lines and even cell phones aren't working. But yes, there is no other woman but you, there never has been since he laid eyes on you."

Lilly didn't know what a cell phone was but

that didn't matter. All that mattered was that Marcus wanted her, had wanted her, and was waiting for her. Her face burst into a smile so radiant that even Baron turned his fixed stare from Sullivan to her and let out a small meow. Sullivan looked at her, almost seeing her for the first time. She was beautiful, and happy. He knew he had lost her forever. He turned his gaze back to the older vampire, noticing for the first time she wore gloves. Probably hiding a judgment mark. What was he getting himself into?

"Ma'am. I can see that Lilly wants to do this, so what are your terms."

"Please, call me Arianne. My terms are this, you agree to spend 150 years with me as my companion and I will let Lilly go to Marcus where he is, starting tonight. You will stay and travel with me, learn with me, and become my progeny. Lilly will relinquish her claim as your maker."

Sullivan didn't even pause to consider her offer. He began to nod his head when she began her terms. He loved Lilly, enough to let her go. "Arianne, I accept your terms. You will send Lilly to Marcus, with Baron, and I will agree to stay with you for at least 150 years." he stood, "Of course, I need to go back to the pub we were staying at and gather my things tonight. If you have a car to take me there and back, it would be appreciated."

Arianne stood as well, putting out her hand and shaking his. "I will have Mitch take you by there on the way to take Lilly to my private plane at the airport. Once she is gone, you will return to me." She smiled. An angel, one turned to a vampire, was going to be a huge asset. And that asset was now hers to wield. This was a coup for the histories.

Lilly spoke up. "Airplane? You are sending me in the air? Oh no, no, no, no. I can't fly. I've never been up in the air." Lilly's eyes widened and she hugged the skull to her tighter in her fear.

Arianne rolled her eyes and tried to smile. The girl was a big pain in the ass at times, her inability to understand or to go along with a plan grated a bit on the older, more experienced vampire. "Oh, ok. I'm sorry. Mitch can take you to my yacht in the Ponchatrain West-end marina; I hope it survived the storm. I know I told the captain to take it to where it would be safest. If it didn't, someone will have to drive you."

Lilly didn't catch the exasperation in her hostess' voice but jumped from her seat and hugged Arianne. "Thank you for this! To see Marcus again, to be able to be with him is such a dream."

"You should be thanking Sullivan too, my dear. He's giving up his love for you and 150 years of his life." Arianne said as Lilly pulled back. The young girl looked at Sullivan, started to put out her hand, then dropped the skull on the chair she had been sitting in and threw her arms around Sullivan.

"Thank you! Thank you!" she squealed, forgetting the fact that she was totally afraid and angry with him of in that moment. She was free, and she would be seeing Marcus again.

Sullivan knew that the hug would probably be

the last contact he would have with her and he tried to put as much energy into it as he could without frightening her again. He could smell her shampoo and the Chanel No. 5 and he hoped he could remember it.

Lilly suddenly stopped hugging him and pulled away, turning her back to him and facing Arianne again. Her heart was soaring, she would be with Marcus, but she also knew that Sullivan was hoping for more. And it was something she never could give him, not after what he had done.

"Mitch, will you ask Eloise to gather Lilly's things and bring them down while you get the car? I would like for her to be on her way to Texas before dawn and I know Sullivan is eager to get his things and get back." She picked up a piece of stationery from her correspondence desk and wrote something on it, sealing it in an envelope. She handed this to Mitch as he left, "See to it that the yacht captain gets this note and that its instructions are followed, to the letter. I will broach no refusals on this from him." Arianne instructed her ghoul and he left the room as she looked at the clock on the mantle. They still had a few hours before dawn, plenty of time to accomplish the things she had started setting into motion. She poured herself another glass of wine.

It wasn't but a few moments of silence between the three vampires before Sarah came into the room and announced the suitcase was in the car and Mitch was ready to take the younger vampires to their destinations. With another hug with Arianne and a heartfelt thank-you, Lilly picked up the skull, walked out of the room and outside, Baron following. Sullivan stood by, then nodded once to Arianne. "I will return shortly." he said and he followed Lilly out the door. They climbed into the back of the limo and it drove out of the driveway and out into the night.

Chapter Twenty-One

THE LIMO WAS large but it felt like a small box to Lilly. Despite her happiness at going to Texas, to Marcus; being in such close contact with Sullivan was daunting. If he tried anything, even Mitch, who was driving, couldn't stop and get back there soon enough to stop him, she didn't know if she could survive it. She wanted to believe Sully was serious about the apology, about the remorse he was apparently feeling, but she was so terrified, even now, it was impossible to trust him completely.

Her only real security, her real protection was Baron. The huge cat was sitting on the seat beside her. Sullivan had taken the facing seat, his back to the driver's compartment.

They sat in stony silence, the air thick with unsaid things between them as the limo slowly made its way through the city, back toward the French Quarter. Lilly quietly pet the top of the skull in her lap with one hand and Baron with the other. Sullivan just sat, stock still, looking at her, trying to memorize everything about her because he probably would not see her again. His heart broken, he was in shock that she had rejected him so completely. He really thought he had a shot of a Happily Ever After with her.

That's what he got for thinking, he thought.

"Sully, I, uh." She tried to begin and stopped. He had leaned forward, arms on his knees that appeared to be too big for the small space. She looked at him, trying not to flinch away like her nerves urged her to do. She closed her eyes and took a deep breath, then opened them and said, "Look, I'm sorry for turning you. I thought I was doing something good. I didn't mean to ruin your life."

That was not what he had hoped to hear. He wanted her to, God, what did he want her to say? That she was sorry for being afraid of him, that she forgave him, that she didn't want him to leave.

No, that wouldn't happen. She was done with him. He was a mean, pathetic...rapist. And she was going to go to the love of her life. He, too, took a deep breath, let it out, and then forced a smile he didn't feel. "It's okay; you were doing what you thought you should do. There was nothing malicious in it."

He looked down, steeled himself, and then continued, "I'm sorry I lost it. I should have listened to you, I should have...."

There was nothing left to say. Anything else was going to be wasted air. Silence built in like a storm front, taking over every molecule of space in the back of the limo. The big car pulled up in front of O'Flaherty's Irish Channel Pub, still locked up from when Sullivan had left. The door opened, Mitch stood by outside. Sullivan slid over to get out. He started to reach out, to touch her hand, her face, just to feel her one last time. But Baron let out a low, vicious warning growl and then hissed at him. Sullivan dropped his hand and stepped out of the limo.

He turned, looked at Mitch, and then ducked his head down, looking back into the car. He looked into her brown eyes for the last time.

"I love you, Lilly. Please. Have a good life."

Then he stepped away and Mitch shut the door. "I'll be back for you once she's on the yacht, be ready," the ghoul said before getting back into the driver's seat. The car pulled away from the pub, leaving Sullivan standing in the road, watching as it went to Royal Street and disappeared around the corner.

Taking his heart with it.

Chapter Twenty-Two

SULLIVAN PUSHED OPEN the door to the little apartment above the pub. It had been a place of such great joy, then horrible violence. He looked around the two rooms. The whiskey glasses still rested on the table. There was a huge dried bloodstain on the bed. There were remnants of glitter. The smell of shampoo and perfume still hung in the air, taunting him. And there were the words Lilly had left for him when she escaped his rampage, still painted in blood on the wall.

"Leave Me the Hell Alone!"

That wall would haunt his nightmares forever. It defined every failure he ever had during the time he had been on this mission. He hung his head and sighed. There was nothing more he could do for the situation. He just had to straighten up and begin again, go back to Arianne's house and become her companion. If the angels came for him, he would have to tell them he wasn't going back. He had an oath to fulfill, a promise made in good faith and he was going to make sure it was fulfilled. He owed Lilly the freedom she now had. It was the one good thing he could hold onto.

He lifted his head, took a deep breath, and then, kicking off his sneakers and stripped off the dirty shirt and pants he had been wearing and pulled out a pair of jeans and t-shirt from the backpack he had left behind. He went into the bathroom to check on the availability of water and found it still off so he returned to the bedroom and slipped on the jeans, putting the contents of his pockets in the dirty ones into the clean ones without thinking. He turned and reached for the shirt when the room lit up with a very, very bright light.

Sully dropped the shirt and put his hands up to his eyes to keep them from burning with the intensity of the light. He squinted through his fingers and could just make out three shapes in the light. Then it seemed to drain away and he pulled his hands away, blinking to get his pupils to work again. There were three angels standing in front of him.

He recognized one of them and smiled. It was his best friend and fellow Enforcer, Essex. The other male was a huge, red-winged Warrior that he remembered was named Helmut. He was known as Mikhail's personal guard and one of the most feared Warriors and he carried a large flaming sword in his right hand. Then he saw the third and his head pounded. It was Nida, the Angel Emissary. She only went on the most dire assignments; she was Mikhail's voice, an Enforcer but with more power than any other, including Ranguel himself. She was here, with Helmut, and with Essex. That could mean only one thing.

This was not an ordinary tuning visit. And it wasn't a rescue. He was in trouble, big trouble. The smile fell from his face.

Helmut stretched out his hand and pointed at Sullivan and said, quietly but forcefully, "Kneel, vampire," and Sully's knees seemed to collapse under him and he landed on them on the wooden floor. "Stretch out your right hand." the Warrior instructed and Sullivan felt his right arm stretch out from his body of its own accord. Eyebrows rose as the angelic ring was found on the hand. Helmut reached out and plucked it from his hand and slipped it onto his smallest finger.

Losing the ring brought home the situation to him, "Essex, tell them..." Sullivan started. Essex held his head up but his eyes betrayed his alarm and pain at what was happening to his friend.

"Silence." The Warrior spoke and the words disappeared from the angel/vampire's throat like they were ripped from him. Nida stepped forward.

"You are the former angel, once named Ei-stered, now called Sullivan, an Enforcer from Ranguel's Unit." It wasn't a question but a statement of lineage. Nida was establishing his identity for the pronouncement she had been sent to make. "You have been turned into a vampire. You knew the rules more than most, even without an attunement. Do you have a defense for your actions since that turning?"

"Speak" Helmut's word released the hold on Sullivan's throat and he opened his mouth. "I was attacked, my wings taken, my ring taken. I was turned by a well-meaning, uneducated and untuned vampire who sought to save my life. I did not willingly submit, I was out cold when it happened."

"While that in itself would have been reversible, your actions after that are what have been a concern to the Angelic Council. You have done things that you knew to be wrong, both for an angel and for a vampire. These actions have been judged and you have found culpable. Even without the attunement, you knew the laws on vampires and you killed. Twice. Once by draining, a strict violation. You have blasphemed, stolen, lied, coveted, and you committed rape. Any one of these could have earned you a strike against you, toward damnation, and you were aware of that. Combined together, they are enough to damn you to the depths of Hell." There was no emotion in Nida's pronouncement, just cold words.

"No!" Sullivan cried out before he could think. "I didn't mean to break..." Red blood tears began to flow from his eyes. He looked from Nida, to Helmut, and finally to Essex who stood stock still, ramrod straight. Then he took a breath and bowed his head, then looked up into Nida's face, "But I did. I did all of the things you say. And I am guilty. I accept the judgment." He bowed his head once again.

"You will be marked for your crimes." Nida pronounced the third of the pronouncements and brought up her left hand. She pointed and began to trace a circle on the back of his right hand with fire.

Sullivan screamed. It was the worst pain he had ever felt and seemed to consume him without taking him. He could not move away from it and try as he would, he could not pass out or look away. Once the circle was drawn, it was divided into three equal parts, the stench of burning flesh filling the room. Then, the Enochian letter M was traced into the first part and the second had the letter R traced within. Sullivan closed his eyes, knowing they stood for his two worst crimes, murder and rape. The last third would hold the mark of condemnation and seal his fate.

He was being sent to Hell. And he could not fulfill the bargain with Arianne. He could only hope that the vampire would not take that fact out on Lilly, the thought strong enough to cut through the pain of the marking.

The intense climax of the pain began to subside into just a fierce burning and he heard Nida ask, "Are you ready for your punishment?"

"Yes, I am ready." He opened his eyes and looked at his hand. But, instead of seeing the completed condemnation mark, the last third of the circle was empty. He looked up into Nida's face. "I do not understand," he managed to say.

"You have been judged, but Mikhail himself has intervened in the Council's judgment. He is giving you a chance to redeem yourself. Because of your self-sacrifice in the matter of the vampire, Lilly Marchantel, you are given the choice to go into Introspection, Retreat, and Retraining or to be given the final mark and take your place with the demons. It is your choice."

Sullivan stayed silent. This was so highly irregular that, in his memory, it had never been done before and he was not sure if it wasn't a cruel trick being played on him, one last humiliation before being sent straight into eternal punishment.

Nida spoke up in his silence. "I do not agree with Mikhail's decision in this case but he says he foresees a need for your services and he is granting this special dispensation."

Essex, who had been silent throughout the entire proceeding spoke, "Take it, Sullivan. It's a chance."

Sullivan slowly nodded his head. "Ok, I accept the chance of redemption, with thanks to Mikhail and to God."

"Then rise." Helmut released the power that had held Sullivan up and on his knees and he collapsed at first, his hands landing on the floor as he crumpled. Then, carefully, he rose, holding his burned hand with his left one.

"I need to go explain my change of plans to someone." He started to explain. But Nida shook her head.

"You have no time and no need. You are to be transported immediately to your destination to begin your IRR." She motioned to the two male angels. "Take him."

Essex took Sullivan's right arm, Helmut his left and in a blinding flash of ethereal light they all disappeared. Only two small charred rings remained in the floor where Sullivan's knees had been.

Chapter Twenty-Three

THE BLACK LIMO swung into Toulouse Street and pulled up to the curb in front of Ralph and Kacoo's restaurant across the street from the pub. Annoyed that Sullivan wasn't out front waiting, Mitch exited and walked up to the door of the darkened pub. He pulled the door and found that it opened. He entered and walked through the first floor of the building, and the patio, then finally winding his way upstairs into the apartment.

As he opened the door, the first thing he noticed was the stench of burning flesh and wood, and something else. He traced through his memory and finally came up with the correct answer; angels. That stink could only be the meddling Heavenly Host.

He took notice of the burn marks on the floor, the dried blood on the bed, the abandoned backpack with the dirty clothing laying nearby, and the words written in blood on the wall.

"Leave me the Hell alone!"

As he walked from the building he knew one thing, he was not going to enjoy returning home and telling Eadwina what he had found and that Sullivan was gone. And he knew she would be furious that he left with angels.

As he shut the pub door, he looked down and noticed a brass key on the ground. He picked it up and inserted it into the lock. It fit. He locked the door and shoved the key under it, climbed into the limo, and left the area.

Chapter Twenty-Four

A BRIGHT LIGHT materialized in the snow deep in a mountain range. As it dissipated, three male figures emerged, two with wings and one without.

Sullivan stood between the two angels and noticed his feet and chest were cold. He groaned as he realized he was barefoot and standing in ankle-deep snow while the angels stood on top of the snow. He should not have felt the cold, as an angel or as a vampire. But he did. He wondered if the attunement and judgment had changed his makeup.

"Vampire," Helmut said, "Since you continue to live, you need to pick a surname."

Sullivan thought for a moment, shivering in the cold, then he smiled. "I know just what. A place-name from Ireland. I will be known as Sullivan Kilcoan." The large Warrior angel nodded.

Essex took Sullivan's left arm at the elbow in a modified handshake and pulled him into his chest. The two men hugged as the large Warrior looked on. "Sullivan, don't mess this up. You have been given a great gift. We were told you were damned and I expected..." his voice trailed off.

"I know. I won't mess it up, I swear." Sullivan looked at his friend and hoped it wouldn't be the last time they spoke. He jammed his cold hands into his jeans pockets and felt something push into his palm.

He withdrew a card and looked at it. It was the information about Arianne Campbell that he had taken from the old man. Sully looked up at Essex and held it out to him. "I need you to do me one last favor, if you would. There's a man at the St. Louis 1 cemetery, an old black man who is the guard there. I took this card from him and I erased his memory of it, of me, and of Lilly. I don't know why I am feeling like there's something important about this card but I need you to go back, return the card, and restore the man's memory for me."

Essex thought about the request and could not find anything wrong with the move. It was one way that Sullivan could make up for some of the things he had done so the angel smiled at his friend. "Ok, I will make sure it is handled." He hugged the vampire one last time, then stepped back and raised his hand to wave goodbye and the light grew bright again as the angels disappeared, forcing him to close his eyes again.

"Good bye my friend." Sullivan said under his breath, almost in a prayer. Then he opened his eyes and looked across the mountains. To the east there was a large, imposing castle-like structure built into the rock. A snowy path lead from where Sullivan stood to the building. Shivering in the cold and looking up at the sky, he tried to figure out how much time he had before sunrise then started walking through the snow toward his destination.

Coming Soon—"Marcus's Vampire"

T HE ELEVATOR DOORS opened into the 25th floor penthouse. Marcus Lancaster exited, followed by his Shetland sheepdog companion, Lance. Marcus had pulled off his bow tie and was unbuttoning the tuxedo shirt as he entered the room. He pulled off the coat and threw it on a nearby chair, the tie fell to the floor, and the shirt just missed the couch. He kicked his shoes off and stepped on the toes of his socks to pull them off while he fumbled with the remote.

The wall panel folded back and a bank of flat-panel monitors appeared, lighting up. As Marcus crossed over to the bar to pour himself a Scotch, he was examining the various news programs that were being shown; he was tied into the satellites so he could watch as many channels as possible from around the world. Most of the broadcasts tonight centered around the devastation on the Gulf coast of the United States in the wake of Hurricane Katrina which had slammed into the area between New Orleans, Louisiana and Biloxi, Mississippi only a week before. The evacuations were mostly over but the damage, the crime, and the trouble were still going on.

"I thought you were going to come home prior to midnight this time." The statement came from the edge of the kitchen. Marcus turned to see the tall blond man leaning against the door, legs and arms crossed in a show of annoyance. Jesse

Cumberlain was Marcus' assistant, his right hand, his confidant, his lover, and a ghoul. He had been turned into one during the Civil War and had been with the old vampire since.

"I had planned on it but the charity auction got a little, shall we say, out of hand and I ended up being there longer than I intended." Marcus bent down and removed the collar from Lance, a collar that looked like the collar and bow tie of a tuxedo. The dog barked his approval at losing the confining apparatus and turned a few spins before wagging his tail and heading for the kitchen in search of a snack.

"What happened?" Jesse watched the dog pass him.

Marcus rubbed his hand across his eyes and sighed. He didn't really want to go into this, these sorts of things usually started arguments with the man in front of him, but he also knew that Jesse was just pushy enough to not give up on finding out what went on and would pester him until he provided details. He looked at the monitors, "Natalie Sherman happened. They talked me into entering the 'slave auction' portion of the event and there got to be a bidding war between Natalie and three other women. The winner would be getting me as a date for an evening to be decided later. Natalie was determined to get that date and pushed the amount to secure it to over $125,000 before the other ladies dropped out. So, she spent the rest of the event following me around and trying to insert herself into my entire life. I don't know whether she was more interested in buying me or showing off to the city just how much money she was willing to part with to do it."

"Really? She paid that much money for you to go out with her? This is just a date, dinner, dancing, or a movie; we're not talking sex here, right?" The frown on Jesse's face told Marcus all he needed to know, his lover was jealous.

"Just a date, baby, just a date. And at least the money will go to help build the south campus of Texas Children's Hospital." Marcus looked over at Jesse, who had changed his demeanor and was actually walking toward him with a big smile.

"I guess that's ok, then, as long as it's for a good cause and you keep it in your pants." The smirk made the younger man's eyes sparkle. He reached the vampire and planted a kiss on his lips that may have started quick but Marcus pulled him into his arms and deepened the kiss, running his hand up under the ghoul's shirt.

As the kiss ended, Marcus opened his eyes and looked over Jesse's shoulder at the monitor for KBQ National News feed. The tag in the upper left corner said "Recorded earlier" and was of a bar in New Orleans. He pulled away and walked up close to the monitor and hit the remote control button for the volume on it. He listened as the reporter, David Jones, talked with the people who sat at the bar. It wasn't the actual interview he was interested in, it was the two people in the background. One was a tall man in jeans and a t-shirt with a white pair of angel wings strapped to his torso with Mardi Gras beads. He stood talking with a strikingly lovely woman in black jeans, a purple shirt, beads, and a tall purple hat. She kept looking at the television on the wall and then back to the camera, gesturing.

"What is it?" Jesse started to ask more but Marcus shushed him.

He hit a button and the feed ran back to the beginning of the segment, then pressed the record button. As the recording played, Marcus took the television into the zoom mode. When the couple were centered in the picture and the woman looking directly into the camera, he paused the picture and zoomed in.

"What?" Jesse stared at the television and then looked at Marcus. He could not remember the last time he saw that particular look on his lover's face. The man was totally and completely surprised, his mouth hanging open, his fangs descending.

Marcus turned to Jesse with red tears in his eyes.

"Who is it? Do you know them?"

He shook his head slowly, "I don't know the man at all but..." his voice trailed off and he stared at the screen again. Jesse put a hand on his shoulder and Marcus turned his gaze back to him.

"It's Lilly. She's alive."

Historical Resources

Storyville, New Orleans: Being an Authentic, Illustrated Account of the Notorious Red-Light District by Al Rose:
barnesandnoble.com/w/storyville-new-orleans-al-rose/1111828145?ean=9780817344030

Dead Spaces: St. Louis One Cemetery, New Orleans (Graduate Program in Historic Preservation, University of Pennsylvania School of Design)
cml.upenn.edu/nola/14history/L1historypgkey.html

"Black Policemen in Jim Crow New Orleans" by Vanessa Flores-Robert. Master's Thesis-University of New Orleans. Page 17-18.

Haunted New Orleans Tour: (includes the ghosts of O'Flaherty's Irish Channel Pub)
hauntedneworleanstours.com/hauntedneworleansbars

Lulu White: The Honest Courtesan:
maggiemcneill.wordpress.com/2011/09/03/lulu-white

1000 Fragrances:
1000fragrances.blogspot.com

Onward Brass Band:
www.onwardbb.com

African-American Registry, St. Augustine Catholic Church-New Orleans
www.aaregistry.org/historic_events/view/st-augustine-catholic-church-new-orleans-founded-first-black-catholic-church

About the Author

Charlayne Elizabeth Denney was born in Amarillo, Texas and lived there until 1991. Now a resident of Houston, she has been a waitress, a DJ, a sports writer, a technical writer, sold knives, swords, and replica weapons, was part-owner of a comic shop, and a perennial student. She has 4 kids, 9 grandkids, 2 Shelties, and a cat who is the inspiration for Baron in "Fangs & Halos." She married her 3rd and final husband, Bruce, in 1993 after a whirlwind six-month romance, having met him at a Science Fiction convention and her sister telling her to "go out with him" (and him overhearing her). She has written many non-fiction articles, has been published in several magazines, and wrote technical training manuals for Compaq. She reviews for Paranormal Romance Guild and loves vampire novels the most. "Lilly's Angel" is her first novel.

Books In the Fangs & Halos Series